"I have a confession," Ellen said as she slid closer and took Jody's hand.

"What?" Jody's voice broke. She wished Ellen would let go of her hand, but somehow she didn't have the strength to remove it. She cursed her decision to have the second margarita.

"I had a terrible crush on you when I was in high school."

Jody stared at her in amazement. "I hardly ever saw you."

Ellen shrugged. "Actually," she said as she leaned toward Jody, "I never got over it." Her lips brushed Jody's.

Jody held her breath and told herself to get up and send Ellen home. Everything in her screamed that she should not be kissing Denise's daughter, but then Ellen's tongue slowly parted her lips.

Jody's mind and body were not working as one. She tried to pull away, but Ellen pushed her back onto the sofa.

"Ellen," Jody finally managed to murmur as Ellen kissed her neck and throat. "We shouldn't be doing this."

"Why?" Ellen asked as she boldly unbuttoned Jody's shirt and captured a firm nipple between her lips.

"I'm old enough to be your mother," she moaned. "Actually, I'm two months older than your mother."

Ellen's hand slipped inside Jody's shorts and stroked her. "This doesn't feel like you want me to stop." She pushed a finger deep inside and slowly removed it.

Despite Jody's best efforts, her body rose up to meet Ellen's hand.

Visit

Bella Books

at

BellaBooks.com

or call our toll-free number

1-800-729-4992

Survival
of Love

by Frankie J. Jones

Bella
BOOKS

2004

Bella Books, Inc.
P.O. Box 10543
Tallahassee, FL 32302

Printed in the United States of America on acid-free paper
First Edition

Editor: Christi Cassidy
Cover designer: Bonnie Liss (Phoenix Graphics)

ISBN 1-931513-55-4

For Martha

Mi Vida, Mi Amor

(My Life, My Love)

ACKNOWLEDGMENTS

Flo Jonas, I can never thank you enough for your courage and willingness to share the details of your own personal struggle with breast cancer. Without your help, I would never have attempted to write this book. Thank you for nudging me out of my own comfort zone.

Cory Matranga, thank you for answering my endless questions. You opened your heart and allowed me to catch a glimpse of the anguish experienced by the partner of a breast cancer patient.

Jean Cassidy, you brave, brave woman. Thank you for reading my first draft and keeping me on "medical" track.

Linda Hill and Terese Orban, I don't believe I have ever met two more persistent women. Thanks for pestering me until I pulled the file cabinet drawer open and dusted off the manuscript, even if I did only keep the first sentence.

Christi Cassidy, thanks for your time, patience and editorial skill.

Peggy J. Herring, thanks for taking the time to read my manuscript while working hard to meet the deadline on your own.

Martha Cabrera, how do I even begin to say thanks? You supported me when I threw away 200 pages and started over, eight weeks before my deadline. During those eight weeks you listened patiently as I ranted about first one snag and then another. You never complained when I woke you up at three a.m. to brainstorm, and you didn't call the guys in white jackets when I rambled around the house talking to myself for hours on end. When the plot fizzled you gave me the courage to throw away yet another four chapters and let my characters choose their own road. I love you, and yes, I will marry you on May 29, 2004.

To all my readers— Thank you for the kind words and support I've received over the years. Mattie, I have so enjoyed your e-mails. For those of you with not-so-kind words, thank you for making me try harder.

CHAPTER ONE

Jody Scott swept mangled leaves and petals onto a piece of cardboard.

"I've finished sweeping the workroom," she called to her business partner, Denise Murray. "Do you need any help in there?"

"No, sweetie, I'm almost through, and we can get out of here."

Jody smiled. It usually took a team of mules to pull Denise out of their flower shop, but her daughter, Ellen, had taken a job transfer back to San Antonio and was due in tonight.

"When did you last see Ellen?" Denise asked her.

Jody frowned and thought for a moment. Ellen was a spoiled brat that she deliberately avoided, but to say so would hurt Denise's feelings. "I guess it was eight years ago when we went to the coast after she graduated from high school." Idly bouncing the broom against the floor, she leaned against the doorjamb that separated the showroom from the workroom.

"It's been that long? Time flies." Denise straightened a stack of catalogs. "You won't recognize her. She's no longer skinny as a stick. She's beautiful, Jody. I don't know where she got those wonderful genes. Her father was no great looker, and they certainly aren't from me." Denise patted her rump.

Jody looked at her lifelong friend. Denise's body had thickened some since high school, and regular appointments with a beautician were needed to keep the gray out of her curly brown hair, but she was still an attractive woman.

"There's nothing wrong with your genes," Jody said. "I remember when you thought Mark Murray was God's gift."

Denise rolled her eyes. "I swear, sometimes I wonder what I was thinking then. I should have stuck to the plans you and I made to go to college together. At least I would've had an education to fall back on when he left me for that twenty-year-old flake."

"Denise, we made those plans when we were thirteen. Things change."

"Yeah, nine months of change. If I had listened to what Mom tried to tell me, I wouldn't have been three months pregnant when I graduated."

"Just remember, you got Ellen as a result of that pregnancy." Jody knew that would calm Denise's regrets.

"You're right." Denise went into the showroom and started rearranging a table of ceramic planters that stood in front of one of the large display windows.

"Denise, go home and rest. You've been cooking and cleaning all week." Jody put the broom away. When she returned, Denise was putting the live flower arrangements into the cooler that ran the length of the end wall of the shop. Jody flipped off the display lights, locked the front door and turned on the fluorescent CLOSED sign. She didn't want to attract after-hours shoppers. "What time does she get in?" Jody asked, referring to Ellen. She began passing the last few arrangements to Denise.

"She wasn't sure since she's never driven out. We estimated between eight and nine tonight." Denise shook her head. "Ellen is so stubborn. She insisted on driving all the way from Los Angeles by herself. I tried to tell her how dangerous it was, but she swears she can't live without her car. I told her she could use mine, and I would hitch a ride with you, but apparently a six-year-old Taurus would cramp her style."

Jody stifled a sigh. To listen to Denise babble about the dangers of traveling alone, you'd think Ellen was coming home in a covered wagon. Would she ever stop babying Ellen?

Oblivious to Jody's thoughts, Denise continued, "She scares me to death sometimes. I don't know why she didn't sell her car and buy another one here, or she could have shipped it home. The company she works for told her they would pay to have her car shipped. But, no, Ms. Independence has to do it herself." Denise placed the last live arrangement into the cooler and scurried to the cash register. She opened the register and sighed. "I still have to balance the register, batch the credit card sales, and go to the bank."

"Bag everything and I'll come in early in the morning and do it for you."

"Are you sure?"

Jody nodded and smiled at the look of relief on Denise's face. Jody held a cash bag as Denise emptied the register tray into it.

"I even offered to fly out and help drive back, but she wanted to do it alone." Denise continued her ranting as she headed to the workroom.

"Sounds like someone I know," Jody said as she zipped the bag and followed Denise.

"Are you crazy? I'd never drive cross-country by myself."

"Maybe not now. What would you have done twenty years ago? Especially, if your mom had said you shouldn't."

Denise snorted and took the bag from Jody. "I see my days of peace and quiet are gone. Between you and Ellen, I will have no chance. Come on," she said and switched off the workroom lights. "I'll put this in the safe. Are you sure you don't mind taking care of this? I could stay and do it."

Jody grinned at Denise's reference to the safe. It was nothing more than an old clothes hamper full of rags they used for cleaning. On the rare occasions when they left money in the shop, Denise would bury the cash bag in the hamper, certain that no burglar would ever think to look there. "I don't mind. The bank is open until noon tomorrow. I'll have plenty of time to run it over."

"Good." Denise took the money to the back of the workroom. She reappeared a moment later. "Let's get out of here."

Jody grabbed her backpack and breathed a sigh of relief. She had a date with Sharon tonight and wanted to get home early. It was almost seven. The shop closed at six, but by the time they cleaned and prepared the days' receipts, they rarely left before seven-thirty.

Denise dug through her purse as Jody locked the back door.

"What are you and Sharon doing tonight?" Denise asked as she pulled out her car keys.

"We're going to stay in with a pizza and watch a movie." She felt a tickle of excitement. Pizza and a movie with Sharon translated into a night of great sex. She had been dating Sharon for almost a month, and things were proceeding smoothly. At least the sex was great. They never got around to talking. She quickly pushed the thought away. To examine their lack of conversation might lead to a conclusion that Jody wasn't yet ready to face.

Jody and Denise crossed the parking lot. Jody gave her a hug and tossed her backpack into the passenger seat of her black Jeep Wrangler.

"I'll see you Monday," Jody said. "Tell Ellen I'll see her soon." Jody was in no hurry to see Ellen. Since the week-long whine-fest she subjected them to after her high-school graduation, Jody had made it a point to be elsewhere whenever she was in town.

"Sweetie, thanks again for working this weekend," Denise called as she got into her Taurus. "Tell Sharon I'll make it up to her."

Jody and Denise took turns working weekends at Petal Pushers, with Eric, their part-time employee. In their original plans for the flower shop, she and Denise had agreed to not hire a full-time employee until the shop's profits could cover a decent salary for each of them and their employee. They had finally hit that goal two years ago, but since their current arrangement had worked so well and the shop's clientele continued to grow they had recently started discussing the possibility of opening another shop. They decided to delay the hiring of a full-time employee until they made their minds up about the new shop.

Jody climbed into her Jeep. Maybe it was time to re-think the decision to delay hiring a full-time employee. Her hasty offer to work for Denise this weekend would severely limit her time with Sharon.

One more reason to not like the brat, Jody thought as she pulled out of the parking lot. She had wanted to spend the weekend in bed with Sharon, but instead she would have to work.

Jody drove to the video store and rented the *African Queen.* They had both seen the movie a half-dozen times. Tonight, Jody didn't want the movie distracting them. Leaving the video store she drove to her home in northwest San Antonio. As she drove, she started to feel guilty about her unkind thoughts of Ellen. Most of the time, Ellen had been a sweet kid. Jody realized she shouldn't continue to judge Ellen by her teen years. Ellen had probably matured into a nice person.

Jody would overlook most of Ellen's shortcomings simply because she was Denise's daughter. Denise had been her best friend since the third grade when Jody's family moved into the house across the street from Denise's family.

The two girls quickly discovered they had a lot in common. They were products of single-child households, a rarity in the late 1960s. Their fathers worked for civil service at Lackland Air Force Base, and their mothers were housewives addicted to soap operas. Denise and Jody loved books and movies. During the summers, they spent most of their free time at the movie theater.

During their junior year, they began trying to decide which college they would attend. Studying came easy for Jody, but Denise had to work to maintain a B average. Jody wanted to go away to college, but Denise wanted to stay in San Antonio. They finally decided to submit applications to Tulane University in New Orleans, Trinity University in San Antonio, and Baylor University in Waco. They agreed they would attend the university that accepted them both. Jody could still remember running to Denise's house when she received scholarship offers from both Tulane and Trinity on the same day. A week later, Denise received her acceptance letter from Trinity, but was turned down by Tulane. With only slight regret, Jody agreed with Denise that Trinity University would make a fine alma mater.

But then Denise met Mark in their senior year and everything changed. Their plans to attend college together fell apart when Denise married Mark two weeks after their high-school graduation.

It had been a difficult time for them. At about the same time Denise began to make plans for her wedding, Jody fell in love with her math teacher, Mrs. Hardin. Confused by the intensity of her emotions, Jody slipped away to the library seeking validation for her feeling. What she found was a handful of outdated references that declared her love a perversion against not only mankind, but God as well. Jody kept her secret. She wanted to tell Denise but was afraid Denise would think she was perverted. Faced with unrequited love and hurt by what she saw as Denise's betrayal, Jody ran from everything familiar. She turned down the scholarship to Trinity and accepted the one from Tulane.

Denise's wedding was a blur of activity. As maid of honor, Jody stood beside Denise and tried to be happy for her best friend. She studied Mark but couldn't see what Denise had found so attractive about him. He was too self-centered. The baby blue tuxedo he wore made him appear even shorter than he really was. Denise looked tired and a little frightened. The newlyweds would be leaving the following morning on their honeymoon, two weeks in Cancun. The trip was a wedding present from Denise's parents. Jody tried to imagine spending two weeks in the same room with Mark and felt her stomach give an uneasy toss. Why had Denise agreed to marry him? Her too-loud sigh of confusion caused the minister to glance her way. Embarrassed, she gave up trying to figure out Denise's actions and turned her thoughts to her own future.

During Jody's second week at Tulane, she met Angie, who would eventually become Jody's first lover. Angie was thirty-seven and owned Riddle's, a popular college hangout. She and Jody were together for almost a year until a tall, lanky cowgirl from Montana named Rita came along and caught Angie's attention.

A few weeks after arriving at Tulane, Jody received a letter from Denise. In the letter, Denise apologized for ruining their plans. She went on to explain that she had gotten pregnant and felt she had no choice but to marry Mark.

At first, Jody was devastated that Denise had not trusted her enough to tell her about the baby sooner, but then she realized that she had been keeping her own secret.

Jody wrote back and announced her lesbianism to Denise. She spent the next week praying their friendship would be strong enough to survive her confession.

The friendship not only endured, it was stronger than ever, Jody thought as she pulled into the garage of her small two-bedroom ranch-style home.

A gush of hot air hit her as she opened the door leading into the kitchen. It was only April, but the days already held hints of the sweltering heat to come. She turned on the central air conditioner and checked her watch. It was almost seven-thirty. She wouldn't have time for her daily run. If she hurried she could shower and maybe catch a quick nap. Since she never got much sleep when Sharon was around, she needed to sleep when she could. She grabbed a pair of shorts and a tank top from her dresser, then raced to the shower. As she washed her hair, she thought about how her life and Denise's often paralleled.

They had continued to call each other on special occasions. When Jody visited her parents in San Antonio, she would always spend at least one day of her vacation with Denise. They would laugh and reminisce for hours or until Mark came home. After he arrived, Jody would quickly find an excuse to leave. She had tried to at least tolerate him for Denise's sake, but there was just something about him that set her teeth on edge. After fifteen years of marriage, Mark left Denise for a younger woman.

Two weeks later, Jody, who worked as an investment advisor for a major brokerage firm in New York, came home to find her Manhattan apartment in disarray. A note from Mia, her lover of nine and a half years, lay on the table. The note informed Jody that Mia had moved to Tucson to live with a young artist whose work had been on exhibit at the gallery where Mia worked. The betrayal shattered Jody's ability to trust and her belief in commitment.

Since their worlds were imploding, Jody invited Denise to New York. After a take-out Chinese dinner and a couple of bottles of wine, they spent the night berating their exes and vowing to never fall in love again.

The next morning they awoke with massive hangovers, but the fires of adversity had forged another link in their friendship. Jody had taken the week off, and they spent the time exploring the city. By the time Denise returned to San Antonio, their shattered hearts were a little closer to mending.

Jody would later learn that Denise had returned home to face not only a teenager but also a pile of unpaid bills. Denise's parents were dead. Her mother had died of breast cancer and her father had been killed in car accident less than a year later. Mark proved useless, since he had been more interested in flying off to Cancun or the Bahamas with his new love than he was in helping to finance the cost of raising a daughter. Denise took him to court to get child support, but at that time, child support laws were a joke. All she received for her effort was a bill from the lawyer.

Jody knew nothing of Denise's financial problems until the bank threatened to take the house, and Denise called Jody asking for advice. After almost a half-hour of arguing, Jody convinced Denise to accept a loan from her. Jody paid off the delinquent bills and sent a check monthly until Denise found work in a flower shop. Over the next few years, Denise had repaid the loan with interest.

Stepping out of the shower, Jody toweled off before slipping into the faded denim shorts and deep blue tank top. She looked into the mirror. The tank top accentuated her sapphire eyes. She smiled, knowing the shirt would serve two purposes, since it was also easy to slip off.

As she combed her short, dark hair, she tried not to dwell on the increasing number of gray strands. Instead, she focused her thoughts on Sharon and found herself growing aroused as she anticipated their upcoming evening. Maybe they should talk before they hopped into bed. If she intended to build a relationship with Sharon there would have to be more than carnal knowledge between them. Did she want a relationship with Sharon? Or was sex the only thing between them?

The clock on the fireplace mantel in the living room chimed. Surprised, she glanced at her watch. It was almost nine. Time had gotten away from her. There was no longer time for a nap. She shrugged. It didn't matter. She was too excited to sleep.

As she brushed her teeth, she noticed the faded postcard of the Hollywood sign taped to her mirror. Denise had sent the postcard on her first trip to visit Ellen at UCLA.

Denise had called, devastated that Ellen had accepted a scholarship to UCLA. Her baby girl was leaving home. Jody secretly thought Ellen had made a wise decision. She needed to be away from Denise's constant mothering if she was ever going to grow up.

In an effort to help Denise deal with Ellen's leaving, Jody made the trip back to San Antonio from New York on the pretense of attending Ellen's high-school graduation. As part of Ellen's graduation gift, Denise arranged for the three of them and Ellen's best friend, Allison, to spend a week together at South Padre Island. Allison had gotten ill just before they left and canceled, but Ellen had insisted she still wanted to go. Jody shuddered when she recalled how much Ellen had whined and complained. The week at South Padre Island had gone so badly, Jody had been tempted to kiss the ground when she finally escaped and flew back to New York. A couple of months later, Jody had received the postcard from Denise.

Jody chuckled at the memory as she rinsed her toothbrush and put it away. She pulled the postcard from the mirror and flipped it over. Instead of the usual "Wish you were here," Denise had written: "Be glad you aren't here. The traffic is horrible and the food is worse. I can't find a decent breakfast taco anywhere."

Jody glanced at her old New York address and experienced a moment of wistfulness. For the most part, she had loved New York. There was always something happening. The memories brought back visions of the constant rushing, the job pressures and the seemingly endless crush of people.

"That's why I left," Jody said and replaced the postcard on the mirror.

After returning to New York from the graduation trip to South Padre Island, Jody quickly settled into her normal routine. Over the next three years, she dated several women, always keeping them at a safe distance. Then she met Lauren, and her carefully guarded world fell apart. *More like I blew it up*, she thought ruefully as she went to the living room and rearranged the pillows on the sofa.

She had been dating Lauren for almost six weeks, which, since being dumped by Mia, was a long-term relationship for Jody. She had no interest in prolonging the relationship beyond the lust stage, but Lauren professed she was madly in love with her.

Lauren, who worked in the publishing industry, was struggling financially, and Jody felt sorry for her. She allowed Lauren's persistence to chip away at her reluctance until she finally gave up and let Lauren move in.

Jody immediately realized she had made a mistake. She didn't love Lauren. She wanted to explain to Lauren how she felt but couldn't bring herself to say the words. Besides, Lauren seemed determined to stay.

Jody never consciously made the decision to sabotage the relationship. But less than a month after moving in, Lauren came home early from work one afternoon and found Jody in bed with a colleague.

Jody didn't probe too deeply into why she had cheated on Lauren. The other woman had held no real interest for her. The one episode was all that ever occurred between them.

At about the same time she split with Lauren, the stock market turned sour. Wall Street firms began to trim their budgets by laying off people. Those lucky enough to keep their jobs found themselves left to absorb the workload. Jody's workday increased from ten hours to fourteen. After a year, she had burned out.

Jody quit her job, sublet her apartment, and called Denise with her flight number and arrival time. She returned to San Antonio financially secure but physically and emotionally exhausted.

Denise fixed up her spare bedroom and listened patiently as Jody admitted her guilt over hurting Lauren and her inability to maintain a relationship. Denise never condemned or judged Jody's actions.

Six weeks later, armed with Jody's finances and Denise's knowledge, they became business partners and opened Petal Pushers. Located on Wurzbach, near the medical center, the shop continued to steadily increase its clientele.

Jody bought a house a few blocks from Denise and less than ten minutes from the shop. She quickly found herself back into her routine of getting in and out of relationships.

Now, three years later, Denise was ecstatic that Ellen was transferring back to San Antonio; Jody was in a relationship that had lasted longer than three weeks; and the shop was doing so well that she and Denise were talking about opening a second one.

At last, it looked as though their lives had settled down and everyone was happy.

CHAPTER TWO

Sharon Larson, a tall, vivacious redhead, was six years younger than Jody's forty-four years and worked as a physical therapist. To relieve stress and keep fit, Sharon lifted weights. She tried to get Jody interested in weight-lifting, but Jody's addiction was running. She viewed lifting weights as a form of punishment, but she did appreciate the result it had on Sharon's body.

Sharon could easily lift Jody, which made for some extremely interesting sex.

Jody's doorbell rang promptly at nine. She opened it to find Sharon dressed in shorts and a halter top that left little to the imagination. Sharon came in with a pizza.

Jody barely managed to get the door closed before Sharon dropped the pizza on a side table and pulled her into an urgent embrace.

"It seems like forever since I last saw you," Jody whispered as she ran her hands along the firm muscles in Sharon's back and nuzzled her neck.

"So it's true. Absence does make the heart grow fonder." Sharon's fingertips traced Jody's jaw. "I've not seen you in four long nights. Are you hungry?" she whispered in Jody's ear.

"Famished." Jody caressed Sharon's small, firm breasts. "But what I need can't be found in a pizza box."

The pizza was forgotten as they made their way down the hallway to Jody's bedroom, leaving behind them a trail of clothing.

It was well after midnight and Jody and Sharon sat in the kitchen sharing warmed-up pizza and wine.

"My parents are having a barbecue a week from tomorrow. Would you like to come?" Sharon plucked a slice of pepperoni off her pizza.

Jody's pizza congealed into a queasy clump in her stomach. Meeting the family was always a dangerous sign.

"Next weekend is my weekend to work," she hedged.

"But you're working this weekend. Why don't you and Denise just switch weekends?"

"She probably would, but with Ellen back home they'll be wanting to spend some time together." Jody picked at her pizza. The excuse sounded as lame as it was.

They ate in silence for several seconds.

"You know," Sharon said, "if you don't want to go, all you have to do is say so. You don't need to make excuses."

Guilt nudged Jody's conscience. She liked Sharon, but she had no interest in meeting her family.

"I'm not ready to get that involved," she admitted. "Let's enjoy what we have."

"You mean until someone else comes along," Sharon said, pushing the pizza aside. "Your reputation is well known. As I hear it, your long relationships last about three weeks."

Jody carried her dishes to the sink. The truth in Sharon's accusations burned.

The San Antonio gay community was worse than living in a small town. Everyone knew your business ten minutes before you did. What difference did it make if she chose to date a few different women? Names and faces of past lovers rushed back to her. All right, so maybe there were more than a few. She had dated them all one at a time—at least most of them. Besides, she never pretended to be interested in renting a U-Haul.

Jody ran water into her wineglass. She didn't want to argue. She liked things the way they were. Why complicate the situation?

Sharon was clearing the table. She wore an oversized shirt that provided a full view of her long legs when she leaned over to retrieve a discarded napkin.

Jody's breath caught at the sight. She knelt behind Sharon and began to kiss the backs of her legs. "Let's not fight, all right?" Her hands and lips worked their way up Sharon's legs.

"I know what you're doing," Sharon protested, but her body was already swaying to the rhythm of Jody's hands.

Still on her knees, Jody turned Sharon toward her and kissed her way up to Sharon's stomach.

"Jody, we should talk. We never talk."

"You talk and I'll listen. Right now, I have something much more important to do with my mouth," Jody murmured. She moved her hands between Sharon's legs and pushed them apart. "Talk. I'm listening." She eased her tongue into Sharon's creamy softness.

When Sharon's only response was a moan, Jody knew the argument was over, at least temporarily. With a smile of relief, she lifted Sharon onto the sturdy, oak table and placed Sharon's legs over her shoulders.

As the night wore on, they eventually made their way to the living room sofa, where they collapsed.

Jody felt as though she had barely closed her eyes when the phone rang. She leaned over Sharon and stretched to reach the handset that was lying on the floor beside the sofa. "Hello."

"I'm glad someone had a night worth remembering," Eric said.

Jody tried to extract herself from the tangle of arms, legs and blanket. "What's up, Eric? It's too early for jokes."

"Oh, honey. It's nine-fifteen. I'm only calling because the cash drawer isn't ready. Should I take money from yesterday's drawer to set up the register, or was there a problem?"

Jody glanced at the clock on the fireplace mantel and groaned. "I'm so sorry, Eric. I forgot to set the alarm. You can set the drawer up. I'll be there in thirty minutes and will balance yesterday's receipts when I get there," she promised as she tossed the handset aside and ran to shower. Jody was too embarrassed to tell Eric she hadn't heard her alarm because she had been sleeping in the living room.

Ten minutes later, she struggled with the last button on her shirt before she grabbed her backpack and headed for the door.

"Hey," Sharon called, her voice thick with sleep.

Jody froze, anticipating a continuation of their earlier conversation.

"Aren't you even going to kiss me good-bye?"

Relieved, Jody ran back and gave her a chaste peck on the cheek.

"That doesn't count," Sharon grumbled.

Jody smiled and shook her head. "Oh, no, you don't. I'm already late enough." She headed for the door to the garage. "Stay as long as you like."

Sharon slid naked from beneath the blanket and came toward her.

"You are beautiful," Jody moaned and silently cursed Ellen for choosing this weekend to come home. "Can you stay? I'll be back around seven tonight."

Sharon shook her head. "I have errands to run." She laughed and said, "You should see the look of disappointment on your face. Don't look so sad. I can stop back by, say, around eight-thirty."

With that promise, Jody raced off. Luckily, she only lived ten minutes from the shop, and with the light early-morning traffic, she made it in six.

Eric was taking displays from the cooler when Jody arrived. As soon as she came in, he started teasing her.

"Look at that smile you're wearing. Somebody had a good night."

"Hush," she scolded, but he was being so silly she had to laugh.

The flower shop was open from nine to six on weekdays and nine to two on weekends. Jody prided herself in never being late in opening the shop. She stashed her backpack behind the counter and started helping him with the displays.

"I'm sorry you had to open by yourself this morning," she said. "I meant to get here early and have the register ready. If I go across the street and buy you a cappuccino, will you forgive me?" She tried to look contrite.

"Perhaps I will, if you include a croissant with that bribe."

"Ouch. Playing hardball this morning." The phone rang as Jody pulled her wallet from her backpack.

"Don't forget you're dealing with an ex-Marine." Eric squared his shoulders, drew his short, stocky frame to attention, and executed a perfect about-face before marching to the phone. "Petal Pushers," he announced in a falsetto.

Jody burst into laughter. "*Semper fi*," she said as she left to get the coffee.

Across the street in the coffee shop, the mouth-watering aroma of fresh coffee enveloped her, making her feel warm and welcome. It was too bad she and Denise couldn't find an aroma to fill Petal Pushers with. The smell of fresh flowers was nice, but there were occasions when the combined fragrances of the flowers could be overwhelming.

She thought about Eric as she stood in line to place her order. He had worked part-time for them for almost two years. He was studying for an engineering degree. Why he had chosen to apply for the position at Petal Pushers baffled Jody at first, but she soon discovered that he truly loved meeting the customers and working with the flowers.

Looking at Eric, with his bristly crew cut and sometimes stoic features, most people would never suspect he was gay. Only after he felt safe with someone did he allow the flaming campiness to show.

He was an honest, hard worker who was always on time. He often stayed late on Sunday evening without complaining, even though he had to be in class Monday morning. He would be missed when he graduated in the fall. She wondered how they would ever find someone as efficient as he was to take his place.

CHAPTER THREE

Monday morning arrived much too quickly. Sharon had stayed over both Saturday and Sunday night. She left at sunrise, after they had spent almost the entire night making love.

Jody pulled on her last pair of clean socks. It was great having Sharon spend the weekend, but unfortunately there was very little time for housekeeping.

She looked around and cringed. The entire house screamed of sex. Clothes discarded in the heat of passion made a pathway from the living room to the bedroom. A jumble of pillows and rumpled sheets lay in front of the fireplace, where she and Sharon had spent several hours the previous night. Dirty dishes filled the kitchen sink.

Disgusted with the mess, Jody started to put things away but stopped. If she took time to clean, she wouldn't have time for her run.

"Tonight," she promised herself as she playfully pulled a pair of Sharon's bikini underwear over the head of a large ceramic cat that sat next to the fireplace.

She moved through her routine warmup exercises and stretches before beginning her run. Jody preferred to run early before the morning commuters filled the air with car fumes and blaring horns. She loved her quiet northwest side neighborhood, with its tree-lined streets named for Hollywood stars—Dean Martin, Gomer Pyle, Cary Grant. Most of the houses had been built in the seventies and lacked the architectural grace of many of the older neighborhoods. The homeowners compensated for this deficit with meticulous landscaping.

As she ran, she made a mental list of everything she would have to do today after work: wash dishes, clean the house, do the laundry and shop for groceries.

"Ugh! There should be a law against Mondays," she said aloud.

As her feet found their natural rhythm, her thoughts slipped back to Sharon. She had never known anyone who could get her aroused so quickly. Just thinking about her caused a delicious tension to start building between her legs. Reluctantly, she pushed the thoughts away. She couldn't go to work feeling this way. To create a distraction, she returned to her mental list-making.

Several minutes later, as she turned the corner of Charlie Chan Drive, she noticed a car pull away from the stop sign. The red Corvette with tinted windows drove slowly behind her. Jody picked up her pace. For the next block, the car stayed behind her. She felt a knot of fear begin in the pit of her stomach, and her side was beginning to hurt. She couldn't maintain this pace much longer. She whirled to face the car, and to her relief it continued its slow journey past her and on down the street. The windows were too dark for her to see the driver. As the car disappeared around the corner, she took several deep breaths until her breathing slowly returned to normal. She shook off the fear the car had caused and walked the rest of the way home.

When Jody arrived at Petal Pushers with ten minutes to spare before the store opened, Denise was already busy working on a large arrangement of gladiolas.

"How was your weekend?" Jody called, knowing Denise would spend every available moment today telling her about Ellen.

"Good."

Surprised by Denise's lack of enthusiasm, Jody turned to stare. "Did Ellen make it in all right?"

"Yeah, no problems."

Jody hesitated. Obviously something had happened, but Denise wasn't ready to discuss it. To give her time, Jody went to make coffee. While the coffee perked, she polished the counter and cooler doors and made some minor adjustments to the window displays.

She poured the coffee and took a cup to Denise. As she set the cup down, Denise turned away from Jody and began to work on a different arrangement.

"So, Ellen got settled in?" Jody waited for a response, but Denise only nodded without looking up from her work. "Denise, is Ellen all right?"

"Everything is fine!" She plunged a red carnation into the arrangement so harshly the stem snapped. "Damn." She flung the broken flower to the floor.

Something was wrong. Denise rarely got upset. Jody placed her hand on Denise's shoulder to calm her.

Denise jumped away, knocking the arrangement to the floor. The clear crystal vase shattered into hundreds of sparkling fragments, and Denise began to sob.

Jody put her coffee down and gently placed an arm around Denise.

"Oh, Jody. I'm so confused. I don't know what to do."

Jody led her to the chair behind the desk and pushed her into it. "What's wrong?"

Denise turned to face her. Jody was shocked to see Denise's eyes were puffy from an obviously long bout of crying. As Denise started to speak, the bell on the front door chimed.

Jody glanced toward the showroom and patted Denise's arm. "I'll be right back. Will you be okay?"

Denise nodded.

Reluctantly, Jody left to help the customer. A steady stream of customers and phone calls kept her busy for almost forty minutes. After the last customer left, she glanced at her watch. She and Eric had worked late the previous day to complete the arrangements for the long list of today's deliveries. She would need to leave soon. She hurried back to the workroom.

The broken vase had been swept up, and Denise was fussing over a long line of bud vases. The shop had a contract with a local restaurant to supply it with small, simple arrangements. The vases would be added to Jody's deliveries.

Jody grabbed a handful of carnations and began placing them in the vases. "Denise, I have a few minutes. Let's talk." The phone rang to prove her wrong. "Blast it! Why does that always happen?" She dropped in the last carnation and went to answer the phone. "I'll only be a minute."

Jody got off the phone to find Denise loading the boxes filled with the restaurant's arrangements into the delivery van. A glance into the van showed the thirty or so arrangements that would need to be taken to the local hospitals and a few individual deliveries that were scattered around the city. The shop's free delivery policy brought in additional orders, but they were often several miles away. The additional orders more than paid for the inconvenience and minor cost of delivery.

"Let's try this again," Jody said as she placed an arm around Denise's shoulders.

Denise sighed deeply. "Jody, I need to talk to you. Are you free for dinner?"

Jody briefly thought of the list of things she needed to do, then pushed it aside. "Sure," she said. "Where would you like to go?"

"We can decide later. It's getting late, and I know you need to get started on these deliveries."

"Can you wait that long?"

Denise smiled slightly and nodded.

Jody gave her a quick hug and hopped into the van.

Jody's day proceeded from bad to worse. Halfway through the deliveries, the front passenger-side tire on the van went flat. Jody managed to change the tire but got filthy in the process. After stopping at a gas station to wash up as best she could, she continued the deliveries. She was on her next-to-the-last stop when a small terrier burst from behind a hedgerow and grabbed her pant leg. Before the owner could call him back, he had managed to tear a large patch from her khakis. To top off her day, the van's air conditioner stopped working.

Exhausted and disgusted, she drove across town to the dealership to get a new tire and have the air conditioner, still under warranty, repaired. The service manager assured her the air conditioner was probably nothing more than a fuse. So Jody waited rather than have to make the trip back for the van later.

The problem turned out to be more than a fuse. A hose had cracked and allowed the coolant to leak out, and of course, to reach the cracked hose, a large number of other items had to be removed. It was almost five before Jody made it back to the shop. She entered Petal Pushers to find Eric dusting the display case.

"Why are you here?" Jody asked, surprised.

"Well, I'm glad to see you, too," Eric replied and arched an eyebrow in surprise as he took in Jody's dirty and torn clothes. "Rough day at the office?" he asked and nodded toward Jody's pants.

"Try total shit. Where's Denise?"

"She called me right after lunch and asked if I could work today. I only have one class on Mondays," he reminded her. "Denise said she wasn't feeling well. She looked like she'd been crying. Is everything all right?"

"I don't know. We never got a chance to talk." Jody gave a silent prayer of thanks that she wouldn't have to have dinner with Denise tonight and instantly regretted her callous attitude. Denise wasn't a whiner. It took a lot to make her cry.

I'll call her later, Jody decided as she flipped through the day's receipts.

Eric finished dusting the shelf. "Oh, yeah. Denise said to tell you she would be waiting for you at your place."

Jody experienced a horrifying flashback of the condition of her house and groaned. She slid down the wall and sat heavily on the floor. She and Denise kept keys to each other's houses, and at any other time Jody wouldn't have minded Denise being there. *Oh, well*, she thought, *it's too late to worry about that now*.

Eric placed a hand on her head. "Honey, are you all right?"

"It's Monday," she said, exhausted. "I'm going home. Close for me, and leave the receipts in the safe. Denise or I will take care of it tomorrow."

Jody pulled her backpack from behind the counter and wondered when things had started getting out of hand. It seemed like recently she was always rushing to catch up.

23

CHAPTER FOUR

Denise's white Ford Taurus was parked on the street in front of Jody's house.

Jody eased into her driveway. As she waited for the garage door to open, she puzzled over what could have happened to upset Denise. It was odd she hadn't gone home, since she only lived a few blocks away. Could she and Ellen already be having problems? Jody doubted it, since they seemed to get along well.

"Only one way to find out for sure," she said as she drove into the garage.

Jody walked through her kitchen door and into a very different house from the one she had left that morning. The scattered clothes, stacks of pillows and rumpled sheets were no longer in sight. The dishes were washed and put away. She looked into the living room and saw Denise lying on the couch.

At the sound of the door, Denise sat up and looked at her strangely.

Jody felt like a ten-year-old who had been caught with a dirty room after having been told to clean it.

"Sorry about the mess," she said, shrugging. "Sharon spent the weekend and we, ah . . . I mean, I never got around to . . ." She trailed off as Denise continued to stare at her. Embarrassed, Jody tried again. "I know the house was a mess, but you didn't have to clean." Exhausted, she set her backpack down and fell into her favorite chair, a deep, overstuffed rocker-recliner.

Denise jumped up and went into the kitchen. "I've made a pot of coffee if you'd like a cup."

Reluctantly, Jody pulled herself from the chair and followed. "Denise, I really wish you would talk to me. I know something's wrong. Is it Ellen?"

Denise sat down at the table with their coffee. "She's a lesbian."

Dumbfounded, Jody stared at her. After several seconds, she cleared her throat and said, "Well, it's not like you don't know any."

"Jody, she's my daughter."

Jody frowned. "Are you saying it's all right for your best friend to be a lesbian, but not your daughter?"

"I don't know what I'm saying." Denise's voice sounded flat and lifeless.

Jody sat in the chair beside her. "Tell me what happened."

"We had a terrible fight. Ellen left. She stayed in a hotel Saturday night. I finally convinced her to come home yesterday, but everything is so awkward. I don't know what to say or do. I'm just so damn angry!" Tears rolled down her face.

"I'm sure it was a shock, but Denise, you've always been supportive of me. What's different with Ellen?"

"She's my baby."

"She's twenty-five. She's not a baby anymore."

"She'll always be my baby."

"Not if you want to keep her. You have to let her grow up and find her own life," Jody said softly.

"Why did she have to hide it from me all these years?" Denise dabbed at her nose with an already damp tissue that she'd pulled from her pants pocket.

"Maybe she just discovered it herself."

Denise shook her head. "She says she has known since high school. How could she have possibly known what she wanted in high school?"

"You knew you wanted to marry Mark," Jody reminded her.

"And look how that turned out. Why didn't she tell me?"

"She was probably afraid of your reaction. It could be the reason she stayed in Los Angeles."

Denise looked at her frowning. "What do you mean? You just said I've been supportive of you. Why would she think I wouldn't support her?"

"Because you're very possessive of her."

Denise started to protest, but Jody held up her hand.

"Don't start in on me, Denise. I'm only telling you the truth. Look at what you're doing now that she has told you. This is probably the very thing she was trying to avoid."

Denise sat quietly for several seconds. "I suppose I do tend to cling to her."

Jody grabbed her own throat and pretended to choke herself.

Denise swatted her arm. "I'm not that bad."

"You're no more clinging than ivy on an English cottage."

Denise eyed Jody's soiled clothes and frowned. "What happened to you? You're filthy."

Jody held up her leg to display her torn pants. "It's that strange effect I have on women."

Denise toyed with her coffee cup. "You know, even with all those women I've known you dated, I never . . ." She let the sentence hang.

"Never what?" Jody prompted, sitting forward.

Obviously embarrassed, Denise looked out the window into Jody's large backyard. "I never thought of your being . . ." She shrugged. "You know, sexual."

Jody stared at her in amazement. "What did you think happened while I was dating 'all those women'?"

"I don't know," she answered. "I guess, I didn't think. Period."

They sat quietly. Jody wasn't comfortable with the turn of the conversation. She wanted to get the topic back to something other than her own life. Before she could think of another topic, Denise started to talk about Ellen again.

"Jody, I don't know what to say to her. I don't have much experience with this sort of thing."

"Gay men and lesbians are no different from you." Jody sipped her coffee. "We want to be accepted for who we are. We want to find someone to love and live happily ever after, just like everyone else in the world. You shouldn't need a lot of experience to understand that."

"Hell, Jody, I don't have much experience at all. I never really dated anyone except Mark. That was high school. I married him a year after I met him. Since the divorce, you know I've avoided becoming involved with anyone."

"That's true," Jody admitted. "Why haven't you ever dated?" she asked, realizing she'd never given the matter much thought.

"Why haven't you settled down?" Denise shot back, avoiding the question. "You're the queen of short-term relationships."

Jody thought about it for a moment. "Maybe we've both been dumped one time too many."

"One time was all it took for me," Denise said, clearly lost in a painful memory.

Jody leaned back in her chair. "Aren't we a pathetic pair?"

Denise laughed. "Sweetie, I knew you would make me feel better." She patted Jody's hand. "I'm just being silly. I guess I really don't care if she's a lesbian, as long as she's happy." She sipped her coffee. "I do worry about her, though. She seems so unhappy. I think she may have moved to get away from someone."

Jody stretched her aching muscles. She wanted nothing more than a long, hot bath and eight hours of uninterrupted sleep. Ellen's love life would take care of itself. "She'll be fine."

"Maybe you could show her around. Introduce her to some people," Denise said. "She's already started working, and she seems to put in a lot of extra hours. I don't want her to be a workaholic. She's young. She should be going out and having fun."

Jody sat upright. "Oh, no, you don't. I'm not about to get involved in Ellen's love life. She's a grown woman. She's perfectly capable of meeting people on her own."

"I'm not asking you to find her dates," Denise said. "Just introduce her to people. She doesn't know anyone here anymore. Can't you at least do that? For me. Please. It would make me feel so much better. I know you could introduce her to some nice women."

"Denise, if she's just broken up with someone, she's not going to be ready to start dating."

"She needs friends, and she's not going to meet them hanging around with me. You can introduce her to other lesbians."

"What are you going to do if she meets someone and gets serious about her?" Jody asked.

Denise sat for a moment before giving a slight nod. "I want her to be happy. I'll be able to handle it."

Jody had her doubts but didn't feel like arguing. It was always easier to give in to Denise than to try to wear her down. "All right, I'll introduce her to a few people, but only if she agrees. If she decides she doesn't want me messing around in her life, then you have to leave us both alone."

"Agreed." Denise smiled. "Now, I have to get home. Come for dinner Friday night, sweetie. Ellen hasn't stopped talking about you since she came home."

Jody rolled her eyes at Denise's exaggeration. She hadn't seen Ellen in eight years; she doubted if Ellen ever thought of her. "Sounds great. I'll bring the wine."

"Good. I'll make my lasagna." Denise stood and gave Jody a long hug. "Thanks for listening."

"Anytime." Jody followed her back into the living room where Denise picked up her purse.

"Oh, by the way, I love your artistic touches," Denise said and motioned to the underwear pulled over the head of the ceramic cat. Denise studied the arrangement as she headed toward the door. "The titles of artistic works have always fascinated me. I would entitle that one, *Pussy in Panties*." Denise laughed.

CHAPTER FIVE

On Friday night, Jody arrived home and checked her phone messages. Two of the three calls were from Sharon. She had told Sharon she had dinner plans tonight and wouldn't be able to see her, but Sharon was still trying to arrange for them to get together over the weekend.

Jody considered inviting Sharon to go with her to Denise's but knew they would end up back at her place, and another weekend would pass without the household chores being done. Besides, Sharon was still pushing her family's barbecue, and Jody's plea of having to work was growing thin. She would never tell Sharon that Denise had volunteered to work this weekend, but Jody had insisted on getting back to their regular schedule.

Another argument over the barbecue had almost erupted over dinner on Wednesday night, but again they avoided the issue by making love. Jody knew Sharon was still upset, so it was best to make herself scarce until after the event was over and everything returned to normal.

Jody changed into a pair of shorts and a light sleeveless blouse. Denise's dinners were always casual, and besides, Ellen was practically family. She grabbed two bottles of red wine from her tiny wine rack in the kitchen, tucked them into her backpack and rushed out.

The warmer than usual weather that had plagued the city the previous week had given way to normal mild spring temperatures. Jody decided to walk the few blocks to Denise's house; it would give her time to think about Sharon and where the relationship was headed.

Instead of thinking about Sharon, Jody found herself enjoying the heady scent of mountain laurel and freshly mowed grass. Birds and squirrels played overhead in the ash trees lining the sidewalks. Before she knew it, the pleasant walk had come to an end, and she was ringing Denise's doorbell.

Denise opened the door, accompanied by the spicy-rich smell of lasagna. She gave Jody a quick hug. "Perfect timing. I was just about to take the lasagna out. Come on into the kitchen."

"Smells great in here." Jody removed the wine from her backpack and followed Denise into the kitchen. "Where's Ellen?"

"She just got out of the shower. She had to work late."

"Already? She's only been here a week." Jody put the wine on the counter, then snagged a carrot stick from a tray and munched on it. "What's she doing?"

"Something to do with training seminars," Denise said as she removed the lasagna from the oven and slid in the garlic bread.

"I train corporate managers on how to manipulate their employees into working harder," Ellen called from the doorway.

Jody turned to the gangly young girl she remembered and stared in shock. Ellen was no longer a girl and she certainly wouldn't be described as gangly. Denise's yearly vacation photos had certainly not done Ellen justice. Of course, Denise was the world's worst photographer. She was the only person Jody had ever known who couldn't operate a simple point-and-shoot camera.

31

Dressed in white shorts and a dark green sleeveless top, and with her short brunette hair combed neatly back from her face, Ellen looked nothing like the brat Jody remembered.

Jody felt her heart skip a beat as Ellen strolled toward her. It was with some difficulty that she managed to tear her gaze from Ellen's long, slim legs. When she did she found pale blue eyes framed by long, dark lashes intently studying her.

"It's good to see you again, Jody." Ellen hugged her.

Jody floated in the enticing fragrance of Ellen's scent. Her breath caught as Ellen's full breasts pressed against her. The hug continued a fraction too long, and Jody pulled away.

What the hell is wrong with me? she wondered as she blurted out a too-casual "Good to see you."

"Jody, would you open the wine, please," Denise said as she pulled the bread from the oven. "We're ready to eat."

Jody drank three glasses of wine and barely touched her food. She couldn't stop staring at Ellen. There was a tiny scar at the corner of her full bottom lip that begged to be kissed. The scar was the result of Ellen's falling on one of her toys and busting her lip when she was three or four. Jody had been there when it happened. She had been on vacation, and she and Denise had been sitting in the kitchen catching up when Ellen toppled over onto the toy. Jody pushed the memory away.

This is sick, she chided herself. *This is Ellen. She's practically family.* Never in her wildest dreams had Jody anticipated being attracted to Denise's daughter. *And that is precisely who she is*, Jody reminded herself as she took a long sip of wine.

She tried to participate in the conversation, but afterward she couldn't remember a single thing they had discussed. All she could remember was Ellen.

After the meal, Jody jumped up. "I'll do the dishes." She needed time alone to sort through her feelings, but Denise refused her offer.

"No, I have plenty of time," Denise said. "Why don't you go show Ellen how much the city has changed since she left?"

32

Jody panicked. She didn't want to spend time alone with Ellen. "She doesn't want to run around San Antonio with an old thing like me," she protested, while a part of her was hoping Ellen would.

"Sure I would," Ellen chimed in. "Unless it's your bedtime," she teased with a smile and a wink that made Jody's heart pound.

Denise laughed, but for some reason Jody was having trouble finding anything funny in the comment.

I'm being a fool, she told herself. *What I should do is leave and call Sharon right now. I won't even call. I'll go home, get the Jeep and drive directly to Sharon's. We can spend the rest of the night in bed. Ten minutes with Sharon and I'll forget all about Ellen.*

But Denise wasn't making it easy. "It's a beautiful night for a drive."

"I have to get up early and work tomorrow," Jody said.

"No, you don't. I'm working this weekend. I need to start placing the Mother's Day orders. We can get back to your precious schedule after the holiday," Denise insisted.

Jody struggled to find another excuse.

"Now, go on." Denise pushed them toward the door.

"Let me help with the dishes and you go with us," Jody pleaded.

"No, I rented a movie. I want to relax and watch it. You two go on. I'll see you later."

"I'm too drunk to drive," Jody said, and in truth she was feeling the wine. Then she remembered. "I walked over!"

"I'll drive." Ellen picked up her keys from a stand by the doorway leading to the garage. "I need to learn my way around the city again anyway. So much has changed since I left." She took Jody by the arm.

Short of chaining herself to the table, Jody saw no alternative but to follow.

When she and Ellen stepped into the garage, Jody gasped. There sat the red Corvette with the deeply tinted windows, the one that had been following her earlier in the week.

Ellen gazed at her over the car. "I hope I didn't frighten you the other day."

Confused, Jody scrambled into the car, bumping both her knee and head in the process.

"Why were you driving so slowly behind me?" she asked as Ellen got into the car. Jody fumbled with her seat belt; for some reason it refused to snap.

"I liked the view," she said softly.

Startled by the bold statement, Jody forgot about the seat belt. It slipped from her hand and slid back around her shoulder. She could think of nothing to say.

Ellen reached for Jody's seat belt, which grazed Jody's breast as Ellen deftly pulled it over and fastened it. She gave Jody's hand a quick squeeze.

Jody told herself to ignore the warm, silky texture of Ellen's hand and the wave of desire washing over her. She focused her attention out the car window as Ellen backed smoothly out of the garage.

Jody struggled to find some safe topic for discussion, but it seemed that everything that came to mind was a potential land mine.

As they drove through Leon Valley and headed toward downtown, Ellen began to reminisce about various places they drove past. She pointed out Bandera Lanes, where she and Denise had bowled on a mother-and-daughter league; the Walgreen where she had worked for two summers before leaving for college.

Ellen pointed toward a side street. "My first girlfriend, Stacy, lived down that street. We were in her room one Saturday afternoon. Her folks were supposed to have been working at some charity thing, but her mom got sick and they came home early. They were already in the hallway before we heard them. There wasn't time to get dressed. I flew out of bed and hid in the closet. I had just barely closed the door when her dad knocked on Stacy's door to check on her. To make a long story short I had to leave by way of the bedroom window. We were so young." Ellen laughed at her memories.

Jody began to relax. "Why did you wait so long to tell your mom you're gay?"

Ellen looked over at her. "Get real. You heard how she reacted when I finally did tell her. I mean, I had to check into a hotel. You can imagine what she would have done if I'd told her when I was sixteen."

Jody chuckled. "Point taken."

"Mom would have totally wigged out and locked me in my room until I was twenty-one. She almost did anyway."

Jody felt the need to defend Denise. "She did what she thought was best for you. She didn't want to see you hurt."

Ellen nodded. "I know, but sometimes it gets to be too much. It's time she realized I'm not a baby anymore."

Jody looked at her. She certainly didn't look like a baby. She forced her improper thoughts away and said, "You will always be her baby."

Ellen finally pulled onto the freeway that would take them downtown. "Tell me about the local gay and lesbian community."

Jody shrugged. "I'm sure it won't be anything like Los Angeles. The military's still here, so a large portion of the community is closeted. But we have a few active organizations and groups like the First Wednesday."

"What's that?" Ellen interrupted.

"It's a group of women who get together for dinner at various restaurants on the first Wednesday of each month. It's a good place to meet women, without having to hit the bars."

"Sounds like a pickup party."

"No. It's nothing like that at all." Jody tried to clarify. "Most of the women are professionals who don't want to go to the bars for one reason or another. The group is a way to meet women with similar interests, like biking, poker, or even going to the movies."

"Do you go to the dinners?"

"Yeah, I make it occasionally."

Ellen looked at her. "Maybe you and I could go next month."

Jody bit her lip. This would be the perfect moment to mention Sharon, but before she could, Ellen changed the subject.

"What else goes on?"

Jody told her about a few of the events that were coming up. "You might want to subscribe to *WomanSpace*. It's a monthly community paper and has a listing of events and organizations."

Ellen turned the conversation back to the First Wednesday group.

Somewhere during the exchange, Jody found herself agreeing to take her to the next dinner. She thought about Sharon. Maybe the three of them could go together.

They parked the car in a downtown garage and slowly strolled along the River Walk. Since it was early in the season, there weren't a lot of tourists yet. As they passed the numerous restaurants decorated with brightly colored lights, a smorgasbord of jazz, salsa, country and rock greeted them. They stopped at an outdoor café with pastel-hued wrought-iron tables and chairs. They asked the handsome young waiter for a table by the river and ordered frozen margaritas with salt. They waved at the people on several dinner barges gliding by. Across the river, mariachis were performing an energetic rendition of "La Bamba." Their waiter returned with their drinks, before rushing off to serve a table of older men wearing American Legion caps.

They sipped their drinks in silence and listened to the mariachis perform a slow, hauntingly beautiful song.

"Has Mom designated you as my official matchmaker?" Ellen asked as the song came to an end.

Embarrassed, Jody hesitated a second too long.

"I thought so," Ellen said with a sigh. "I relieve you of all responsibility." She sipped her margarita.

"She's worried about you. It's only natural, I suppose."

"*What* is she worried about?"

Jody sipped her drink to stall. Should she mention what Denise had told her? She finally decided Denise wouldn't mind. "She thinks you may have moved back here to mend a broken heart or perhaps to escape a love gone wrong."

Ellen laughed softly. Her laughter was deep and throaty and Jody found herself wishing Ellen would laugh more often.

"Mom is something else. I could never get anything by her."

Except the fact that you're a lesbian, Jody was tempted to add. She said instead, "So it's true?" She tried to ignore the bitter stab of unexpected jealousy that shot through her.

Just then the waiter reappeared. "Another margarita, ladies?"

Jody nodded.

As he walked away, Ellen leaned forward and crossed her arms on the table. "It's not exactly a broken heart. I moved back for a lot of reasons. I missed Mom. I missed San Antonio. The transfer here puts me in line for a great career opportunity, and I used the move as a way to end a two-year relationship that should never have happened."

"Why do you say that?"

Ellen shrugged and turned her attention to the jazz ensemble performing at the café next door.

The waiter arrived with their margaritas, gathered their empty glasses and glided away.

Just when Jody had decided Ellen wasn't going to tell her about her relationship, she began to speak.

"Beth works for one of the firms I went out to evaluate. I broke my one cardinal rule and we started dating. We became lovers." She hesitated. "Beth is very needy. At first, I found it rather flattering, but it got old fast. I broke off the relationship after a few weeks, but she kept coming around. Eventually her persistence wore me down. I was renting an efficiency apartment at the time, and she owned her own home, so I moved in with her. I tried to make it work. I asked her to get help, but she refused. She insisted I was the problem. She said I was cold and uncaring. I finally realized that no matter what I did, it would never be enough. When a job opened up in San Antonio, I snatched it and ran." She hung her head. "I'm such a coward. I waited until I had already accepted the position and it was too late to back out before I told her."

They sat in comfortable silence for several minutes, sipping their margaritas and listening to the jazz ensemble perform a toe-tapping "Sweet Georgia Brown."

"You probably think I'm a real louse," Ellen said after the song ended.

Jody studied her margarita glass and shrugged. "We do what we have to. Have you heard from Beth since you got here?"

"She calls on the cell at least a half-dozen times a day. I refused to give her the home number. Although a couple of rounds with Mom might send her fleeing."

They both laughed.

"Enough about me. I want to hear about you," Ellen said, gazing at her.

"Nothing much to tell."

The waiter approached and saved her from having to make further denials. "Ladies, I'm sorry, but we're closing." He gave Ellen a brilliant smile as he handed Jody the check.

"We'll return to this conversation," Ellen warned as they each placed money on the table.

"I'll take heed of the warning," Jody teased back. She considered asking Ellen if she wanted to spend more time on the River Walk, but she was already tired and the alcohol was making her sleepy. She'd be mortified if she were to doze off during a lull in the conversation. They headed for the car.

Jody settled into the passenger seat and looked out at the city she loved. She couldn't remember the last time she had laughed and talked so much. They drove toward Denise's house.

"You live near Mom, don't you?"

Soothed by the alcohol, Jody replied, "Yes, I live on Charlie Chan Drive. It's only a couple of blocks away from you."

"I'd like to see your house."

"Now?" Jody asked, surprised.

"Sure, why not?"

Jody hesitated. Common sense told her to send Ellen home, but the alcohol had mellowed her and her hormones were finally under control, so why not?

"Okay." She settled back and enjoyed the ride in silence.

Ellen parked in Jody's driveway, and they went up the walk. It seemed strange to Jody to enter her house through the front door, since she always used the door in the garage. Jody could smell Ellen's perfume as she unlocked the door. Maybe this wasn't such a good idea, she thought as she fumbled with the key.

Once inside, Ellen studied the room and nodded. "It's you. I love the fireplace and what you've done with the colors."

Jody looked around, pleased. She had spent months looking for just the right shades of color and the perfect furniture.

"I wouldn't have thought it possible to blend these shades of gray, blue and peach so well." Ellen sat on the sofa, kicked her shoes off and tucked her feet beneath her. "Sit by me," she said and patted the sofa beside her.

Jody sat down but kept to the far end of the sofa.

"I've been talking about myself all night. Tell me about you. What makes Jody Scott tick?"

Jody hesitated. She never liked to talk about herself. She decided she would tell a few anecdotes of her New York years, and then she would tell Ellen about Sharon. But to her surprise, she found herself telling Ellen about Mia and Lauren. She tactfully omitted the part about her infidelity to Lauren, and somehow she never got around to mentioning Sharon.

"I have a confession," Ellen said as she slid closer and took Jody's hand.

"What?" Jody's voice broke. She wished Ellen would let go of her hand, but somehow she didn't have the strength to remove it. She cursed her decision to have the second margarita.

"I had a terrible crush on you when I was in high school."

Jody stared at her in amazement. "I hardly ever saw you."

Ellen shrugged. "Actually," she said as she leaned toward Jody, "I never got over it." Her lips brushed Jody's.

Jody held her breath and told herself to get up and send Ellen home. Everything in her screamed that she should not be kissing Denise's daughter, but then Ellen's tongue slowly parted her lips.

Jody's mind and body were not working as one. She tried to pull away, but Ellen pushed her back onto the sofa.

"Ellen," Jody finally managed to murmur as Ellen kissed her neck and throat. "We shouldn't be doing this."

"Why?" Ellen asked as she boldly unbuttoned Jody's shirt and captured a firm nipple between her lips.

"I'm old enough to be your mother," she moaned. "Actually, I'm two months older than your mother."

Ellen's hand slipped inside Jody's shorts and stroked her. "This doesn't feel like you want me to stop." She pushed a finger deep inside and slowly removed it.

Despite Jody's best efforts, her body rose up to meet Ellen's hand.

Ellen removed Jody's shorts and dropped them to the floor. "If you really want me to stop, just say so and I will." Ellen's voice grew huskier. Clearly, she was aroused. Her lips traveled across Jody's stomach and continued downward until she leisurely ran her tongue through Jody's wetness. "Do you want me to stop doing this?" she asked as she deftly pushed her tongue into Jody.

Jody lost all control. She wanted to stop Ellen and send her home, but at the same time, she wanted to feel her own tongue plunging into Ellen.

"Tell me what you want me to do," Ellen said as she pulled Jody's clitoris into her mouth and began to suck greedily.

Jody found herself gathering Ellen's soft hair in her hands and yelling, "Harder," before Ellen's fingers slammed back into her. As her body exploded with sensation, Jody was only vaguely aware of her own voice screaming Ellen's name.

Afterward, Ellen moved up to snuggle against her.

"What have I done?" Jody moaned as she covered her eyes with her arms.

"You've made me very happy," Ellen answered as she placed an arm protectively across her.

Jody dropped her arm from her face and was shaken by the look of adoration flowing from Ellen's eyes. Never had she felt such a multitude of emotions wash over her. She felt strong, yet weak, and both protected and protective.

"I know this is wrong." Her hand trembled as she brushed a lock of hair from Ellen's face. "I want to make love to you." *God help me in the morning*, she thought as she pulled Ellen against her.

The sun was tinting the eastern sky pink before they finally fell into an exhausted sleep.

CHAPTER SIX

The phone's ringing pulled Jody from slumber. She extracted herself from the tangle of limbs and stumbled off the sofa to the phone.

"Hello," she croaked, her voice heavy with sleep.

"Ellen didn't come home last night and I'm concerned. Is she with you?" Denise asked.

Jody rubbed her eyes and was greeted by the heady, musky scent of Sharon on her hand. Still trying to shake the cobwebs of sleep from her head, she glanced toward the sofa and came sharply awake as she gazed at the brunette hair showing from under the blanket that she had pulled over them sometime during the night.

That's not Sharon's head and it's not Sharon's smell on my hands. It's Ellen, Jody thought as she grabbed the chair for support.

"Jody. Jody, are you there?" Denise asked.

"Y-Yeah," she stuttered. "I was asleep. What did you say?" She glanced at the clock. It was a little after eight.

"I'm worried about Ellen. When I went out to go to work, her car wasn't in the garage. Is she with you?"

"Yeah." Jody's mind scurried for excuses. How was she going to explain this to Denise? *I'm not*, she decided cowardly. *I'm going to lie.* "She had a couple of margaritas, and I was worried about her driving home. Since it was so late, she stayed here. She slept on the sofa," she added quickly. At least that much was true.

"Oh, I'm so glad. If she's with you, I know she's safe."

Jody cringed.

"I was just concerned. People are so crazy these days. You never know what they're going to do." Denise launched into a long diatribe on crime. Jody missed most of it because Ellen had poked her head from under the blanket. The smile she flashed practically stopped Jody's heart.

Ellen crawled from beneath the blanket and walked naked toward her. Jody couldn't take her eyes off her.

Sharon had small breasts and hard muscles; Ellen was long-limbed, with full breasts and soft, rounded contours. To her mortification, she realized she was comparing her girlfriends as she would fresh fruit at the supermarket.

Ellen's smile changed from one of sweet innocence to one that practically shouted, "Here I am. Come and take me."

Jody dropped the phone. As she scrambled to pick it up, she heard Denise demanding to know what had happened.

"I fell asleep listening to you complain," Jody lied. Ellen was behind her running the tip of her tongue across her shoulders. Denise was still talking. Jody tried to ignore the effect Ellen's tongue was having on her, while she struggled to think of a way to get Denise to hang up. Ellen stepped in front of her and slowly ran her tongue down Jody's stomach.

"I made a breakfast casserole. Why don't you and Ellen come over for breakfast? I have to leave in a few minutes, but I hate to see it go to waste," Denise said as Ellen's hands pushed Jody's legs apart.

"Can't. I have to go." Jody gave up trying to find a diplomatic way to get Denise off the phone and simply hung up.

Ellen's mouth found its way between her legs.

"I can't stand," she moaned as Ellen's tongue made longer and broader strokes.

Ellen ignored her.

Jody was forced to brace her bare back against the wall to keep from falling. She cried out as Ellen's tongue and hands took her over the edge.

Two hours later, dressed in robes, they sat across the table from each other and waited for the coffee to perk.

"What am I going to tell Denise?" Jody rubbed her hands across her eyes.

"What would you tell her if I was someone you'd met at a party?"

"But you're not," Jody replied more harshly than she intended. She dropped her head onto her crossed arms. "God, I can't believe I've done this."

Ellen caressed her hair. "I'm not going to say I'm sorry. I've dreamed of this for too long."

Jody raised her head and took Ellen's hand. "My real problem may be that I'm not sorry either," she replied, staring into Ellen's clear blue eyes.

Ellen smiled and again Jody experienced the sharp twisting sensation inside.

I'm sleeping with my best friend's daughter. A sudden vision of Denise's face caused her to jump up.

"This can't be." She began to pace. "It'll never work. Think of the pain we'll cause Denise."

Ellen sat quietly as Jody continued to vent.

Jody was on her third lap around her tiny kitchen when she saw Sharon's photo on the refrigerator.

"Oh shit." She cringed and covered her face with her hands.

Ellen's arms slipped around her. Jody hadn't heard her approach.

"It's going to be okay. I'll explain it to Mom." Ellen turned Jody around and pulled her head to her shoulder. She began to caress Jody's hair.

Jody suddenly remembered the gray in her hair. What if Ellen didn't like it? For the first time, she wished she had done something about the gray.

"We'll work it out," Ellen said.

"I'm too old."

Ellen cupped Jody's face between her hands. "Jody, I've been thinking about you for a long, long time. I've tried forgetting you through work and with other women, but I couldn't. I didn't mention it earlier, but you were a major factor in my decision to transfer back here. I was tired of wondering if what I felt for you was just a childhood crush."

A stab of fear shot through Jody. She didn't like the possibility that she was only a "childhood crush" for Ellen. She quickly reprimanded herself. It would be better for everyone if Ellen came to her senses and left.

"Now that I know for sure, I'm not letting you go without a chance to get to know you." Ellen was gazing intently at her. "I love Mom. I don't want to do anything to hurt her, but she'll have to understand that she can't dictate my life." She shrugged and continued, "Jody, I don't know if what I feel for you will last past the initial lust, but I know I've had one hell of a crush on you since I was fifteen. Last night did nothing to alleviate those feelings. I want the chance to get to know you better."

Jody stared into her eyes. She should send Ellen home. The last thing she needed was someone in love with her, especially if that someone also happened to be her best friend's only daughter. Why didn't she just tell her to go home? She opened her mouth, but the words wouldn't come. She turned away and gazed out the window. The previous night had been special, not just the sex, but the talking and laughing too. She threw up her hands in surrender. "This is total insanity. Denise will kill me."

"It's not about Mom. This is between you and me. If I wasn't your best friend's daughter, would you see me again?"

In a heartbeat, Jody told herself. "The fact remains, you *are* Denise's daughter. Not to mention that I'm nineteen years older than you. How can I possibly explain this to Denise?"

Then there was the matter of Sharon. She couldn't date them both at once. She felt trapped. Half of her was yelling, "Send the kid packing," and half of her was saying, "Do whatever it takes to keep her."

"Perhaps I've assumed too much," Ellen said. "I guess my first question should be, do you want to see me again?" She reached out and took Jody's hand.

Jody hesitated. She liked Ellen. She enjoyed her company and wanted to see more of her, but there were problems. First, Denise was not going to be happy. She would surely read Jody the riot act. Second, there was the age difference. How long would Ellen stay interested in her? The novelty of a ten-year crush might keep her curious for a while, but eventually Ellen would notice the gray hairs. Then she'd start to see the sags, and no matter how much Jody ran or exercised, she no longer had the same taut suppleness as that of a twenty-year-old. At some point, Ellen would move on to someone nearer her own age.

"What are you thinking?" Ellen asked.

"I'm thinking that getting involved with you could be emotionally dangerous for me."

"How?"

"I'm not a young woman anymore."

"No, you aren't, but you certainly aren't as old as you try to sound. You're forty-four. I know there's a sprinkling of gray in your hair, and I can see these." She touched a fingertip to the fine lines at the corner of Jody's eye. "I'm enchanted with the heart and soul of the woman inside, not the shell." Ellen gazed into Jody's eyes. "I may be young, but I'm not that shallow. If things don't work out between us, it will be because of something other than the way you look."

"But you are so beautiful. You could have anyone you want. There are hundreds of women who are much younger than me who would fall all over themselves for a chance to date you. I saw how men and women both looked at you last night."

Ellen leaned back, obviously impatient with the turn of the conversation. "Is that all you see?" she asked. "Are you only interested in me because of my looks?"

"No," Jody protested. "Of course not."

"Then why are you assuming I would grow tired of you simply because of your looks?"

Jody bit her lip and thought about what Ellen had said. She slowly reached a decision. She'd tell her the truth. The complete truth, not just the varnished version she gave her last night. She'd tell her about Sharon and her own inability to commit not just to Sharon but to anyone. If Ellen stayed, then she'd face Denise. *But if she leaves, what will I do?*

Jody went to pour the coffee and handed a cup to Ellen. "We have to talk." She led Ellen back to the table. "Ellen, my longest relationship lasted nine and a half years. Mia walked out on me for someone else. I loved her, but I couldn't make myself go after her. Maybe she would've changed her mind if I had bothered to let her know I still cared for her. But I wasn't able to do it. Since then I haven't been able to make a commitment to anyone. There was one time when I thought I could. Lauren was sweet, loving and fun to be with. But something in me wouldn't allow her to get too close. I cheated on her, and she caught me. When she left, all I felt was a sense of relief. Almost as though I had escaped from something." She rushed on before she could chicken out. "I'm sort of seeing someone now. Sharon is her name. We've been dating for a few weeks." Jody didn't know what else to say about Sharon.

Ellen stared into her coffee.

Jody tried to ignore the tension building in her stomach as she waited for Ellen's response.

Finally, Ellen took a deep breath. "I wish you would have mentioned Sharon last night, before—" She stopped and looked out the window.

"I'm sorry."

"Do you love her?"

"No." The speed of her answer surprised Jody, but she knew it was true. "Sharon and I have never discussed where our relationship is going. Our time together was spent—" It was Jody's turn to stop short.

"Kind of like last night." Ellen grinned and looked toward the rumpled sofa.

"No. You and I talked more last night than Sharon and I ever have."

The doorbell rang. They stared at each other.

"It's going to be Mom," Ellen stated flatly. "What do we tell her?"

They sat a moment longer.

Jody stood, took a deep breath and retied her robe. "The truth. She deserves to know what's going on."

Together they walked to the front door holding hands. No one was prepared when the door opened, clearly not Ellen, not Jody and certainly not Sharon.

CHAPTER SEVEN

Sharon's fury started at tornado force and swiftly escalated to a full-blown hurricane. When she stopped shouting long enough to take a breath, Jody quickly stepped in.

"Sharon, I know I have a lot of explaining to do, and I will." She turned to Ellen. "I think it would probably be best if you went home."

Ellen nodded. "I understand." She gathered her clothes from the living room floor and headed for the bedroom to get dressed.

Jody took Sharon to the kitchen. "I'll be right back and we'll talk."

"Are you going for one last quickie?" Sharon spat as Jody walked away.

Jody stopped, ready to argue the accusation, but decided not to. Sharon's anger was valid.

Ellen was already dressed and in the process of slipping her shoes on when Jody came into the bedroom.

"I'll see myself out," she said.

"Ellen, I want to see you again." Ellen seemed as surprised by the statement as Jody was. They stood staring at each other.

"I think you need to get things straightened out with Sharon first." Ellen froze. "You know where to find me."

Jody walked her to the front door. "I'll call you."

Ellen turned to her. "Just make sure you know what you want. I don't play games." Without waiting for Jody to respond, she left.

Jody turned back to the kitchen, but Sharon had come into the living room.

"Dinner with an old friend!" Sharon snapped. "Jody, she's young enough to be your daughter. How old is she anyway? Eighteen? Nineteen?"

"She's twenty-five," Jody said defensively.

"You're nineteen years older than her? What is it with you? Are you trying to recapture your youth by chasing younger women? Each new girlfriend gets a little younger." Sharon began to pace back and forth by the rumpled sofa. "I shudder to imagine what you'll be doing by the time you're fifty."

"Sharon, please sit down so we can talk." Jody fell into her recliner.

Sharon stared at the sofa, the only other place to sit.

Embarrassed, Jody got out of the recliner and motioned for Sharon to take it. She pushed the pillows and blanket off the far end of the sofa, hoping the nightmare rapidly developing here might disappear if the evidence did.

Jody pulled her robe closer and folded her hands, while Sharon waited for her explanation.

"I'm sorry you found out like this. I was going to tell you."

"How sweet of you." Sharon's sarcasm cut deep.

"Sharon, we never agreed to monogamy. We never agreed to anything, actually." A silence fell between them.

"What happens now?" Sharon's voice had lost all its fury.

Jody wished it would return. She could handle anger much better than she could the look of hurt that shadowed Sharon's face. She remembered a similar look on Lauren's face from years before, when she had walked in and caught Jody. Experience had taught her that a clean cut would be less painful in the long run.

"I don't think we should continue to see each other."

Sharon began to sob softly.

Jody left the sofa, knelt in front of her and hugged her. "I'm sorry. I never meant to hurt you," Jody said as Sharon continued to cry.

Sharon clasped her tightly. "I thought we were doing so well. Can't we make this work?"

Jody had some difficulty extracting Sharon's arms from around her. "Don't do this. You're a wonderful woman. I wouldn't want you to change. We're just not right for each other."

Anger flashed in Sharon's green eyes. "You're a cold, manipulating bitch." She shoved Jody harshly away. Jody fell onto the floor and lay there staring as Sharon left, slamming the front door so hard a picture on the front wall crashed to the floor.

Jody lay on the floor and struggled with her emotions and conscience until her back began to hurt. When she finally stood and glanced at the clock, she was surprised to find it was almost eleven.

She changed into shorts and went for a run. She was halfway through her route before her mind began to clear and she was able to think.

Eighteen years on Wall Street had taught her to trust her instincts, and Ellen felt right. If she and Ellen continued to see each other, they had to ensure that Denise would not be hurt. Jody needed to talk to Denise right away. Maybe she could find a way to explain things so that Denise would understand.

She completed her run and took a long, hot shower before dialing Denise's home number. She breathed a sigh of relief when Ellen answered.

"It's me. Jody."

"I've been worried about you. I wasn't sure you would call. How did it go?"

"We decided it would be best if we didn't see each other anymore."

"Are you sure that's what you really want?" Ellen asked.

Jody thought about it before replying. She wanted to be sure she could make Ellen understand. "My relationship with Sharon wasn't about love or forever. It was two people having a good time while it lasted."

"Did Sharon feel the same way?"

Again, Jody hesitated. "I don't think Sharon was ready to break things off, but I believe she would have been soon."

Silence hung between them.

"Where's your mom?" Jody asked to break the tension.

"She's still at work."

Jody shook her head as she glanced at the clock. "Of course. I must be losing my mind. It's not even one yet."

"You took so long in calling, I was afraid you had changed your mind," Ellen said.

"I've been thinking."

Ellen remained silent for several seconds. "And?" she prompted.

"I want to see you. I don't know what's going to happen between us. I don't have a very good track record in relationships, but I want to try."

"Jody, I want to make love to you." The statement raced through the wires like a flash fire.

Jody knew she should say no but found herself saying, "Leave your mom a note and come over."

"Okay. I'll be there in half an hour."

After hanging up, Jody got dressed and started putting her house back in order. Girlfriends sure played havoc with her housekeeping routine.

Jody and Ellen spent the remainder of the afternoon making love and talking. Afterward they went to a small, neighborhood restaurant that Jody recommended and enjoyed a quiet dinner of seafood.

After the waitress brought them coffee, Jody sat back in her seat and said, "I think it's best if we tell Denise right away. The longer we wait, the worse it will be for her."

"I agree, but do you think she's going to be that upset? I mean, you're her best friend. It seems to me, she'd be happy."

Jody shook her head and fidgeted with her silverware. For the first time in years, she wished she hadn't quit smoking. Everything was happening so fast. She hadn't had time to come to grips with her mercurial emotions. How could her feelings for Ellen be so strong in such a short time?

"I honestly don't know how she's going to react, but I don't think we should expect her blessing for a while. She's going to need time to adjust to the idea."

"When are we going to tell her?" Ellen asked as she pushed her empty coffee cup away.

Jody sighed. "I guess there's no time like the present." She took her time in counting out a large tip, hoping some brilliant line of reasoning would come to her. All she got for her worrying was a smile from the waitress and a severe case of heartburn.

There were three cars parked in front of Denise's house when they arrived.

"Shit!" Jody hissed. "I forgot she was playing Bunco tonight." Denise got together with her Bunco club once a month to roll the dice and eat. The few times Jody had attended as a sub, there was a lot more eating and gossip than playing.

"It'll keep," Ellen said, placing a hand on Jody's arm. "Do you want to come in?"

"No, it's getting late. I'd better go on home. Can you come with me?" She ran her hand through Ellen's hair.

"I could. But should I?"

They both looked toward the brightly lit house.

"I'll come over tomorrow, and we'll tell her then." Jody kissed her softly. "Call me when you get up."

✑✐✑

Early Sunday morning, the phone pulled Jody from her sleep. Her first thought was that she needed to start unplugging the phone before going to bed. Then, maybe she would be able to sleep.

Her palms began to sweat when she heard Denise's voice, and for an instant she feared Ellen had already told her.

"Sweetie, I'm sorry to wake you, but I just received a call from my cousin. Aunt Alice died. I have to go to New Jersey." Her voice broke.

Jody sat up. "What happened?"

"Remember? She's the one who was diagnosed with breast cancer a few months ago. She refused all treatments. She told the doctors she was seventy-four and didn't want to go through the agony my mom did. Jody, sometimes I get so scared."

"Denise, don't think about it."

"First Mom and now Aunt Alice. You know they say breast cancer runs in families."

"You've got nothing to worry about. Things have changed a lot since your mom died, and you're always good about doing your self-exam and going to the doctor."

"I guess, but I still get scared. I have to go," Denise said. "Oh, I almost forgot. I managed to get everything ordered for Mother's Day. It'll be delivered on the Thursday prior to that Sunday, but I'll be back by then. Sweetie, I'm really sorry to leave you alone with the shop again."

"Don't worry about it. Just do what you have to do. I can handle the shop," Jody said. She breathed a guilty sigh of relief that she had been given a reprieve in telling Denise.

"I'll probably be gone a few days," Denise explained. "She made me executor of her will, and I have to get all of that taken care of."

Realizing she wouldn't be able to see Ellen for several days, Jody experienced a slight pang. She tried to hide her disappointment. "Don't worry about the shop. Eric will be there, and I'll arrange for a temp to come in if things get too crazy. Is there anything you need for me to take care of at the house while you're gone?"

"I don't think so. Well, maybe you could do something to keep Ellen company. She's not going."

"She won't be attending the funeral?" Her heart soared.

"No, since she's just started this new position we thought it best she stay here. I really have to go. Ellen is going to drive me to the airport. I managed to get an early flight out. I'll call you as soon as I know how long I'm going to be gone."

Less than two hours later, Ellen stood in Jody's doorway. "I hope you don't mind my dropping by."

Jody took in the long tanned legs and smiled. "You can drop by any time you want." She pulled Ellen into the living room and closed the door. "I'm sorry about your aunt." She hugged Ellen.

"I feel bad for Mom," Ellen said. "I should have gone with her."

"Is it horrible of me to say I'm glad you didn't?" Jody pulled back and gazed at Ellen. "I've missed you," she admitted as she kissed her deeply.

"I missed you, too. I came by to see if you would go to the zoo with me."

"I haven't been to the zoo in years."

"It's time you went. Come on. It's going to be a beautiful day."

"I need to run by the shop first and spend a couple of hours there, but I could probably break away this afternoon."

Ellen tilted her head and smiled. "A half a day is better than nothing. Pick me up when you're ready." She gave Jody a quick kiss. "Hurry up and get to work so you can rush back to me."

It was a beautiful afternoon. They arrived at the zoo a little after lunch and as usual, Jody started feeling sorry for the animals and had to leave before making it halfway through the exhibits.

"I'm sorry the animals upset you," Ellen said as she took Jody's arm.

"It's not the animals that upset me. It's the cages. It's cruel to lock the animals away like this. They look so defeated." Jody took a deep breath and decided not to let her sadness ruin their afternoon. "We'll find something else to do."

"Let's go ride the train," Ellen insisted as they pushed their way through the zoo's revolving exit door. "I've not ridden it in years."

They rode the *Brackenridge Eagle* miniature train through Brackenridge Park twice before buying hot dogs and sodas from a vendor. They found a vacant picnic table by the river. While they ate, they watched a group of kids feed the ducks.

"I've had a great day." Jody wadded up the paper from the hot dog and leaned forward on the bench. "Thanks for inviting me."

"Spend the night with me," Ellen said as she caressed Jody's hand.

Jody's stomach did a series of somersaults. "I wouldn't feel comfortable being in Denise's house," she admitted. "Stay with me."

"I want you," Ellen whispered.

Jody felt her body respond and jumped up. They quickly gathered their trash and headed for Jody's Jeep.

The estate proved much more complicated than Denise had anticipated. It took her nearly two weeks to clear things up. Eric came in between classes, and between the two of them Jody and Eric were able to keep up with the orders.

While Denise was gone, Ellen spent most of her free time at Jody's, only returning home early each morning to shower and dress for work.

On the Saturday morning that Denise was due to return, Jody and Ellen lay in bed talking.

"We have to tell her when she gets back," Jody said as she stroked Ellen's back.

"I have to go to Midland on Monday to give a seminar. I'll be back on Wednesday. Let's wait until I return. I don't want to tell her and then leave," Ellen said.

"All right, but we tell her Wednesday night. I'll invite her over for dinner, and we'll tell her then."

CHAPTER EIGHT

When Jody arrived at Petal Pushers on Monday morning, Denise was in the workroom stacking supplies. Jody had meant to straighten out the supplies before leaving the previous evening, but it had slipped her mind. With college graduations and Mother's Day only six days away, they were already swamped with orders. In an attempt to keep up, Jody and Denise had agreed to start coming in two hours earlier each morning. They would use the extra time to prepare arrangements to cover their day-to-day walk-in customers and phone orders.

"Good morning," Jody called. She tried to sound as natural as possible. "Glad to have you back."

Denise turned and it seemed to Jody that she took a moment longer than usual to respond. Jody felt sweat pop out on her neck. Had Ellen already told Denise?

"I'm sorry," Jody said, her conscience already getting the best of her.

Denise gave a small snort as she picked up a box of bud vases. "Jody, please. You don't have to apologize. I'm only cleaning this out to prepare for Thursday's large shipment. I know how busy you've been. I saw the receipts. You've had to cover for me so much lately, I'm the one who should be saying I'm sorry."

Jody reached for the countertop to steady herself. She had almost blurted out her guilt. *Get a grip*, she told herself.

It was stupid to wait until Wednesday to tell Denise. Of course, with Ellen in Midland, they didn't really have a choice, if they wanted to tell her together. The next three days were going to be hell. As she tucked her backpack under the counter, she considered telling Denise she wasn't feeling well and hiding out until Wednesday night, but that would leave Denise in a serious pinch. The next few days would account for over a fourth of the shop's yearly income. Most of that income would come from Mother's Day sales. *Hectic* wouldn't come close to describing the next few days.

If only all of this had happened two weeks later. Eric would be out of school, and Denise would be on vacation for a month.

With Eric working at the shop full-time during the summer, Denise normally took off the month of June and Jody took off July. It gave Jody an opportunity to spend time with her parents in Missouri and still have time to fly back to New York to visit old friends.

"I've made coffee already. As soon I finish setting these up, we can grab a cup. I want to talk to you."

"I'll get the coffee while you do that," Jody said, eager to escape.

The pot shook in Jody's hand as she poured the coffee. What did Denise want to talk about? If Denise asked her point-blank about Ellen, what would she say? She wished she and Ellen had discussed the possibility that Denise might find out before they told her.

Jody gave herself a good mental shake. Denise couldn't find out if neither she nor Ellen told her.

Everything will be fine, Jody told herself. *All I have to do is keep my cool.*

"How is Sharon?" Denise asked, appearing at Jody's side.

Startled, Jody leapt aside and yelped. Her leg knocked against the table and caused coffee to slosh over the rims of both cups.

"Jody, what is wrong with you? You scared the crap out of me, jumping like that."

Unable to meet Denise's eyes, Jody grabbed a handful of paper towels and began to wipe up the spilled coffee. "I'm a little tired and you startled me."

Denise clucked her tongue. "Sweetie, you're getting too old for these all-night escapades. You need to find your Ms. Right and settle down."

"You're probably right," Jody agreed, pitching the soggy paper towels into the trash can. She could feel Denise watching her. To avoid meeting her gaze, Jody busied herself with refilling their cups.

"Are things with Sharon all right?" Denise asked.

Jody hesitated. Denise never settled for a simple statement. When she told her she was no longer seeing Sharon, there would be questions. Wednesday night seemed like an eternity. Again she cursed their decision to wait.

"I'm no longer seeing Sharon."

"I see. Your choice, I guess."

Irritated by her correct assumption, Jody looked up. "What's that mean?"

Denise held up her hands filled with rolls of florist tape. "Don't get mad. I only meant that when one of your relationships end, it's usually because you decided it was time to move on."

Jody shoved the carafe back onto the coffeemaker with a loud crack. "What the hell do you mean? You make me sound like some female Don Juan who hops in and out of every available bed in town."

As if to dodge Jody's anger, Denise took a step back. "Jody, I'm sorry. That's not what I meant at all."

Ashamed of both her outburst and the fact that it had stemmed from guilt, Jody turned away. She heard the sound of the rolls of florist tape dropping onto the display case.

"Jody." Denise touched her arm. "Please, look at me. I'm sorry. Sweetie, I swear I didn't mean to hurt your feelings. I was rude and out of line. Please, forgive me."

Jody bit her lip, struggling not to spill out the secrets held in her own black heart. What kind of friend was she anyway? She should have sent Ellen home and never let any of this get started. There was still time. She could end things with Ellen before they told Denise. If they ended it now, Denise would never have to know.

"Please don't be angry with me," Denise begged. "You know I can't stand it when we argue."

Jody's guilt deepened. Denise, who was almost in tears, was the best friend she had ever had. It was stupid to do anything that would endanger that friendship. Ending this thing with Ellen was the right thing to do. So why did she feel like crap just thinking about ending it?

"It's not you," Jody said. "I'm just being an asshole. Maybe I am trying to be a female Don Juan."

Denise gave her a quick hug. "No, you're not. You just haven't found the right woman yet. As soon as she comes along, you'll settle down."

"Do you really think I'm capable of settling down?"

Denise took her coffee cup from the table and seemed to give the question some serious thought. "Do you want my honest opinion?"

"Yes." Jody's hands felt clammy, and she caught herself drying them on her slacks. She grabbed her coffee cup and wrapped her hands around it, even though it was almost too hot to hold.

Denise gazed into her coffee as though it were her crystal ball. "I think you're basically a homebody who wants to settle down."

"Then why did I cheat on Lauren?"

"Because she scared you, and I don't believe you ever really loved her."

"What do you mean, she scared me?"

Denise took a sip of coffee before answering. "Lauren was too much like Mia."

"No way," Jody protested.

Denise looked at her and smiled. "Think about it. They were both wrapped up in their professions. Both were very persuasive. You told me yourself that you hadn't been ready to settle into a relationship when they each came along, but they were. Look at how hard you tried to avoid further involvement with Lauren, but she kept ragging until you gave in. You're a pushover for a sad story."

"I am not."

Denise chuckled and said, "Remember the pens?"

Jody rolled her eyes. "He was a con artist."

Denise would never let her live that fiasco down. The shop had only been open a couple of weeks when a man wearing wraparound sunglasses and carrying a white cane and a beat-up briefcase slowly tapped his way into the shop. He told Jody a sad story about losing his eyesight during a boating accident with his son, and now he had to sell pens for a living. She bought all six dozen of the pens he had with him, most of which she would soon learn were inkless.

Denise had been pulling into the parking lot as the man left the shop. She saw him fold up the white cane and tuck it into the brief-case. Intrigued by his curious actions, she watched him walk to the bus stop on the corner where he removed a paperback from his hip pocket and began to read.

Jody had been appalled when Denise told her about the odd scene she had witnessed. When Jody finally admitted her gullibility, Denise laughed until tears rolled down her cheeks.

"I am not a pushover." Jody would have liked to be able to offer a stronger-sounding denial, but deep down she knew Denise was correct. She was a sucker for a sob story. Both Mia and Lauren had given her one about their budding enterprises. She had fallen in love with Mia, but the only reason she allowed Lauren to move in was because she felt sorry for her. Lauren had struggled so, trying to work her way up in the publishing industry.

"Enough psychoanalysis for now," Denise said. "I need to talk to you."

Jody's heart pounded. "What about?"

Denise looked at her and frowned. "Don't look so scared. I'm not going to ask for a kidney."

Jody tried to relax. There was no way she could continue with this charade.

"Come on back. We can work and talk at the same time." Denise motioned for Jody to follow her into the workroom. "As you know, sales are up almost twenty-five percent from this same time last year. I think the free city-wide delivery has helped. Plus, the contracts with the restaurants have really increased. I believe we are ready to expand. I know we've been talking about opening another shop," Denise rushed on, "but I was talking to Mrs. Jimenez this morning. She was opening up when I came in."

Jody nodded. Mrs. Jimenez owned the card shop next to them.

"Since her husband died last year, you know she's been thinking about retiring. Well, her daughter has convinced her to move down to Corpus Christi and live with her, so Mrs. Jimenez is going to sell the shop. What do you think about buying it?"

"A card shop?"

"No, just the building. We would need to talk to her, of course, but the way I see it, we could do it one of two ways. We could either let her dispose of the inventory and we buy the building or, if she doesn't want to do that, we could buy the inventory and building. We then sell the inventory to another card shop. Mrs. Jimenez invited me in to look the inventory over and everything is in good condition and it's current. I don't think we would have any trouble selling it."

"You want to open another shop next to this one?" The lack of sleep, plus worrying about Denise's reaction to her involvement with Ellen, was making Jody slow in catching up with Denise's enthusiasm.

"No, we expand this one." Denise waved her hands. "I've had longer to think about this, so let me tell you my vision and then you tell me what you think." She went back to working on the funeral spray she was arranging. "Okay, overhead, our biggest worry. If we open a new shop, we'll have to hire two full-time employees, one for each shop. You and I work so well together, I hate the idea of us working separately, but that's the only logical choice. We can't put the newbies in charge of a new location. Even if we're lucky enough to find someone with experience, one of us needs to be there."

Jody nodded as she manipulated a strand of ribbon into a large bow. There were so many things they wanted to do to expand the business. She had been pushing the idea of them taking on corporate accounts. She was sure they could pull in more restaurants. If there was anything San Antonio had plenty of, it was restaurants. And Denise had been wanting to start carrying gift baskets. They were always receiving requests for them, but they didn't have the time to prepare them. They had looked into the possibility of buying them from a vendor, but the real cash reward came in putting the baskets together themselves. Jody kept silent, eager to hear Denise's ideas.

Denise pushed on. "Then there's the concern of finding the perfect place for the new shop, the expense of setting it up, will the new employees work out, and all the other things we've talked to death."

Denise took the completed bow from Jody, inserted it into the spray and set it aside. She began to gather her materials for the next arrangement.

The business had grown so that they were struggling to keep up with orders. They needed to hire at least one full-time person and maybe even another part-timer, but the shop was already too cramped.

As if reading her mind, Denise said, "We're bumping into each other now. Imagine what it'll be like with two more people. That's why I thought we should buy the shop next door. All we'd need to do is knock out the common wall, put in a door and move the workroom over there. Then we could use this space as the showroom."

Jody thought about the plan. It did make a lot of sense, but she wanted to look at the numbers. The phone rang, giving her a chance to delay making a comment.

"Let me think about this while I'm making deliveries and we'll talk about it later. In fact, why don't you and Ellen come to dinner Wednesday night? We will talk about it then."

"Sounds good. Do you mind if I talk to Mrs. Jimenez about the price and how she's planning to sell?" Denise picked the phone up before Jody could reply.

She was still trying to process the fact that she had tossed out the invitation as though it were nothing more than a simple dinner invitation. In reality, what she had to tell Denise might seriously damage their friendship. It suddenly struck her that she was still thinking about telling Denise.

So much for my determination to end the relationship with Ellen, she thought.

When Denise took the phone from her ear and reached for a sales receipt pad, Jody said, "Let's wait on Mrs. Jimenez until after we talk Wednesday." She could see the disappointment in Denise's eyes as she nodded and went back to the phone.

CHAPTER NINE

Later that night as Jody tossed and turned in bed, she tried to concentrate on Denise's plan for the shop. It was a good plan. It made sense to expand their current location and keep their work force combined. There were issues and questions to be addressed, but on the surface it was the logical choice. Would the hassle of the renovations cause them to lose customers? Would new employees change the feel of the shop? What were the tax implications? If they increased the restaurant contracts would the one van be able to keep up with the deliveries, or would they have to purchase another one? How would the shop look afterward? She tried to imagine how the two shops would look as one, but thoughts of Ellen intruded.

Jody's pillow felt as though it was stuffed with tennis balls. She pounded on it until her arm grew tired, but it still felt lumpy. She finally gave up pummeling the pillow and admitted there was nothing wrong with it. She couldn't sleep because she felt so lousy about deceiving Denise. Why couldn't she just accept the fact that dating Ellen wasn't possible?

Disgusted with her restlessness, she got up and went into the kitchen to get herself a cold beer. Maybe Denise would surprise them and not object to their dating.

"Yeah, and maybe I'll win the lottery without buying a ticket," she grumbled as she dropped into her recliner. She sipped the beer. "No one dates her best friend's daughter. Especially not one that's nineteen years her junior. I'm lower than a worm turd."

She slowly realized that as rotten as she felt about deceiving Denise, she felt worse about not seeing Ellen. She missed her. She never dreamed she could miss another person as badly as she did Ellen. A dozen times that day she had remembered things she wanted to tell her, only to realize she wouldn't be seeing her until Wednesday. While grocery shopping, she bought several items— which included a basket of fresh strawberries, a rich blend of Mexican coffee, a small stuffed puppy that barked and wagged its tail whenever you squeezed his foot—simply because she thought Ellen might enjoy them.

She pulled her feet under her and tried to get comfortable.

I must be losing my mind, she thought. Why else would she be getting herself into this crazy mess? The intelligent thing to do was to end the relationship before it went any further. It was crazy to jeopardize her friendship with Denise over something that was bound to end in disaster anyway. Ellen would eventually realize that her feelings for her were nothing more than a schoolgirl crush. The crush had only lasted this long because Ellen had been away all those years. She would see her mistake and move on to someone nearer her own age. This was just a fling for Ellen, Jody reasoned.

Besides, everyone knew she wasn't capable of maintaining a long-term relationship. How long could they possibly last as a couple?

She would end it when Ellen returned on Wednesday afternoon, Jody decided. That was the wise thing to do.

The phone rang, jarring Jody from her rationalizing. Who would be calling so late? It was after midnight. She glanced at the caller identification display. In spite of her decision to end the affair, her heart soared as Ellen's name flashed across the screen.

Jody snatched up the handset and forced her voice to sound calm. "Hello."

"Hi."

That was all it took. One simple word and Jody's resolve to break up with Ellen faded away.

A sense of warmth rushed over her. She was surprised to find there was more comfort than lust in the feeling. Each of her relationships since Mia had been physically passionate and short-lived, lacking the easy comfort of a real relationship.

"I know I'm being inexcusably selfish, waking you in the middle of the night, but . . ." Ellen hesitated and Jody thought she heard a small sigh.

"What's wrong?" Jody asked, glancing at the clock on the mantel. It read twelve-seventeen.

"You'll laugh, or worse, think I'm being silly."

"Try me."

"I miss you."

A smile crossed Jody's face. "That's pretty amazing. I was just sitting here thinking the same thing."

"Yeah, right. You were probably sound asleep."

"You know we older people actually require less sleep."

"Don't talk like that. You aren't old."

"I'm no spring chicken, but I have to admit, when I'm talking to you, I feel much younger."

"Good. Then you'll have to keep talking to me."

Jody laughed and asked, "How is Midland?"

This time Ellen's sigh wasn't so subtle. "Don't ask. Sometimes I wonder why I keep doing this."

"I thought you enjoyed your work."

"I don't know. When I first started this job, I justified the layoffs and cutbacks by telling myself that in the long run we were helping people. Sure, a few people lost their jobs and I felt bad for them, but the majority kept working and were able to do so for a healthier company. I felt our recommendations help put the company in a better position to compete."

"What changed your mind?"

"I came to Midland to do a twelve-month follow-up on an evaluation that my predecessor did. It's one of the stipulations in our contract. The company took my predecessor's advice to cut the work force by three percent, but on its own, it also cut the salaries of the remaining workers by six percent. There was no need to do that. They got greedy and used our evaluation as an excuse to screw their employees."

"Businesses are hurting everywhere."

"They weren't hurting that bad. The CEO still managed to take home over a million dollars last year."

Jody hesitated, not knowing what to say to make Ellen feel better.

"I walked through a few of the offices to interview some of the remaining workers and, Jody, they hated me. I tried to explain that I wasn't there to reevaluate their jobs, but simply as a follow-up. They didn't believe me."

"Explain to them that their company went beyond your recommendations."

"I can't. It would violate our contract. We aren't allowed to disclose any of our findings to employees."

Jody kept silent. There was nothing she could say. Ellen was still young. She hadn't yet become completely jaded with the real world.

"I'm sorry," Ellen said. "I didn't call you to cry on your shoulder about work. I missed you and wanted to talk to you. Tell me about your day."

Jody hesitated. "Actually it was kind of rough. I feel like I'm lying to your mom. It made things awkward. Are you sure we aren't making a horrendous mistake?" She hadn't planned to blurt out that last bit; it just happened.

It was Ellen's turn to be silent.

Jody was beginning to fidget before Ellen finally spoke. "Mom isn't going to be happy when she finds out about us. But it's not just because it's you. She would be upset no matter who I got involved with. You know how possessive she is."

"She's trying not to be," Jody said, feeling as though she'd betrayed Denise's trust. She was certain Denise had trusted her not to reveal confidences. "She cares for you."

They both fell silent.

After several seconds, Jody said, "We're getting ourselves all worked up for nothing. After all, we're only dating. It's not like we're renting a U-Haul or adopting children together."

"Not yet," Ellen replied calmly. "I normally date someone six to eight months before moving in, and I never discuss adoption until we've been together two or three years. Of course, with you I might make an exception."

Jody laughed and braced for the heart-pounding, shallow-breathing, palm-sweating reaction that always occurred whenever a girlfriend started talking, even in jest, about moving in. Strangely, none of these things happened. She chalked it up to exhaustion.

"You can start breathing again," Ellen said. "I was joking."

"I know." Still, she remembered Ellen's ex-girlfriend who continued to call her on the cell. "Are you still hearing from . . ." She struggled to recall the name. "Beth?"

"Yes, it took her a while but she finally managed to get my work number somehow. I had messages on my voice mail at work. I delete them. I don't bother to call her back and try to explain it's over. She doesn't listen."

"You don't seem to be worried about it, so I assume she's not the stalking type."

"Beth? No. She's actually a sweet person most of the time, but she clings to the point of suffocating. I think she'll keep calling for a few more days, but she'll meet someone soon enough. She won't have any trouble finding someone else. With the distance between Texas and California, she'll lose interest."

"So, your primary reason for returning to San Antonio has worked?"

"No. The primary reason I came back to Texas was because I kept thinking about you, and I had to get you out of my system once and for all."

A trickle of disappointment wormed its way through Jody. "Have you gotten me out of your system?"

"Quite the opposite. You're more embedded than ever. Now, I walk down a hallway and pass by some woman wearing your perfume and I get weak in the knees. I hear a funny story and I want to call you and tell it to you. Love songs that used to disgust me with their mushiness have taken on a whole new meaning." She stopped and laughed. "Who's being codependent now?" she asked.

"I don't think that qualifies. I believe those symptoms result from a bite of the infamous love bug."

"I see. Do you think this wily little insect could ever penetrate that thick wall of armor around your heart?"

Jody hesitated. The phone grew slippery in her hand. She quickly switched the phone to her other hand and dried her palm on her T-shirt. It would be easy to blurt out a simple yes, but it was important that she not let herself become infatuated by the idea of falling in love. She had to maintain rationality about this relationship with Ellen. She said slowly, "I care for you a great deal. I believe I could fall in love with you."

Jody could almost feel Ellen's disappointment seeping though the phone line.

"I want to be honest with you, Ellen. I don't want to hurt you or mislead you."

"Why is it so hard for you to let yourself trust your feelings?"

"I trust my feelings." Jody leapt from the chair and began pacing.

"Tell me about Mia. I only know the bare bones that you and Mom told me."

"What's to tell? She met someone else and moved on."

"And you haven't trusted anyone since."

"It's too late at night for all this melodrama. She moved on and so did I. There's nothing else to say."

"I'm sorry. I didn't mean to upset you. I had no right to judge your feelings or reactions."

Jody returned to the recliner and sat down. "No. I'm the one who's sorry. As you can tell from my reaction, I still have some issues with Mia's leaving." Without warning, Jody yawned. She tried to stifle it, but Ellen heard her.

"I'm keeping you up," Ellen said. "I should let you go back to sleep."

Jody found she didn't want to stop talking to Ellen. *All the more reason to do so*, she thought.

"I probably won't get a chance to call tomorrow. I'll be busy compiling my data. I'll see you Wednesday."

"Good night," Jody replied, and wished she had the courage to ask Ellen not to hang up.

"Sweet dreams."

Before Jody could respond, Ellen had hung up. Jody held the silent phone and looked around her living room. Why did it suddenly seem so empty and so lonely?

"This is crazy," she said as she set down the phone. "This is what happens when you drink beer in the middle of the night." She took the beer bottle to the kitchen. "The next thing I know, I'll be listening to country music and pulling out old photos."

She headed for her bedroom. *This is precisely why you don't get too involved*, she thought. All she needed was a good night's sleep. Tomorrow she'd tell Denise that she agreed with her idea for expanding the shop, and Wednesday she'd tell Ellen she didn't want to see her anymore.

Renovating the shop would keep her too busy to worry about girlfriends. Maybe she'd stop dating altogether. She could convert to Catholicism and become a nun. "Great. Then I'd be surrounded by women." She gave up trying to figure it all out, and crawled between the rumpled sheets.

Despite her determination, sleep was slow in coming. When she finally drifted off, vague images of Mia, Lauren and Ellen danced into her dreams.

When the alarm finally rescued her, Jody came fully awake, confused and terrified. She might never say the words aloud, and she might be able to keep the truth from Ellen, but she couldn't lie to herself. Jody Scott the proclaimed queen of love-'em and leave-'em had been sucked into the relationship pit. She closed her eyes and moaned. How had she allowed this to happen? How was she going to tell Denise that she was falling in love with her daughter?

CHAPTER TEN

By Wednesday evening, Jody was a nervous wreck.

The hectic rush of the upcoming holiday had become her saving grace. The shop was a madhouse. The phone rang all day with orders for Mother's Day. Even the deliveries to the hospitals increased, but no matter how tired Jody was, Ellen continued to creep into her thoughts and dreams.

When she wasn't in the delivery van running around the city, she answered phones, waited on walk-in customers or helped Denise prepare the arrangements.

Exhausted from working another fifteen-hour day on Tuesday, Jody and Denise had neither the time nor energy for normal conversation. They had been so busy, Jody hadn't even had a chance to talk to Denise about expanding the shop. She finally decided the conversation would have to wait until after Mother's Day.

Ellen called the shop shortly after five on Wednesday afternoon. Jody, just in from a third round of deliveries, answered the phone in the showroom.

"I just got back. I'm off the rest of the day," Ellen said. "Can you get away?"

Jody hesitated. Now was the time. She should tell Ellen no and call off the dinner plans. She could plead exhaustion. She had opened the shop at six that morning in order to change the air conditioner filters and wipe down the insides of the coolers. Denise would never question the change in plans. On the other hand, they were almost caught up with the orders for tomorrow, and she could come in early again tomorrow to finish them off as well as any orders that might come in during the night. People often left orders on the shop's voice mail. She found herself agreeing. "I'll be home in twenty minutes."

"I've missed you so much."

Unsure whether Denise could hear her on the phone, Jody said, "I'll see you soon," and hung up.

In the workroom Denise was wiping off her worktable. "Thank goodness. I just finished the last of the orders for tomorrow," she said.

Jody breathed a sigh of relief. At least her leaving early wouldn't throw them behind. "I think I'm going to run on home. I want to stop by the store and pick up a few things for tonight," Jody lied. She had everything she needed for the dinner, but she couldn't very well tell Denise she wanted to leave early to see Ellen.

Denise looked up, surprised. "All right. I can close up."

"I'll see you at eight then." Jody turned to leave.

"Jody, I've been meaning to ask. Is everything okay? You've been rather quiet the last few days."

"Yeah, everything's fine. We've been so busy, and I have a couple of things on my mind."

"Does this have anything to do with your breakup with Sharon?" Denise put down the cleaning rag and gazed at her.

Jody's heart pounded. "No, I'm fine with that. I'm kind of getting involved with someone else, and it's not going as smoothly as I'd like," she said and instantly regretted her choice of words. How could Denise ever approve of Ellen's getting involved with her? No mother would want to see her daughter get involved with someone with a track record like hers.

Denise shook her head and sighed. "I'm sorry to hear that. I wish you could find what you're searching for."

"What would you say if I told you I thought I might be falling in love?"

Denise gave her a tired smile. "I'd say it was about time, and whoever you fall in love with will be a lucky woman." She shook her head. "Jody, I don't care how hard you pretend to be beyond Cupid's reach, at heart you're a big old softy. Honey, you're a born romantic, pure and simple." Denise came over and gave her a quick hug. "You have so much love to give. You deserve someone who'll love you in return."

Tears sprang to Jody's eyes. She quickly turned away and blinked the tears back. If she started crying now, as tired and confused as she was, she would go on a crying jag that would rival Niagara Falls.

She tried to speak, but the words got stuck in her throat. She attempted to swallow the pain lodged in her throat, but it refused to budge. She coughed and forced herself to say, "I hope you truly mean that." Her voice sounded thin and strained.

"Of course I do. You're like a sister to me, sweetie. Who you fall in love with won't change my love for you."

Jody grabbed her backpack to escape. If they continued to talk, she would tell Denise everything. Instead she changed the subject. "I think you should go ahead and talk to Mrs. Jimenez about us possibly purchasing the card shop. You're right. It makes more sense to expand rather than splitting up our resources."

Before Denise could respond, Jody rushed out the door.

Safely enclosed in her Jeep and trapped in rush-hour traffic, Jody slowly allowed herself to admit she wasn't going to end the relationship with Ellen. She wanted a chance to see how far they could take it.

She refused, however, to allow herself the luxury of envisioning a future with Ellen.

They would take it day by day, and see if the relationship survived. Denise would be fine as long as Ellen was happy. She'd have doubts at first, but when she saw they were happy together, she'd come around.

With a new sense of determination, Jody gripped the steering wheel and inched the Jeep forward.

"We'll take everything slow. We'll give Denise time to see that we care for each other. When she sees I'm not playing games, she'll be supportive," Jody said aloud. Denise even said it wouldn't matter whom she fell in love with.

But she didn't know you were talking about Ellen, her conscience nagged.

"All the more reason for me to show Denise how much I care for Ellen."

A horn blared behind her and Jody realized the line of cars in front of her had already started moving forward. She forced her attention back to driving.

The trip home took closer to thirty minutes than the twenty Jody promised.

The sight of Ellen waiting for her on the front porch steps warmed Jody's heart. Jody waved as she pulled the Jeep into the garage and rushed through the house to open the front door.

Of all the women I've dated, why is it you I'm falling for? Jody wondered as Ellen stepped into the house and embraced her.

It felt so right. This was what she wanted to come home to every day. *God*, she prayed, *please help Denise understand.* She didn't want to lose her friendship, but she wanted a chance with Ellen.

Ellen kissed her softly. "I've missed you."

Jody could only smile and gaze at her in wonder.

Ellen blushed under her close scrutiny. "You think I'm being silly."

"No, I think I'm . . ." A fist closed around Jody's heart and she panicked. *My God*, she thought. She couldn't even say the word out loud. Was she losing her mind? One minute she couldn't wait to get home and tell her she was falling in love with her, and the next minute she couldn't even speak.

"You're what?" Ellen prompted.

"A fool for pain."

"Why does it have to be pain? Why can't we have something wonderful between us?"

"Because we're too different."

Ellen pulled away and led Jody to the sofa. "Jody, we aren't so different. We both like jazz, lazy nights at home and eating ice cream in bed. We like a lot of the same authors and movies. Although I'm not so sure about those animated films you seem to enjoy so much," Ellen teased, referring to their first date when Jody had admitted that *Bambi* was her all-time favorite movie. Ellen pushed a lock of hair from Jody's forehead. "But I'm willing to give *Bambi* a try if it means that much to you."

Jody took Ellen's hand. "I'm scared. What if everyone's right, and I can't make a commitment?"

Ellen put a finger over Jody's lips. "Stop it. There are no guarantees in life. With all the craziness in the world, we could all be blown away before morning. You and I are going to take this one day at a time and see where it leads. I'm not asking for forever, but be warned," she said as she stared into Jody's eyes. "I'm falling in love with you. I intend to do everything in my power to be right here by your side, and I intend to stay until you make me leave."

"You could get hurt," Jody said.

Ellen tilted her head to one side, carefully studying her. "Or we could both be surprised." She grinned. "I don't believe you're the womanizer you like to imagine you are. I suspect you were hurt by

Mia's betrayal and never got over it. I think you're scared to commit to anyone because you're afraid of getting hurt again."

A stab of irritation struck Jody. Ellen's words hit close to home.

Before Jody could respond to the accusation, Ellen cuddled against her. "Hold me," Ellen said. "I can't stay long. I need to get back to Mom's and do some work before we come back for dinner tonight. I have so much to do, but I had to see you for a while."

Jody pulled Ellen deeper into her arms and stroked her hair. "We need to talk about tonight and how we're going to handle telling your mom."

"Let me tell her," Ellen said. "It'll be easier on you if I tell her before we come over."

"No, we both tell her. We're in this together, and she should hear it from us."

They sat in comfortable silence. As the seconds ticked away, Jody realized she was holding a vibrant, attractive woman in her arms, and for possibly the first time in her adult life, she was perfectly content to merely be sitting and holding her. There was no lust, just satisfaction. As she stroked Ellen's hair, she couldn't help but wonder what the next few hours would bring.

The clock on the mantel chimed the half-hour.

"It's already six-thirty," Jody said. "I need to start cooking."

"What can I do to help?"

Jody hopped up and offered Ellen a hand. "You can chop the cilantro and tomatoes while I start the beans." After pulling Ellen up, she kissed her deeply. "Don't give up on me," she whispered, her voice thick with desire. "I just need to go slow."

Ellen kissed the tip of Jody's nose. "If we had more time, I'd show you exactly how slow I can go."

"Oh, that was mean," Jody said with a moan. "Now I'll have these images running through my mind all night."

Ellen's hand eased between Jody's legs. "Here's a little preview to go with your mental images."

Jody's breath caught, and despite herself she began to rock to the movement of Ellen's hand.

"It's too bad we don't have more time," Ellen murmured, her hand moving slightly faster.

"I'll order take-out," Jody said, kissing her.

As Jody's tongue sought the tender recesses of Ellen's mouth, Ellen's hand slipped into Jody's slacks and pushed aside the damp underwear. When Jody's knees threatened to buckle, Ellen pushed her against the doorjamb and used her knee to push Jody's legs apart.

Jody's head dropped to Ellen's shoulder as Ellen's fingers continued to work their slow, wonderful magic.

It was after seven before Ellen left. At the door, she hugged Jody tightly. "No matter what happens tonight, I'm not giving up on you." She kissed Jody lightly and rushed off.

Jody drove to a nearby Mexican restaurant and ordered three Mexican dinners to go. The enchiladas, with sides of rice and beans, weren't as good as her own, but they'd suffice.

CHAPTER ELEVEN

Denise and Ellen arrived promptly at eight. In a nervous frenzy, Jody had set the table, cleaned the bathroom, and was in the process of cleaning her sock drawer when she saw Denise's car pull up in front of her house. Jody met them at the front door. Her heart pounded as Ellen gave her a small hug and a modest kiss on the cheek.

Feeling like the worst of louses, Jody turned for Denise's customary hug. As Denise hugged her, Jody was struck with the horrible feeling she was about to lose something very dear. She hugged Denise so tightly in return that Denise peered at her for several seconds afterward.

Jody ushered them inside. "I didn't get a chance to cook," she apologized as Denise set her purse down.

"What happened? I've been looking forward to your enchiladas all day. I thought that's why you left early," Denise said.

Jody glanced at Ellen just as Ellen ran a hand through her hair. Jody experienced a flashback of what that hand had been doing to her only a couple of hours ago. She felt her face flame as her body responded to the image.

"Are you all right?" Denise asked. "You look flushed."

Ellen gave Jody a sly smile as she approached her. "You look like you might have a fever." Before Jody could escape, Ellen's hand was on her forehead. "You feel warm."

Jody jerked away and headed for the kitchen. "I picked up take-out from Casa Verde. I'm keeping the food warm in the oven, so let's eat before it dries out."

"Well, I hope you remembered to get beer. You know how I enjoy a cold beer with my Mexican food," Denise said.

Jody relaxed slightly. "Denise, would I serve you Mexican food without a cold beer?"

"Of course not, sweetie. That's why I love you so much," Denise teased.

"Let's hope you always do," Jody muttered as she stuck her head into the refrigerator to retrieve three cold Coronas.

"What did you say?" Denise was pulling the dinners from the oven.

"Mom told me you two were thinking about possibly expanding the shop," Ellen cut in.

Jody sent her a silent thank-you as Denise began talking about her plans for renovating the shop. As she rambled on about demolishing walls and redecorating the display cases, Jody glanced at Ellen. She was nervously pushing her food from one side of the plate to the other.

As Jody continued to watch, she began to get concerned. What if Ellen had already changed her mind?

Jody reached for her beer and knocked over the salt shaker.

Denise stopped talking and looked from Jody to Ellen. "What's wrong with you two?"

Jody and Ellen exchanged glances.

"Denise, we need to talk to you." Jody saw Ellen's face pale slightly.

"What about? You both are so jumpy, flies won't land on you."

Jody tried to remember the brilliant rhetoric she had been practicing, but none of the illuminating explanations came to mind. "I think I'm falling in love with your daughter," she blurted out.

Denise stared at them. "Of course, you love Ellen," she said in a small voice. "She's like a niece."

"No, Mom," Ellen said as she reached for Denise's hand. "Jody and I are dating."

Denise flew out of her chair and held up her hands. "I don't want to hear any more. This is a sick joke. It's not funny and I don't want to hear another word."

Jody stood. "It's not a joke, Denise."

"It had damn well better be," Denise hissed, staring at Jody.

"Mom, listen to us," Ellen pleaded. "I've had a crush on Jody for years."

Denise turned to her. "Ellen, you are not getting involved with Jody. There are things you don't know."

"Denise," Jody said, "I'm not that bad. You make me sound like an ax murderer."

She looked at Jody and said, "You are my dearest friend. I don't want to hurt you, but there's no way in hell I'm going to stand by and let you get involved with my baby girl."

"Mom, I'm grown. That decision isn't yours to make."

"This is not open for discussion. Get your things. We're going home." Denise started toward the living room.

When it became obvious that Ellen wasn't following her, she stopped and looked back. The room grew deathly silent.

Ellen was the first to break the silence. "I'm not going anywhere. I'm staying with Jody. We want to talk to you."

Denise whirled and stormed back toward them. For a moment, Jody thought she might strike Ellen, but instead she turned on Jody. "I trusted you. How could you do this to me? You were like a sister to me."

"I've not done anything to you, Denise. I never meant for this to happen. I didn't just say, 'Oh, today I'm going to fall in love with my best friend's daughter.' You know that."

"Don't you talk about love. What do you know? You hop in and out of beds like they were shoes."

"Mom, stop it." Ellen's voice held a slight tremor.

"Honey." Denise took Ellen's hand. "You'll just be another number. She'll keep you around until someone else comes along." She glanced at Jody. "Someone younger."

"Denise!" Jody exclaimed. "You can't seriously believe that."

"I've known you for almost thirty-five years. I watched you go from woman to woman. How many women *have* you been with?"

Jody was too stunned to respond. She had expected Denise's show of concern for Ellen, and even disapproval of their relationship, but not this open hostility.

"Let's go, Ellen." Denise started toward the door once more.

Ellen stepped next to Jody. Again, Denise stopped to look back.

"I'm staying here, Mom."

Jody saw the pain rip through Denise. She wanted to say something that would ease her anguish. She wanted to comfort Ellen, who was trembling and trying not to cry. Most of all, she wanted to be somewhere far away from the wave of pain and anger that swarmed the room like a colony of angry bees.

"Denise, please," Jody pleaded. "Be happy for us."

Anger flooded Denise's face. "Happy that you're going to destroy my daughter? Happy that you're tearing her away from me?" She turned to Ellen. "You're too young to understand. Now, let's go home."

Tears glittered on Ellen's lashes. "Please, don't do this."

"You put yourself in this position." Denise stood waiting for Ellen to join her.

As tears began to stream down her face, Ellen dropped her head against Jody's shoulder.

Jody pulled her closer and saw Denise sway as though she had been physically struck. Jody reached out to her. For the briefest of moments, she thought Denise was about to relent, but instead she shook her head, clearly defeated, and left. The soft closure of the door was more painful to Jody than all the preceding anger.

"I can't just let her walk away," Jody said as she started for the door.

Ellen placed a hand on her arm and stopped her. "She needs time. Let's give her a couple of hours, then I'll go home and talk to her."

Jody stared at the door in stunned disbelief. She had never seen Denise so angry or so hurt. Not even when she discovered Mark was cheating on her.

Jody realized Ellen was crying. "I'm sorry," she said.

"Why can't she be happy for me?"

Jody hugged her close. "Honey, it's not you. She's scared I'm going to break your heart."

"It's not you who's breaking my heart."

Jody led her to the sofa and sat her down, then knelt down in front of her. "You need to remember that your mom has seen me walk in and out of a dozen relationships. I can't really blame her for not wanting you to get involved with me."

"But she's wrong. This time will be different."

"How can you be so sure?" Jody asked. "What makes you think this time I'll be different?"

Ellen leaned back and rested her head against the sofa. "I don't," she admitted.

Jody froze. She had hoped to hear Ellen announce some profound reason why this relationship would be special. Disappointed and somewhat angry at her gullibility in wanting a simple answer to explain away all her problems, Jody went to the recliner, sat down and dropped her head into her hands. She had to find some way to make things right with Denise.

You know what you have to do, she told herself as she raised her head and gazed at Ellen. Her heart clenched as she watched a tear slide down Ellen's face.

"Are you going to use this as an excuse to bolt?" Ellen asked.

Startled that Ellen seemed to know exactly what she had been thinking, Jody stuttered out a denial.

Ellen sat up and stared at her. "I apologize. I was out of line asking that. I'm angry with Mom and taking it out on you."

Jody shrugged, not trusting her voice to conceal her deceit.

Ellen glanced at her watch. "Mom should be home by now. I'm going to go over and talk to her."

"Do you think she'll talk to you?"

Ellen smiled slightly. "She'll talk to me, but you'll probably be subjected to a very long session of Mom's famous cold-shoulder treatment."

Jody cringed. "Yeah, I've experienced it a time or two in very mild doses."

"I suggest you wear a heavy parka tomorrow, because the shop is going to be frigid."

"Maybe I'll get lucky and we'll have a lot of deliveries."

Ellen came over and kissed Jody's forehead. "Call me if it gets too bad, and I'll call and request a delivery every hour."

"You're sweet," Jody said as she walked Ellen to the door. "Call me later and let me know how she's doing."

"I will."

Ellen kissed her softly. "Try to get some sleep."

Jody watched until Ellen, on foot, was out of sight. Back inside, she threw away the remnants of the disastrous dinner. To kill time, she washed the few dirty dishes and scrubbed the oven, all of the appliances and countertops. She had just finished cleaning out the refrigerator when Ellen called.

She glanced at the clock as she raced for the phone, and was shocked to see it was nearly midnight.

"Did I wake you?" Ellen asked.

"No. I was cleaning out the refrigerator."

"At midnight?"

Jody ignored the question. "How did it go?"

Ellen was silent for a long second. "Not good. I'm moving out tomorrow."

"What!"

"She won't listen. When I told her I intended to keep seeing you, she told me she wouldn't allow me to live under her roof. My transfer from California provided me with housing reimbursement until I could locate a place. I'll get the paper tomorrow and start looking for an apartment. I should've started looking sooner, but I let Mom convince me to stay with her so I could save more money for a down payment."

"You could stay here," Jody said, praying she wouldn't accept the offer. If Ellen moved in with her, Denise would be twice as angry. Besides, the relationship was still too new. Jody needed time to adjust to this sudden change.

"No," Ellen said. "When or if I move in with you, it'll be because you want me to and not because I have to."

Jody breathed a silent breath of relief. She didn't want to rush things with Ellen. It was too soon for them to live together. "Let me know if you need any help moving."

"Thanks, but I don't have much. My furniture is still in storage. I don't want to take it out until I find a house. Now stop cleaning and go to bed. You have a long day ahead of you."

"I don't suppose you're talking about deliveries and all those orders coming in for Mother's Day, huh?"

Ellen chuckled. "Good night."

CHAPTER TWELVE

The next day proved harder than Jody could have ever imagined. She arrived a little before seven and already there were twenty-seven call-in orders waiting to be filled. Of the twenty-seven, eighteen had requested morning delivery. Jody filled out work tickets for each order and started a pot of coffee. She was gathering supplies for the first arrangement when Denise arrived a little after seven.

"Good morning," Jody called. She was determined to try to act as normal as possible.

Denise quickly squelched that thought with a curt nod. Denise picked up a handful of the order tickets and went straight to her worktable and began working.

Jody decided to try again. "I made coffee."

Denise continued to work.

"Fine. We're going to act like children today," Jody growled as she snatched up a wedge of floral foam and smashed it into the bottom of the pot she was arranging.

Things didn't improve as the morning progressed. Denise refused to talk to her unless she absolutely had to for the sake of the shop. Several times Jody glanced up and caught Denise glaring at her. Whenever Jody tried initiating a conversation, Denise would simply walk away. Jody was relieved when the arrangements were finally completed and she could escape the shop to make the deliveries. She took her time with them, in no rush to return to the shop and Denise's hostility. After the last arrangement had been dropped off, she reluctantly returned to Petal Pushers but remained in the showroom, waiting on customers or taking phone orders.

She couldn't prevent the smile that burst forth when she answered the phone and heard Ellen's voice.

"I didn't have any luck apartment hunting. I'm going to be staying at the downtown Holiday Inn for a few days," Ellen said, then rushed on before Jody could speak. "I'm working late tonight, but I thought maybe we might be able to have lunch together tomorrow."

"It will depend on deliveries," Jody reminded her.

"I have an appointment at ten-thirty. Why don't I call you afterward and see how you're doing then?"

"Sounds good."

"I'll call you later tonight," Ellen said. "I've got to go. The boss is bellowing."

Jody hung up the phone. It rang immediately. She grabbed it, hoping it was Ellen calling back. Jody wanted to talk to her. She didn't want to wait until tomorrow night.

The woman on the phone had the soft, slow-spoken drawl of West Texas. "Yes, my name is Patsy Caldwell. I'm on the board that's hosting the American Physical Fitness banquet that's being held at the St. Anthony Hotel tomorrow. We need sixty table arrangements by no later than six tomorrow night. We told the hotel we'd get the flowers ourselves, and now I'm sorry we did. The florist we contracted with caught his boyfriend . . ." She paused. "Well, suffice it to say he's no longer worrying about filling our order." She took a deep, shaky breath. "I'm sorry, but it's been a horrendous day. A friend of mine, Sharon Larson, suggested I contact your shop. I understand this is a hectic time for you, with Mother's Day coming up, but I'm desperate. Do you think you can possibly help?"

Jody was trying to process the idea that Sharon had made the referral. Was this a sick attempt to get even with her for breaking off the relationship? Jody shrugged off the thought. Sharon would never do anything that underhanded. Maybe there was hope they could become friends after all? She realized the woman was waiting for her to answer.

They were so busy, Jody considered turning the order down outright, but she could almost feel the woman's desperation through the phone.

"What kind of arrangements are you looking for?" she asked.

"At this point, we aren't going to be too demanding. If possible, I would like for them to all be about the same size and have some color coordination. The room is burgundy and beige."

"Can you hang on a minute? I need to speak with my business partner." Jody went to the worktable where Denise was putting a bow onto an arrangement. "I have to talk to you." Before Denise could say no, Jody rushed on to explain the situation. "Can we help her?"

Denise frowned. "We don't have enough flowers for that many arrangements."

"I'll tell her no." Jody tried to hide her disappointment. She gave one last try. "Such a large order could give the shop a lot of publicity. If we save their butts, the committee will certainly remember us the next time they need flowers."

"Wait a minute," Denise said.

Jody could almost see the number-crunching going on in Denise's head.

In the excitement of the challenge, Denise had temporarily forgotten about her anger. "If I can get the flowers, would you be able to stay late tonight? I'll call Eric and see if he can come in to help us. His classes ended yesterday."

"Sure, I don't have any plans tonight."

Jody saw the look in Denise's eyes the minute Denise remembered who Jody should be having plans with.

"Denise, we can't let our personal differences get in the way of the shop. If you want to be angry with me, fine, but do it after hours." Jody's anger surprised them both.

Denise nodded. "Tell her you'll call her back in a few minutes. I need to call Manny and see if he can get me the flowers."

Jody nodded. Manny was their main distributor, and knowing him, she was certain he could get them what they needed. "I'll get prepayment on a credit card," she said, "and double-check the hotel delivery hours."

Three hours later, a large delivery truck pulled up to the back door with the flowers just as Eric came in through the front.

Jody walked into the showroom to greet Eric as Denise left to deal with the delivery man.

"Hi ho," Eric called as he strolled in. "School is out, and I'm officially yours for the summer." He held out his arms and said, "So where do I begin?"

"We'll start with the sixty arrangements as soon as Denise finishes with the delivery."

Eric stepped closer and gazed at her. "Are you sick?"

"No."

"What's with the raccoon eyes?" he asked, pointing to the black circles under Jody's eyes.

Jody tried to shrug off his curiousity. "I've been having trouble sleeping."

"Oh, I see. Miss Sharon still keeping you up all night?"

"Sharon is old news. Jody has moved on to a much younger prospect," Denise snapped from behind them.

Jody groaned. She hadn't heard Denise come back into the room. She had hoped she would be able to explain the situation to Eric before something like this happened.

Eric quickly held up his hands. "Ladies, I don't know what's going on here, and quite honestly I don't want to. We have a lot of flowers to arrange. I think we should probably get started." Without waiting for either of them to respond, he scurried back to the workroom.

Jody turned to Denise, but she was already following Eric to the back. Jody glanced at the clock. It was a quarter after six. "It's going to be a long night," she muttered as she locked the front door.

The trio worked together in near silence until after one Friday morning, when Jody realized that at least one of them would have to get some sleep if deliveries were to be made the following day.

"Eric, you go and get some sleep. You can make deliveries tomorrow, and Denise and I will finish up here."

"Are you sure?" He looked at the mess around them. "I can miss a few hours of sleep and still function."

"I don't want you to be up all night and drive tomorrow. Or today, rather," Jody said with a wave of her hands.

"Good point," he agreed. "I'll be back by seven with bells on."

"Forget the bells and bring food," Denise called without looking up from her work.

Eric issued a sharp salute. "Until we meet again, fair ladies."

Jody walked him to the door.

"What's going on?" he asked when they were out of earshot.

"I'm dating Ellen."

"Denise's *daughter*?"

"Yes, and keep your voice down."

"Are you crazy? Surely there was at least one more lesbian in town you haven't dated. Why Ellen?"

Jody stopped and took a deep breath. "I think I'm falling in love with her."

"Christ in a handbasket." Eric rubbed his knuckles over his short, bristly hair. He noticed Jody's distress and shook his head. "Oh, Ms. Thing, you do know how to complicate your life."

91

To Jody's surprise, he gave her a long hug before he leaned back and looked at her. "If you really love her, don't screw this up. Let go of whatever it is from the past that keeps getting in your way. Sometimes, we only get one chance at the real thing."

Tears kept Jody from speaking, but she managed to nod.

"Good luck with the new mother-in-law," he whispered before he sped out the door.

Jody grinned in spite of herself and locked up behind him.

"We're lucky to have him helping us," she said when she returned to her worktable. "We're going to miss him when he graduates and moves on."

Denise didn't answer.

"Denise, how much longer are you going to stay mad at me?"

Again Denise didn't answer.

"You know, if you intend to act like this, maybe we should forget about attempting to renovate the shop, because at this rate, we won't have a shop in three months."

Denise's childish behavior and Jody's exhaustion sparked the outburst, but once said, the statement lay between them like old dynamite, one wrong move and everything could explode.

The phone rang shortly after two. Denise was closer to it and picked up. Jody knew by the sudden straightening of Denise's shoulders that Ellen was on the line.

"It's for you." She handed the phone to Jody and left the room.

"Hi," Ellen said. "I hope I didn't make things worse."

"No, it's about as cold as it can get here."

"I tried calling you at home. When I didn't get an answer, I assumed the shop must have gotten swamped with orders today." Jody told her about the large rush order.

"Do you want me to come down and help?"

"No, we should be able to finish in plenty of time. We have to deliver them before six tomorrow evening." Jody glanced at the clock. "Make that six this evening." She stifled a yawn. "Even if we get behind, Eric will be back around seven and he can make an

92

arrangement faster than Denise and me put together. The guy is amazing to watch."

"It's a good thing he's majoring in engineering and won't ever be in competition with the shop," Ellen teased.

"Tell me about it." Jody could smell coffee perking. "Why are you up so late, or early? Whichever the case may be."

"I'm still tweaking numbers. The home office wasn't happy with the results of one of our assessments, so I'm having to look at other options."

"Sounds boring."

"I usually enjoy it, but I seem to be distracted by something and can't keep my mind on work."

"Sounds serious. What's the source of this distraction?"

"As though you don't know."

Jody could see Denise standing at the front window looking out. She realized Denise wouldn't return until she got off the phone. "I'm sorry to cut you short, but I need to get back to work."

"I don't guess there's much chance of me seeing you at lunch."

Jody groaned; she had forgotten about the possible lunch plans. "No. In fact, I probably won't be able to see you until Monday. The next three days are going to be really hectic."

At that moment, Jody could not have guessed what an understatement her prediction would be.

CHAPTER THIRTEEN

The phone at Petal Pushers started ringing at eight Friday morning and didn't stop until after seven that night when Denise finally took it off the hook.

Eric came back a few minutes later and dropped into a chair beside a worktable. "I'm exhausted."

"It hasn't exactly been a tea party here," Denise said as she trimmed the stem of a yellow rose.

"Did you have any trouble getting the delivery to the banquet hall?" Jody asked. She was arranging a funeral spray. She hated making funeral sprays. They depressed her, but they accounted for a substantial portion of their sales.

Eric went to the utility closet and got a small whisk broom and dustpan. "I got to the hotel with no trouble," he said as he began sweeping up the snippets of stems and discarded petals from Denise's table. "The banquet hall was located in one of those odd stand-alone additions they have downtown. There are only two ways in. You know the kind I mean. It's a long room that usually hangs out over one of the pools, and it only has the one elevator and a single flight of stairs." He dumped the debris into the trash can and started cleaning Jody's table. "Jody, you should be so glad you weren't delivering today. The elevator was being repaired, and I had to carry the arrangements up the stairs to the hall."

"You had to carry all sixty of them by yourself?" Denise asked, looking over her shoulder.

"I had about half of them upstairs before two of the banquet organizers appeared and started helping. As God is my witness, I'll never take another flight of stairs," he groaned in his best Scarlett O'Hara drawl. When no words of sympathy came his way he peered at the two women. "You two look like crap."

"Thanks for your intelligent observation," Jody growled. She couldn't remember the last time she'd slept, and Denise looked as though she might topple off her stool with the slightest push.

"When was the last time you ate?" he asked after returning the broom to the closet.

"I'm not hungry," Denise said as she shaped yet another bow.

"I'm too tired to eat," Jody said.

Suddenly, someone started pounding on the front door. Jody was so startled she dropped her scissors.

"Who the hell is that?" Denise asked. "Eric, please go tell them we're closed."

"Sure. When I get back we will begin our conversation about you two going home and getting sleep."

"Too much to do," Jody and Denise mumbled in unison.

Jody retrieved her scissors and went back to work. She heard the bell ping as Eric opened the door. She slid off the stool to stretch her back, but she had been standing so much during the day that her feet began to throb almost instantly. Choosing the lesser of the two aches, she crawled back upon the stool.

"I'm so tired," Jody said. "After Sunday I don't want to see another flower for—"

"A month," Denise finished for her.

Jody looked up, surprised. She had for the most part spent the day silent or talking to herself. Denise's response gave her a brief shot of hope. Maybe she was calming down.

Denise turned to her. "Since Eric has started full-time for the summer, I think you should start your vacation on Monday."

Jody frowned. "You always go on vacation first, besides it's only May. I don't normally go until July or later."

"I can't leave now. I think it would be best if we had some time away from each other, so I'd really appreciate it if you took your vacation early."

"Well, tough petunias. I don't want to take my vacation early." Jody threw the scissors down. "If you are so damn disturbed by my presence, you can leave."

Denise jumped from her stool and planted her hands on her hips. "If that's the way you want it, fine. We can dissolve this partnership and move on."

Jody heard a startled gasp and turned to find Ellen and Eric standing in the doorway. For a moment, Jody forgot her exhaustion. She couldn't stop the smile that appeared with seeing Ellen. She wished she could hold her.

Jody saw Eric glance from Ellen to herself and back to Ellen. He rolled his eyes and smiled.

"What are you doing here?" Denise snapped at Ellen.

"I've brought everyone something to eat."

"I'm not hungry," Denise and Jody snapped in unison.

"You're right," Ellen said to Eric. "They are cranky as a couple of old sore-tail cats. His analogy not mine," she said as Denise turned on her. "I think you both should go home and get some sleep."

"There's too much to do," Jody explained. "The order for the banquet put us behind in our orders today. If we don't catch up tonight, we'll never be able to get through tomorrow."

Ellen walked to the desk, which at the moment was about the only area in the workroom that wasn't covered with flowers and floral supplies. She began to pull containers from the bag. "I picked up Chinese. Since I wasn't sure what everybody liked, I got a hodge-podge, so there's a little bit of everything here."

"I'll start another pot of coffee," Eric said.

Without waiting for Jody and Denise to join her, Ellen began to put together two plates. She set a plate at each end of the desk. "Do you two think you can remain civil to each other long enough to eat? Or should I put one plate out front?"

Jody hung her head. Denise's threat to dissolve the partnership frightened her. Surely, Denise wasn't that angry at her, was she?

The delicious smells from the Chinese food began to fill the room. The loud rumbling of Jody's stomach embarrassed her, but she smiled when she heard Denise's stomach growl too.

"I guess I'm hungry enough to sit with the devil himself." Denise went to the far end of the desk.

"Too bad you'll have to settle for little old me," Jody shot back as she moved to the other end of the desk. For several seconds there was silence as the two of them attacked the stack of egg rolls.

At some point, a cup of coffee appeared in front of Jody, who continued to devour her lemon chicken.

After they had eaten, Eric and Ellen began to clear away the food containers. Jody stood to go back to work.

"Where are you going?" Ellen asked.

"Back to work."

"No, I want you both to sit here for at least another half-hour and rest. You're no good to anyone if you're too exhausted to work."

"Jody, I'll finish the spray you were working on," Eric offered.

"And I can complete the arrangement you were making, Mom," Ellen said.

"You can't finish that," Denise protested.

Ellen's hands went to her hips in a manner so much like her mom's that Jody smiled. "I don't suppose you remember that I spent my summers helping out at that little flower shop you used to work at on Culebra," Ellen said. "Nor the fact that for four summers during college I worked in a flower shop in Los Angeles. I'm perfectly capable of completing an arrangement, Mom."

Jody leaned back in the chair and propped her feet up on a stack of boxes. She wasn't going to look a gift horse in the mouth. Thirty minutes of rest was all she needed to get herself through the night.

When Jody awoke her neck and back ached. She slowly lowered her feet to the floor and moaned. The squeak of a chair made her turn in time to see Denise raise her head up from the desk. There was a large red circle on her forehead where it had been resting on her arm.

"I guess we fell asleep," Jody mumbled as she looked around the workroom. Ellen and Eric were nowhere to be seen. The worktables were filled with completed arrangements.

"Good lord, it's after seven," Denise said looking at her watch.

"The orders. It looks like they finished them," Jody said.

They went to look at the massive display of flowers. "They must have worked all night," Denise said, gently touching one of the arrangements.

Jody suddenly remembered the comment Denise had made about dissolving their partnership. The thought made her ill.

"You wouldn't really dissolve our partnership because I'm dating Ellen, would you?"

Denise paused. "I can't begin to tell you how much I hate this rift between us, but as a mother, I can't just stand by and let you hurt Ellen."

"How can you be so sure I will?"

Denise looked at her. "How can you think you won't? You're nineteen years older than her. Even if you were to make a go of the relationship, which I don't think you will, in twenty years you will be sixty-four and Ellen will be forty-five. Is it fair to her to be saddled with that kind of burden? What happens when you're seventy? Do you want her to be stuck caring for you, when she'll still be a vital, active woman?"

Jody had no response. How could she argue with the numbers? Ellen would be hitting the prime of her life just as Jody was beginning to settle into the comforts of old age.

"I need time, Jody. We all do. You need to think about what you're doing."

Jody nodded. "I'll start my vacation on Monday," she said. "I can go to Missouri to visit my parents."

Jody's parents had moved back to Missouri after her dad retired from civil service. He'd been stationed at Lackland Air Force Base in San Antonio when Jody was small. After one enlistment in the Air Force and with no prospects waiting for him back in his small Missouri hometown, he took a civil service position at Lackland and stayed in San Antonio until he retired. He'd told Jody many times that his job was in San Antonio, but his heart was in Missouri.

Denise nodded. "Thanks. I appreciate your making the effort, and I really can't get away now."

"What about the partnership?" Jody asked, praying Denise would say she'd made a mistake.

"If you insist on continuing to see Ellen, I'm afraid that may be our only option."

Jody was about to protest when the front doorbell chimed.

It was Ellen. She was carrying several brown paper bags. Upon seeing the two of them, she smiled.

"Good morning, sleepyheads. Bringing you two food is getting to be a habit. I borrowed your keys, Mom." Without waiting for them to answer, she gave Denise a quick peck on the cheek. "Mom, I'm ignoring the fact that you didn't return my greeting and that you may have even attempted to turn away from my kiss." Without breaking stride, she turned to Jody and gave her a hug and a peck on the lips.

Jody froze, uncertain what Denise's reaction might be. Denise's only response was to quickly avert her eyes.

"Obviously, I'm not going to get a response from anyone this morning. Oh, well, I'm going to feed you breakfast anyway," Ellen said as she headed toward the back. "Then I'm sending you both home to rest and, well . . ." She stopped and looked back at them. "I don't mean to be rude, but it's growing extremely obvious that neither of you has been home in way too many hours."

"What do you mean?" Jody asked.

"She means you're rancid," Eric called out.

Jody turned to find him behind her. She hadn't heard him come in.

Denise pulled at her shirt and grimaced. "I guess I could use a little freshening up."

"Honey," Eric chirped, "chipped paint needs a little freshening up. You two need a full renovation."

He ducked as Jody hurled a sales pad at him.

CHAPTER FOURTEEN

They cleared a section on one of the worktables and sat together to eat their breakfast tacos. Eric and Ellen kept up a steady conversation with little input from her or Denise. As they planned their day, Jody wondered how she was going to tell Ellen that she would be leaving on a month-long vacation in a few days.

"I'll be back around ten," Denise announced as she stood and threw her paper plate into the trash.

"Mom, stay home and rest," Ellen said. "Eric will do the deliveries and I can help out at the shop today."

Denise and Jody smiled. "It's the day before Mother's Day. You have no idea how busy it's going to get," Denise said. She took her purse from the desk, and with a small wave she left.

Eric eyed the arrangements. "Speaking of deliveries, I'd best hit the saddle."

"I'll help you load the van," Ellen said as she joined him by the table.

Eric shook his head. "No, thanks. I have my own system, and besides, I think you're needed more in here."

Jody looked up in time to see him nod toward her. "I'm neither dead nor deaf, Mr. Eric. Let's get the van loaded so I don't have to look at your smiling face all morning." She tried not to groan as she pulled herself up from her chair.

With a lot of direction from Eric, they finally had the van loaded exactly as he wanted it. After he drove off, Jody and Ellen went into the shop where Jody plopped into her chair.

"I've never been so tired in my entire life," she said, rubbing her hands over her face.

"Two more days," Ellen said. She planted a kiss on Jody's head before pulling a chair over next to her. "Then Eric will be here, and you and Mom can start taking a few days off."

No time like the present, Jody thought. "I'm starting my vacation on Monday."

"That's great," Ellen said and smiled. "A few days of sleeping late, and you'll be back to your old self in no time."

"Denise requested I take my full vacation. I'm going to take a couple of weeks to go see my folks in Missouri, and I may go on to New York from there."

Ellen nodded. "Of course."

Jody sensed Ellen's disappointment. "If I skip New York, could you take a few days off when I get back? Maybe we could get away for a long weekend. Or if not, we can just lock ourselves in my house and not come out until Monday morning."

Ellen smiled. "Maybe I'll have my own place by then."

"Any prospects?"

"I looked at an apartment off of Thousand Oaks yesterday, but it faced the street and the traffic noise was horrible."

"Oh, no. Thin walls will never do. You're way too noisy."

"I'm glad to see you remember that. I was beginning to get a little nervous."

Jody took Ellen's hand and kissed it as she gazed into her eyes. "If I weren't so tired, I'd refresh your memory."

Ellen moaned and ran her fingers through Jody's hair. "Then by all means, go home and sleep. I'll stay here and help Mom. After the store closes, I'll come by and you can rub my poor tired feet."

Jody's fingers trailed up Ellen's leg. "It won't be your feet you'll be begging to have rubbed."

The phone started ringing.

Jody sighed and shook her head. "I'll be back by ten."

"Jody," Ellen started to protest.

Jody held up a hand to stop her. "You'll be glad to see me by then."

Ellen gave her a quick kiss. "I'm always glad to see you."

Jody went home. Even though she was exhausted, she ran for the first time in days. It took her longer than usual to find her natural stride, but when she did, the stress of the previous few days began to melt away. She ran a shorter, easier route than her usual one, and took a slow leisurely stroll back home where she showered in the hottest water her body could tolerate. As the water pounded the tiny kinks and knots out of her muscles, she thought about what she would do if Denise insisted they dissolve the partnership.

During her eighteen years as an investment broker, she had managed to build herself a sizable portfolio. Through careful planning and low-risk investments, she hadn't taken the financial beating that many had when the stock market turned sour, but most of her investments weren't liquid assets. Dipping into them would incur severe tax consequences. She kept a reasonable emergency fund set aside that she could fall back on, but it wouldn't last long.

As the water pounded down on her, she allowed herself to admit that money wouldn't be the issue. Losing Denise's friendship would be. Denise had been her best friend for nearly thirty-five years. What would she do without Denise in her life?

How could she make things right between them again? Stop seeing Ellen was the obvious answer, but that was not an option.

She turned the shower off and stepped out. She toweled herself dry while trying to decide what to do.

As she used the end of her towel to wipe away the steam on the mirror, it struck her full force that Denise could disappear from her life. She held on to the vanity for support.

Losing Denise wasn't an option. She turned the faucet on and splashed her face with cold water. She would do something to change her mind. There had to be a way to save her friendship with Denise without giving up Ellen.

When Jody returned to the shop shortly before ten, Ellen was on the phone and two customers were waiting. Jody dropped her backpack behind the counter and began helping the customers. There was a steady stream of walk-ins, and the phone would ring almost as soon as Ellen hung up. Things were still hectic when Denise came in a few minutes later.

The day became a blur of a ringing telephone and people. Jody and Denise worked nonstop in a futile attempt to keep up with the incoming orders. When the rush became too heavy for Ellen to handle alone, they took turns helping her with the walk-in customers and the telephone. When Eric came in from the morning deliveries, they quickly loaded the van for another round. By three they were so backlogged with deliveries, Jody loaded up her Wrangler with arrangements destined for a nearby hospital.

It was after four when she returned. Eric was in helping Denise. The four of them worked together until after seven when Denise finally took the phone off the hook. Jody saw the last customer out and locked the door behind him.

Denise removed the cash drawer from the register and started the cash register tape, while Jody submitted the credit card batch. Eric and Ellen moved the live arrangements to the cooler.

The cash register receipt was still running when the exhausted group made their way to the workroom. They collapsed wherever they could find a spot free of flower debris or floral supplies. Jody looked around. Everyone looked shell-shocked.

"I don't know what I would have done if you and Mom hadn't come back," Ellen said as she removed her shoes and rubbed her toes.

"Tomorrow will be worse," Denise predicted. "The last-minute shopping is always hectic."

They all groaned.

"Well," Jody said. "I should have turned down that big order for the hotel. If we hadn't spent so much time on it, we would've had most of the FTD arrangements already."

FTD blitzed the airwaves just before Mother's Day. When people saw an advertisement for a certain arrangement on television or in a print ad they tended to request that specific item. She and Denise usually prepared a few of the featured arrangements and kept them on hand.

"This is the first time I've worked Mother's Day," Ellen said. "I didn't usually start working until June."

"It's usually not this bad," Jody said. "It's just hard playing catch-up all weekend." Jody slowly stretched her arms over her head.

"That order will bring us four times the business those individual sales will," Denise said.

"You're probably right," Ellen said. "Those organizers won't forget how you saved their butts."

The cash register finally stopped printing. No one moved.

"Should I go get the tape for you?" Ellen asked.

Jody already knew that this had been the busiest day the shop had since Valentine's Day. "No, rest. I'll get it." She pushed herself up. Was it her imagination or did her muscles and joints ache more with each major sales holiday? She ripped the tape from the register, rolled it into a loose bundle and read it. She smiled tiredly as she waved the tape. "This might make everyone feel better."

"How'd we do?" Denise asked.

Jody studied the total. "I'd say roughly ten percent over last year and we still have tomorrow."

105

"Now that's a cause for celebration." Denise raised an imaginary glass.

"Let's celebrate with food. I'm starving," Eric said. "What are we bringing in tonight?"

"You and Ellen go home and rest," Denise said. "Jody and I can finish the orders for tomorrow morning and close up."

"I don't think so," he said, standing. "We're in this together. I'm in the mood for a big, juicy hamburger. How does that sound to everyone?"

There was a chorus of agreement.

"I'll go pick up the food and we'll eat. Afterward, we'll get started and get a jump on tomorrow's madness. Then we'll all go home and enjoy a good night's sleep."

"Sounds like a plan to me," Ellen said.

Denise followed Eric to the front to lock the door behind him, and Jody sat down beside Ellen. "Spend the night with me," she whispered, brushing Ellen's hair away from her face.

"Do you think you can stay awake long enough to show me that good time you promised?"

"Probably not, but I always wake up fully energized after a couple of hours of sleep." Jody winked at her suggestively.

Jody heard Denise returning and moved away from Ellen.

"Christ, I feel like a teenager again," Ellen complained. "This has got to stop."

"What has to stop?" Denise asked as she came through the door.

"Eating out," Jody said quickly. "She thinks all this takeout food is unhealthy."

"She's right," Denise said as she headed toward the restroom.

When she was out of earshot Ellen turned to Jody. "Why did you do that? She has to face the fact that she can't keep trying to control my life."

"Tomorrow will be hard enough. Let's try to keep everything as calm as possible, at least until closing time tomorrow."

"Yeah, about the time you take off on vacation," Ellen said.

"You're welcome to come with me," Jody said.

"You know I can't take vacation now. I haven't been here long enough to ask for vacation. Besides I'm sick and tired of living in a hotel. I've got to find a place to live."

"I've been meaning to ask. Can you afford to continue living in a hotel?"

"The company gets a corporate rate and that helps a lot, but I hate staying there. I want to get settled into a place of my own."

Jody gazed into her eyes. "I can't believe you've only been back three weeks. So much has happened."

"Jody, I'm scared," Ellen said, taking Jody's hand. "What are we going to do if she doesn't change her mind?"

"She will. She has to." Jody stopped and looked toward the restroom. "I don't want to lose you or her, and I don't want a rift between you two, but if she doesn't change her mind, I'm afraid we're all going to lose."

Neither of them spoke as the uncertainty of their future stared them in the face.

CHAPTER FIFTEEN

Ellen followed Jody home. It was after one o'clock when they fell naked into bed.

"I'm so tired," Ellen said, snuggling into Jody's arms.

"Sleep," Jody urged, fighting to keep her own eyes open.

"But I want to make love to you," Ellen protested in a voice already softened by sleep.

"You will." When Ellen's breathing slipped into the steady rhythm of sleep, Jody relaxed and allowed her eyes to close.

A few hours later, she was coaxed from her slumber by fingertips trailing up her spine. She shuddered with delight and moaned. "Don't you dare stop," she said as kisses were planted across her shoulder blades.

"No chance of that," Ellen said as she ran her fingertips back down and over Jody's hip.

Jody remained still, enjoying the delicious feel of Ellen's hand until she could no longer stand the tension. She pulled Ellen into her arms and kissed her deeply.

As she made love to Ellen, Jody felt something shift within her. It was as though a hollowness in her had begun to fill. She let the new sense of well-being engulf her as Ellen slipped her hand between Jody's legs and granted the release Jody so desperately needed.

As she drifted through the final waves of pleasure, Jody slid down between the long, slender legs and nudged them apart. She buried her face in Ellen's wetness, rubbing and pressing until her face was wet with her lover's desire.

Ellen was crying Jody's name when Jody pushed her tongue deep into Ellen's center, holding her until nothing else in the world existed. She held tightly and rode the explosive wave of Ellen's climax.

Ellen pulled Jody up and snuggled into her arms.

I love you, Jody thought as Ellen once again drifted off to sleep. As Jody held her, she thought about the long, stressful day that was ahead of them.

And then I start my vacation, she told herself. She made a mental note to call her parents to let them know she would be coming for a visit. There was so much to do. She still needed to notify her parents, make airline reservations, stop the newspaper delivery. At some point in her mental list-making, she drifted off to sleep.

By two Sunday afternoon, the phone had finally quit ringing and the walk-ins had stopped.

"Eric, go home. We have the beast whipped," Denise said as she covertly examined the jade bracelet that Ellen had given her for Mother's Day. "In fact, if we go thirty minutes without a customer, I say we close and all go home."

"Sounds good to me," Jody said.

"If you're sure you won't need me," Eric said.

"No, go on. I'll see you next month," Jody said as she stood to give him a hug.

He looked at her, puzzled. "Next month?"

"Yeah. I'm taking an early vacation."

His back was to Denise and he gave Jody a questioning look.

"Long story," she whispered as she hugged him.

After he left, Jody turned to Ellen. "You should go home and relax, too. You have to work tomorrow."

"Rub it in," Ellen said and turned to Denise. "Happy Mother's Day, Mom." She gave Denise a quick hug. Denise was still angry and took a step back as if to avoid the hug, but Ellen was too quick. "I know you're angry with me, but I love you, Mom."

Denise turned away.

Ellen looked at Jody and shrugged. "Walk me to my car?" She grabbed Jody's hand.

Jody followed. "You know this is only going to piss her off more."

Ellen turned away and looked across the parking lot. "Jody, I told you. I don't want to hurt her, but she has to learn that she can't keep trying to run my life."

Jody stepped around Ellen in order to see her face. Ellen quickly brushed away tears.

"That's what I thought," Jody said pulling Ellen into her arms. "I'm sorry you're hurting."

Ellen embraced her. "Why does she have to be so stubborn?"

"Honey, that's a question I've asked myself a hundred times."

"When are you leaving?" Ellen asked, trying to dry her eyes.

"Wednesday, I guess. I'll call my parents and the airlines tomorrow. But there are a couple of things I want to take care of first, so I probably won't leave until Wednesday afternoon."

"Good. You can have lunch with me tomorrow then," Ellen said.

"Okay. What time?"

"Is it all right if I call you tomorrow? My schedule is so unpredictable."

"Sure. Just give me a call at home."

With a last quick kiss, Ellen climbed into her car. "Until tomorrow," she said with a wave.

Jody watched until the Corvette was out of sight before she returned to the shop. Denise was busy straightening the supply cabinet. Jody took the broom and began to sweep. With Eric and Ellen gone, the shop was suddenly too quiet. She looked around at the piles of wilted petals on the floor and the few discarded flowers slowly dying and suddenly shivered.

I do need a vacation, she thought as she swept up the piles of trash.

CHAPTER SIXTEEN

Jody slept in Monday. At noon, when she still hadn't heard from Ellen, she called Ellen's cell phone.

Ellen answered on the second ring.

"Is this a bad time?" Jody asked.

Ellen hesitated.

"I'm sorry to bother you. I was calling about lunch. Just call when you're ready," Jody said.

"I don't think I'll be able to make lunch," Ellen replied.

Jody felt a finger of dread sneak across her scalp. "What's up?"

"It's probably nothing."

"What's nothing?"

"The doctor found a lump in my breast while doing my exam."

"What exam?"

"My annual physical. I waited until I got out here to take it, and Dr. Chavez found a small lump during my breast exam."

"You hadn't noticed the lump?" Jody asked.

"No."

"So, what happens now?"

"She wants me go for a mammogram."

"When?" Jody asked around the dread in her throat.

"I'm on my way to the imaging center now."

Jody sat down on the side of the bed. "She was that concerned?"

"I think she was a little concerned, you know, after Grandma and Aunt Alice." Ellen paused. "Anyway, she called the imaging center and got me in this afternoon."

"Do you want me to meet you there?"

Ellen paused. "No. I'm fine. You know how these things go. They'll run the test and I'll end up waiting for days to hear the results.

"Have you told Denise?"

"No. I'm not going to say anything. I'm sure it's nothing more than a cyst. There's no need in getting her upset."

"I think she would be pretty upset that you didn't tell her."

"Why worry her needlessly?"

Jody decided to keep her opinions to herself. It was up to Ellen if she wanted Denise to know. "Will you call me as soon as you're finished with the appointment?"

"Yes."

"I'll be at home. Call me if you change your mind and want me to meet you."

"Thanks. I'll be fine."

By three o'clock, Jody had cleaned every room in her house and was sick with anxiety. She tried not to think about the history of breast cancer in Ellen's family.

Jody considered calling Denise but stopped herself. Ellen would have to decide if she wanted her mom to know what was going on.

At three-thirty Jody lost her battle with waiting. She called Ellen's cell phone. There was no answer.

Jody picked up the phone to call her parents but changed her mind. She wasn't in the mood for chitchat. She loved her parents dearly but once her mother started talking about the garden and the neighbors it would be an hour before she could escape. She started cleaning out a closet instead.

Ellen called a little after four. "I'm on my way back to the hotel. Can you meet me for dinner?"

"Yes. What did you find out?"

"Nothing. The tech told me the doctor's office will call me as soon as she gets the results."

"Well, how long are they going to take!"

"Jody, calm down. You know it's always a waiting game with doctors."

"I know, but still."

"Let's not talk about the tests. I don't want to spend the next week worrying about them. Spend the night with me."

"At the hotel? Wouldn't it be more comfortable coming here?"

"Hey, people pay good money to sleep in hotels. Bring your jammies and spend the night with me," Ellen said.

"I don't own jammies." Jody wanted to ask more questions about the tests but felt she had to respect Ellen's wishes.

"All the more reason for you to spend the night," Ellen teased.

"What time shall I be there?"

"I'm only twenty minutes away from the hotel. I'm in Room twelve-oh-seven."

"It'll take me at least thirty minutes to get downtown."

"I'll be waiting."

Jody pushed the speed limit and cut the thirty-minute drive to twenty-five.

As promised, Ellen was waiting for her and wasted no time once Jody was through the door. She kissed Jody and led her to the bed. As they made love slowly, Jody found herself being overly cautious of bumping Ellen's breast.

After Jody's third apology, Ellen grabbed Jody's hand and placed it gently against her breast. "It's all right to touch it."

"I don't want to hurt you," Jody said, pulling her hand away.

Ellen looked at her closely. "Is that all it is?"

"Of course. What else would it be?"

Ellen hesitated. "Not that I expect them to be or anything, but would it make a difference if the tests were positive?"

Shocked, Jody sat up. "Of course, it makes a difference. I care for you very deeply."

"That's not what I was asking. I mean would it make a difference in the way you see me? Would you still . . . care for me?"

Jody pulled Ellen closer and wrapped her arms around her. "Yes, I'd still care for you. But we aren't going to have to worry about that, because I'm sure the tests are going to come back negative. As you said, it'll probably be a cyst." As she held Ellen, Jody imagined she could feel heat radiating from Ellen's breast. She suddenly recalled a science experiment she had witnessed as a child. The experiment demonstrated the effects that heat had on yeast. In her mind she saw the ball of dough start to expand, more than doubling in size. She fought the urge to break contact with Ellen's body, to reduce the body heat generated between them.

They talked about Ellen's work and reminisced about things that had happened in their past. Dinner was forgotten as they made love again, and fell asleep in each other's arms.

The following morning, Jody woke to Ellen's stirrings.

"Go back to sleep," Ellen whispered. "I'm going to shower."

Jody squinted at the red dial on the clock. It was five in the morning.

"Why are you up at this hour?" she asked.

"I need to go in early and try to get some work done. I was out of the office most of the morning yesterday, and I had planned on going in during the weekend but didn't."

"You shouldn't have put in all those hours at the shop." Jody started to sit up.

"No, don't get up. I enjoyed those hours working with you and Mom at the shop. Now, go back to sleep. You're on vacation, so rest."

Jody slipped back under the blanket. "Wake me before you leave."

"I will," Ellen promised and kissed her cheek.

A few seconds later, Jody heard the shower turn on. She snuggled deeper into the bedcovers, but it was useless. She was awake. She gave up trying to sleep and started planning her day. The first thing she should do was call her parents and let them know she would be visiting for a couple of weeks. Then she needed to call the airline for reservations. Jody sat up in bed and pulled the blanket up around her shoulders. Maybe she should postpone the trip to see her parents until the results from Ellen's tests were back. Even though Ellen didn't seem concerned over them, Jody would feel better if she waited until the results came back. Besides, it wasn't like she would be wasting the time. There were several things around the house in need of attention.

The rose garden, she decided. She'd been wanting to put a rose garden in her backyard for over a year.

She heard Ellen in the shower and thought about joining her but knew if she did, Ellen would be late for work. So instead, Jody called and ordered breakfast.

By the time Ellen came out of the bathroom Jody had breakfast arranged on the small table.

"What's this?" Ellen asked, smiling. She was dressed in a pale blue linen suit.

"Breakfast is the most important meal of the day," Jody mimicked the popular television commercial from her childhood.

Ellen laughed.

"I thought you might be hungry since we never got around to having dinner."

"As a matter of fact, I'm famished. What do we have to eat?"

"The all-American heart-attack-producing breakfast of eggs, toast, bacon and a pot of coffee."

"Um, let's start with the coffee."

Jody leaned over and kissed Ellen quickly. "Your wish is my command."

"I'll have to remember that," Ellen said, wiggling her eyebrows.

After Ellen left for work, Jody took a quick shower and dressed. Since her favorite garden center didn't open until nine, she had a couple of hours to kill. She dug through the desk drawers until she found a piece of hotel stationery and began sketching a rough plan for the rose garden.

CHAPTER SEVENTEEN

Leti and Maricela were still arranging the outside displays when Jody pulled into the parking lot.

Leti, a tall, lanky woman in her mid-fifties, glanced up as Jody approached. "Hello," Leti called. She set a tray of petunias down and waved.

Maricela's short, heavy-set form was bent over a water fountain that she was in the process of assembling. She saw Jody and frowned. Jody waved and said hello anyway. Maricela had been angry with Jody ever since Jody dated Maricela's sister, Pat, a few years before. The short affair hadn't ended well, and Maricela still blamed Jody.

Only a pleading look from Leti budged Maricela away from the fountain long enough to be civil.

"I haven't seen you two since the Christmas party at the community center," Jody said as she gave Leti a hug.

"We've been here," Maricela said, heading into the store.

"What brings you out so early?" Leti asked as she watched Maricela disappear inside.

"I want to put a rose garden in my backyard, but I'm not sure how much room I need for the plants. I thought I'd drop by to see if you had any suggestions as to which varieties I should plant and how much room they'll need."

Leti pulled her cap off and brushed her arm across her forehead. "The size will depend on the number of plants you want. It's best to decide how large you want the garden to be and use that to determine the number of plants. You can plant any of the varieties we carry. Some do a little better in certain locations but, of course, drainage is the big issue. Along with how much sun will be hitting the plants during the heat of the day, and how good your soil is."

Jody pulled her crudely drawn plans from her pocket. She used it to point out where the trees and other flower beds were in her yard, and which area of the rose bed would get afternoon sun.

"The house will shade the entire plot until about midmorning," Jody explained.

"How's your soil?"

"Not very good. I'll probably have to dig out the area and then fill it in with a topsoil mixture like you recommended I do for the flower beds."

"Why don't we start you off by preparing the soil and after you get it ready, you can choose the rosebushes. People don't realize that roses are hardy plants. They'll grow almost anywhere." Leti motioned for Jody to follow her. "Let me show you a few things you can use to enhance your current soil, and if you don't care for them, then I'll load you up with some topsoil and get you started."

After listening to Leti explain the various fertilizers and soil products, Jody decided to stick with her original plan to dig out the area and replace it with a much more fertile topsoil. She rented a garden tiller from them and purchased several bags of sand, topsoil and mulch. Since the tiller would not fit into Jody's Wrangler, she made arrangements to have everything delivered. Leti promised the items would be delivered before noon that day.

Jody went home and changed into an old tank top and shorts. She walked out onto the flagstone patio and surveyed the backyard. She loved the yard. Her property consisted of a double lot. The house stood on one lot and the backyard was the other. A large portion of the yard was covered in St. Augustine grass, which provided a deep, rich carpet of green. To her left was an oak tree that had stood there well over fifty years. Toward the back of the yard were two towering pecan trees and several smaller fruit trees. Since moving in, Jody had added four small flower beds scattered throughout the yard. Some had been planted merely for color, but the majority were for the purpose of attracting butterflies and hummingbirds. The rose garden was to be purely for her own enjoyment. She wanted it to be visible from both her bedroom window and the large bay window in the kitchen. She went back inside to check the view from both windows and to ensure she'd chosen the perfect location. She then measured off the garden's dimensions and used a couple of garden hoses to mark the layout. As a final precaution, she went back inside to view the area outlined by the hoses. Satisfied with the layout, she got a shovel and began digging the grass from the area. She would save the grass and transplant it to the far side of the tool shed where the St. Augustine hadn't yet reached. The removal of the grass was back-breaking, but she already had a large section removed by the time Maricela backed the truck up to the side gate.

Grateful for the break from digging, Jody went to help her unload the tiller and bags. They worked in silence.

After they finished unloading the truck, Maricela handed her a copy of the delivery receipt.

Jody decided it was time to get the problem between them out into the open. "You're never going to forgive me for breaking up with your sister, are you?"

Maricela braced her solid frame against the back of the pickup. "You really hurt her."

"Maricela, we only dated for a couple of weeks."

"She thought you were serious. She didn't realize it's all a game to you."

"I'm sorry she was hurt, but I never pretended it was forever."

"She was at a bad spot in her life and your breaking up with her didn't help. I'll pick up the tiller tomorrow. If you decide you'll need it longer, just give Leti a call. If you aren't going to be home, leave it by the gate." Without waiting for Jody's response, Maricela climbed into the truck and drove off.

Why did things always have to be so complicated? Knowing there was no answer to her question, she went back to work on her rose garden.

By late afternoon, she had removed all the grass and several inches of dirt from the designated area. She was ready to replace extracted soil with the more fertile mixture and begin tilling.

Before beginning that task, she decided to take a break and made herself a sandwich. She took her lunch out to the patio to view the work she'd accomplished. As she studied the area, she suddenly envisioned a swing in the middle of the garden, with an arbor covered by lush climbing roses shading the swing. She raced inside for a pencil and pulled the sweat-dampened plans from her pocket. She added a crude sketch of a swing with an arched arbor over it. She realized the new additions would require a larger area. Her back ached as she thought about the additional digging that would be required, but she knew the extra work would be worthwhile. She tossed the half-eaten sandwich aside, picked up the shovel and went back to work removing more grass. It was late afternoon before she ripped open the first bag of sand and dumped it into the enlarged area. Leti had explained to her that the sand would provide drainage for the plants.

After dumping in all the sand, Jody realized she only had enough for the original smaller version.

She glanced at her watch. It was after six. Leti and Maricela's shop stayed open until eight, but they were all the way across town from her. Feeling slightly guilty, but determined to complete the soil preparation today, she jumped into her Jeep and headed for the nearest home-improvement center.

When she returned home, she checked her messages and experienced a stab of disappointment that Ellen hadn't called. She toyed with the idea of calling her but decided to wait and call later. She unloaded the additional bags of sand and topsoil, then went back to work.

It was after eleven before she smoothed out the last of the topsoil. Exhausted, yet filled with a sense of accomplishment, she dropped into a lawn chair. The rich, warm fragrance of fresh soil filled the air.

She watched the bugs hovering around the large reflector light she'd hung from the tree to illuminate her work area and again thought about calling Ellen. She couldn't wait to complete the garden and invite Ellen over to see it. She angled her watch around until she could see the time. It was only a little after eleven. Ellen would probably still be up.

Jody went inside, grabbed the phone and a cold beer and took them back to the patio. She sipped the beer as she dialed Ellen's cell number and waited.

When Ellen answered, Jody heard the music of mariachis in the background. "Where are you?" Jody asked.

Ellen was a little slow in answering. "I'm having dinner with a friend from Los Angeles."

"Oh, I'm sorry to disturb you. I didn't realize you had plans tonight. Not that you have to tell me if you have plans," Jody added, flustered. "I just meant that . . ."

"I didn't know she was going to be in town. We kind of bumped into each other."

"I see," Jody said, although she wasn't sure she did. She could sense Ellen's discomfort. "Look, I'll let you go. I was just calling to, you know, say hi. I'll talk to you later."

Jody hung up before she could make a bigger fool of herself. Immediately, she wished she could call back and ask Ellen why she was out with some other woman until nearly midnight. Maybe Ellen was already tired of her and was looking for someone younger. A mosquito buzzed around her ear. She gave a half-hearted swipe at it and wondered who the woman was. How did they happen to bump into each other? The mosquito buzzed against her cheek. Was it a friendly dinner? Maybe she was an ex-lover. The back of Jody's arm began to itch. She reached back and was numbly aware of a half-dozen welts from mosquito bites.

It's nothing, she told herself. If Ellen said she was only having dinner with a friend, then there was nothing else going on. Relationships required a certain amount of trust and distance, she reminded herself. Besides, she and Ellen were only dating. No commitment had been made. She felt a sharp stab over her eye. The mosquitoes were eating her alive. She swatted at the one above her eye and only succeeded in slapping herself.

She gathered up the phone and the now-warm beer. With a last glance at her rose garden, she turned out the light and escaped into the house.

As she dumped out the beer, she made a decision. She wasn't going to allow herself to get all psyched out over Ellen having dinner with an old friend.

She focused instead on her rose garden. Tomorrow, she would start looking for the swing and arbor. When she had them, she could start choosing her plants.

She showered and fell into bed exhausted but satisfied with the day's accomplishment. It took some effort, but she finally pushed away the nagging thoughts and doubts of what Ellen was doing and fell asleep.

CHAPTER EIGHTEEN

The following morning, Jody sat on her patio, having her first cup of coffee. She attempted to count the number of hummingbirds that were swarming the feeders. The phone rang, interrupting her futile efforts.

"Did I wake you?" Ellen asked.

"No. I'm outside enjoying my coffee and counting the humming-birds."

"I'm jealous."

Jody watched a hummingbird approach one of the numerous feeders filled with sugar water. She wanted to ask about Ellen's dinner date but knew she shouldn't. To her relief, Ellen brought up the subject.

"I wanted to call and talk to you about last night. I couldn't really talk when you called, and it was too late to call after I got back to the hotel."

What time did you get back to the hotel? Jody wanted to shout. While traveling in Midland, Ellen had called Jody after midnight. Jody stiffened when she heard Ellen take a deep breath. She braced herself and waited for the bombshell that she instinctively knew would drop.

"Beth is in town."

Jody struggled to recall the name. Who the hell was Beth? She bit her tongue and waited for Ellen to continue.

"She remembered my telling her about Petal Pushers. She went there and Mom told her where I was staying. She was waiting for me when I got to my room yesterday," Ellen said.

Before Jody could stop herself, she blurted out, "What does she want?"

"She wants us to try again. She says she still loves me and she's willing to see a counselor to work on her codependency issues."

"What did you tell her?" Jody cursed herself for asking a question to which she didn't really want an answer.

Ellen sighed and Jody felt her heart skip a beat.

"I told her I was seeing someone else, and that she and I didn't have anything to work out."

"So she's going back to California?" Jody prayed she was.

"Not exactly."

Jody knew she was going to regret asking, but a naughty streak of masochism forced her to. "What does 'not exactly' mean exactly?"

"She's taken a leave of absence from work and is staying here in San Antonio."

Jody breathed a sigh of relief. "Living in a hotel, as you well know, isn't cheap. How long can she possibly stay here without working?"

"She's not staying in a hotel."

"Where is she?"

"She's staying with Mom."

"What?"

"She went to see Mom and pleaded her case. My guess would be, Mom saw it as the perfect means of separating you and me and has joined forces with Beth."

"I don't believe this."

"Mom is going to do whatever she feels is necessary to get you out of my life," Ellen reminded her. "You know that's why she insisted you take your vacation early. She thought you would go visit your parents, and by the time you came back, you'd be ready to move on to someone else."

Jody tossed her cold coffee into the grass and set the cup on the patio table beside her. "What do *you* want?" she asked.

"I want the same thing I wanted yesterday."

"Which is?"

"Stop pretending to be so dense. I love you, Jody Scott, and I want to try to make a life with you. If I can ever get you to stop thinking of *commitment* as a dirty word. I think the question now is, what do *you* want?"

Jody stared at the fresh, rich soil of her rose garden. She was glad she'd gotten rid of the old depleted dirt, so the new roses would grow. Maybe it was time to make a fresh start herself, to let go of the distrust Mia's desertion had instilled in her. She took a deep, shaky breath and slowly exhaled. "I love you, Ellen Murray, and I want you in my life for as long as you can stand me."

"That could prove to be a very long time."

"Is that a promise?"

"Yes. Can you handle that?"

"I think so," Jody said.

"Is that a promise?" Ellen asked, mimicking her.

"No, that's a commitment."

"I knew you had it in you." She laughed.

"Are you free tonight?" Jody asked.

Ellen groaned. "No, I'm having dinner with a client. I would reschedule, but it's a new client and my boss asked me to attend. I probably won't be free until after ten and then I'll have some work to do afterward. I'll need to type my preliminary report while everything is still fresh in my mind."

Jody looked at the garden again. If she could find the bench and arbor today, she could set them up and plant the roses tomorrow. She could then show Ellen the completed project. "How does tomorrow night look?"

"I'll make it a point to keep tomorrow evening free," Ellen said. "There's only so many nights with you that I'm willing to give up."

"Good. Come by after work. I'll make us a nice dinner and show you my latest creation."

"What creation?"

"No. You have to wait and see the final product."

"All right. I'll come by right after work."

"Make sure you forget your jammies. You won't need them."

"Promises, promises," Ellen teased and said good-bye.

Jody sat on the patio for several minutes. She waited for the regret in uttering those three scary words to set in. When it failed to appear, she felt the vise around her heart loosen. Maybe this time really would be different.

With a new wave of hope, she went into the house and grabbed a pad of paper and the phone directory. Pouring a fresh cup of coffee, she began to make a list of all the home improvement and garden centers in the area. After organizing them by location, she set off to find the perfect swing and arbor for her rose garden.

It took two hours and six shops before she found exactly what she was looking for at a small family-owned outdoor furniture shop. The redwood swing displayed a carved rose on its crossbeam. The three-inch vertical slats of the seat would provide more comfort than the usual one-inch slats. She chose a matching redwood arbor that was wide enough to fit over the swing. She purchased the two pieces and arranged for delivery. The owner agreed to set the items in the back-yard if Jody was not home when they arrived.

From the furniture shop, Jody drove directly to Leti and Maricela's garden center. With Leti's help, she chose a dozen rosebushes in various shades of red, pink, white and yellow. Some of the bushes already had several small buds. While there, she picked out a few basketball-size landscaping rocks and a small birdbath. With all of her purchases complete, Jody headed home to finish her project.

Impatient to begin, she planted the roses that would be along the back edge of the bed and then mowed the yard to kill time. The furniture arrived late, but the deliveryman helped her set the swing and arbor into place and showed her how to attach and drive in the stakes that would anchor the arbor.

An hour later, with the arbor securely anchored, she planted the remaining rosebushes, four of which would eventually climb over the arbor. With the roses in place, she arranged the landscaping rocks. The rocks were heavy and she was glad she only had a few to handle. The birdbath was easy to set up.

Darkness set in before she was satisfied with the arrangement of the rocks and fountain. Once again, she was forced to hang a light from the tree in order to finish up.

After everything was complete, she turned out the light and sat in the swing. It felt so comfortable, she stretched out and stared up at the thin sliver of a crescent moon, and the faint glow of stars. The night sky was the only thing she disliked about city living. She couldn't see the stars clearly.

It didn't take long for the mosquitoes to find her and drive her inside. She made a note to find something that would repel them enough for her to enjoy her new outdoor creation.

She wanted to call Ellen and tell her all about the rose garden, but it was after ten. She settled for a shower and fell into bed. She was too tired, or maybe just too excited, to sleep. She tried to watch a movie, but thoughts of Ellen and the fact that they had made a commitment of sorts kept sneaking in and distracting her. She finally gave up on the movie and turned the television off.

The neighbor's security light cast shadows of tree limbs dancing on her wall. Would Ellen move in with her? Or would Ellen want to have her own place? She tried to imagine Ellen living in her house and was surprised to find it wasn't hard to do. As a test, she tried to imagine one of the various other women she had dated living with her, and she couldn't form a mental picture.

Was it too early to ask Ellen to move in with her? Ellen was miserable at the hotel, and even with the corporate discount, it must be costing her a small fortune. How was Denise going to react if they decided to live together? As she mulled over the questions, she fell asleep.

CHAPTER NINETEEN

A loud ringing pulled Jody from sleep. Disoriented, she fumbled for the alarm clock, trying to turn it off before she realized it was the phone. She squinted against the brightness of the room. The long ray of sunshine dancing across the foot of her bed startled her. She glanced at the clock on the bedside table as she reached for the phone. It was almost ten. She couldn't remember the last time she had slept so late.

"Hello," she answered, still staring at the clock. There was silence. "Hello."

She was about to hang up when Ellen spoke. "I need to talk to you."

"What's up?"

"Nothing really, I just . . ." She hesitated.

"Are you all right?" Jody froze. Had Ellen already changed her mind about Beth?

"Not really." Ellen took a deep breath. "The doctor just called with the results from the tests I had on Monday."

Jody shivered suddenly and pulled the blanket up across her shoulder. "That was quick."

"Apparently Dr. Chavez requested a rush."

"And?"

"She's scheduling me for a biopsy at eleven tomorrow morning."

"A biopsy? Shouldn't you be getting a second opinion or another mammogram?"

"Why? She can feel the lump and the mammogram confirmed it was there. What good will another mammogram do?"

Jody tried to think of something positive to say, but all she had were questions. "Who's doing the biopsy and where is it going to be done?"

"Dr. Chavez will do the procedure in her office. She said she would make a small incision and insert a biopsy needle to remove a sampling from core tissue of the lump. Afterward the incision is closed with a stitch or two."

Jody could tell Ellen was reading the information.

"Would you like me to go with you?" Jody asked.

"The doctor said I would be able to drive afterward. It's really no big deal."

"It is a big deal, Ellen. You should have someone there with you. If not me, at least call Denise."

"No. I don't want to tell Mom yet. I don't want to worry her."

"Then let me go with you."

Ellen hesitated. "You can pick me up at work tomorrow around ten-fifteen, if you like."

"Thank you. I'll bring you back here and you can rest for the day."

"No. I'm going back to work afterward. Dr. Chavez says I'll be fine. I can take Tylenol if I need to after the local wears off. In fact, I'm going to have to cancel our dinner engagement this evening. I'm sorry, but I've got so much work to do, and the doctor appointments are putting me further behind."

"Ellen, you need—"

"Jody, don't tell me what I need. I called you because I thought you'd understand. I'm going back to work afterward, and I intend to spend the night at the hotel, alone. I have a lot of work to do. It seems like ever since I've gotten here it has been one thing after another. I'm behind in my work and I don't want someone else to have to pick up my slack."

Jody realized Ellen was scared. With her family history, Jody thought, who wouldn't be? "I'm sorry. You're right. I got a little overprotective. I'll pick you up at ten-fifteen. I'll sit in the waiting room at the doctor's office, and I won't even hold your hand on the way over."

Ellen laughed at Jody's absurdity. "All right, I got a little melodramatic. I'm starting to feel overwhelmed, I guess."

"I'll be around if you want to talk."

"Thanks for being so understanding. I really am sorry about all this drama. Please don't be upset with me about canceling our dinner plans."

"Don't worry about me," Jody said and sat up. "I'll see you tomorrow."

Jody slipped into shorts and a red T-shirt and made coffee. As it brewed, she stood at the kitchen window watching a pair of ruby-throated hummingbirds darting between feeders. The morning sun reflected off their iridescent backs. She watched the male, with his brilliant red throat, as he veered away from the feeder and hovered outside the window as though he were gazing at her. It took her a minute to realize that her red shirt was the source of his attention. She moved away from the window. If she continued standing there, the hummingbird might fly into the windowpane in an attempt to investigate the red object.

She poured herself a cup of coffee and carried it out to the rose garden where she sat in the swing. The morning sun hadn't yet cleared the roof of the house, but already she could feel its warmth. The earthy smell of the topsoil rose up to greet her. Somewhere in one of the trees behind her, a cardinal chirped for its mate. Several mourning doves cooed from various locations around the yard. She needed to refill the bird feeders.

Without warning, it hit her. Ellen could have breast cancer. *I could lose her before we even have a chance to know each other.*

You don't have to put yourself through this, a voice whispered. *You can leave now.*

Jody ran her fingers over the tender leaves of the rosebush nearest the swing. There were several small buds that would soon be bursting open. She caressed one of them with her fingertip. As she stared at the rosebud, she realized Mia's leaving hurt her so badly, she had hidden her heart away as a means of protecting herself. She hadn't loved Lauren or any of the other women she had dated. She hadn't allowed herself to love them. She let go of the rosebud and took a sip of her coffee.

I'm in this for the long haul, she thought. If Ellen had cancer, they'd face it together. Jody ignored the cold fist of fear that began to settle deep in her stomach.

CHAPTER TWENTY

The following morning, Jody parked the Jeep in front of Ellen's office building and waited. The sun beaming through the windshield reminded her that the hot, humid days of summer were only a few weeks away. She rolled down her window and inhaled the sweet smell of mountain laurel. A dozen or more of the sturdy plants lined the sidewalk, yet only one was still blooming.

She gazed at the drab glass and brown brick multistoried building, glad that she no longer had to do the normal nine-to-five routine. She put in a lot of hours at the flower shop, but for the most part the time was enjoyable.

The large number of people who hustled in and out of the building soon convinced Jody why time-motion studies were a booming business.

Ellen walked out precisely at ten-fifteen, dressed in an expensive-looking cream-colored suit.

Jody smiled when she saw that Ellen was wearing matching heels. Grateful for her own freedom, she wriggled her toes inside her comfortable loafers. Giving up the job on Wall Street had been the best decision she had ever made.

"Good morning," Ellen said as she slipped into the Wrangler and gave her a quick kiss on the cheek.

"It's a good thing I haven't gotten around to removing the top yet," Jody said, giving it a thump. She normally removed it around the first of May, but with so much going on, she hadn't gotten around to it. "The wind would have messed up your hair."

Ellen stuck her tongue out at Jody, then ran a hand vigorously through her short brunette hair. It simply fell back into place. "I'm completely low-maintenance," she declared.

They were silent until Jody pulled onto the freeway that would take them across town.

"How are you doing?" Jody asked.

"All right. I guess I'm a little nervous."

Jody reached for her hand. "I'll be there if you need me."

"I appreciate that. I'm trying not to get ahead of myself and worry for nothing. The doctor said that eighty-five percent of the time lumps aren't cancerous."

There it was. The word Jody was fighting to avoid. A sudden jolt of rage shook her. Why did Ellen have to say it? Now it existed. Now it could invade her life. It could invade Ellen.

"I guess you'll be working this coming weekend," Jody said, hoping to change the subject.

Ellen took a moment before she responded. "I really should. I'm so far behind. It seems like I get a new account every day. I don't even have time to wrap up one project before they give me another one."

"You have to rest sometime. Remember, the more you do, the more they'll find for you to do. You're part of the corporate fodder, and they won't mind eating you alive."

"I guess I feel guilty that I just got here and all of this stuff is happening. I've not had time to get established. I'm not normally this . . . this . . ." She stopped and sighed.

"It's all right. You're just in one of those cycles where everything turns to crap. We all get stuck in them sometimes. Things will settle down soon." Jody squeezed Ellen's hand. Despite the warmth of the day, her hand felt cold. "Are you sure you're all right?"

Ellen glanced out the window. "Truthfully, I'm scared, but I can't talk about it right now. I need to not think about the biopsy or the results until later."

Jody nodded. "Okay."

Ellen seemed content to sit quietly and stare out the window of the Jeep. Jody decided to wait for her to break the silence. Ellen was still gazing out the window when they pulled into the parking lot at the doctor's office.

As they stepped out of the Jeep, Jody struggled to think of something to say to reassure her, but nothing original came to mind.

Inside the crowded office, Ellen went to the desk to sign in, and Jody made her way to the far corner where there were two empty seats. Three small boys and a young girl sat on the floor staring at a Disney movie. The girl looked up and smiled as Jody sat down. She was missing a front tooth.

Jody smiled back and the child giggled.

"What happened to your tooth?" Jody asked.

"The tooth fairy came and got it," she replied. "But she left me a dollar."

"A dollar. That's a lot of money for a tooth."

"Hush. I'm trying to hear the movie," the oldest boy snapped.

Jody stared at him. He was no more than seven and already he clearly felt he had the right to talk to her as he pleased.

"I see you've made a new friend."

Jody looked up to find Ellen standing next to her.

"Hush," the boy said without looking up.

Ellen grimaced and took the empty seat next to Jody. "Was I ever that rude?"

Jody chuckled. "Do you remember when we went to the coast for your high-school graduation?"

Ellen groaned and covered her face. "I had such a crush on you, I nearly died. Five entire days with you sleeping in the next room. It was almost more than I could stand."

"I don't believe it."

"It's true. I thought you were absolutely the hottest thing."

Jody looked at her and frowned. "I don't like the past tense of that statement."

A loud burst of laughter erupting from the television temporarily distracted them.

"Why didn't you tell me?" Jody asked as the noise died down.

Ellen looked at her with raised eyebrows. "Get real. How could I tell you? You were Mom's best friend. I mean, I knew you were gay, but there was no way I could have said anything."

"So you were serious about having a crush on me all these years?"

"Yes."

"Why were you such a brat?"

Ellen looked embarrassed. "I guess I thought you would think I was cute or something. You were so hot."

Jody smiled and sat a little straighter.

"Look at you," Ellen teased. "Before your head gets so large you won't be able to get out the door, I should remind you that I did go on with my life. It wasn't like you were in my every thought."

"Oh," Jody said as her ego deflated.

"It's just that you kept coming back."

Just then the nurse called Ellen's name.

Jody heard Ellen take a deep breath as she reached for her purse. "I'll be right here," Jody reminded her.

Ellen nodded and headed toward the door.

"Now maybe I can hear," the little boy muttered.

Jody saw an empty seat across the room and decided to move. She found an investment magazine on the rack and tried reading an article on IRAs, but every time the door separating the waiting room from the back offices opened, she would sit forward. After starting the article for the fourth time, Jody finally gave up and set it aside.

Jody had never been a nail-biter, but by the time Ellen emerged from the doctor's office over an hour later, she had gnawed three nails and was working on the fourth.

Ellen looked pale as she gave a small smile and patted Jody's arm. Jody managed to control her questions until they were in the Jeep and she had the motor running.

"What did she say?" Jody asked.

"She won't know anything for twenty-four to thirty-six hours." Ellen pulled the seat belt across her and carefully fastened it.

"Are you hurting?" Jody peered at her. There was a fine film of sweat on her face.

"No. It feels a little odd, but it doesn't hurt. The local hasn't worn off yet."

Jody started out of the parking lot. "Are you sure you want to go back to the office?"

Ellen nodded. "I have to get caught up."

Reluctantly, Jody drove her back. They rode in silence.

When she pulled the Jeep up to the curb, she said, "If you need anything, you call me."

"I'm fine, and thank you for going with me."

Jody shrugged. "I'm glad you asked. When will I see you again?"

Ellen tilted her head and said, "What if I came by after work today? You can show me that big secret you're hiding."

It took Jody a moment to realize that she meant the rose garden. "I'll fix dinner. What would you like?"

Ellen shrugged. "Let's wait and see what we feel like eating." She stepped out of the Jeep and gave Jody a small wave.

Jody waited until Ellen disappeared inside the building before she pulled away from the curb. She drove home and made herself a sandwich. She sat at the kitchen table and picked at her food as she battled the fear building within her.

In the last few days, her world had started to implode. Somehow, she had to find a way to repair the rift with Denise. A frightening thought struck. What if the rift was already beyond repair? What would her life be like without Denise?

Jody dumped the mangled sandwich into the garbage disposal and went outside. She retrieved a pair of clippers from the toolshed and pruned the new shoots emerging from the crepe myrtle trees. She edged the grass and filled the half-dozen bird feeders around the yard.

She was putting away the extension cord for the edger when the phone rang.

Jody grabbed the phone and smiled when she heard Ellen's voice. "This is a nice surprise. I wasn't expecting to hear from you."

She heard Ellen sigh. "Jody, I'm not going to be able to come by tonight."

Jody tried to swallow her disappointment. "What happened?"

"I've got to work. We're being hit with an internal audit. They're always a royal pain. They come in and pull our recommendations and we have to justify how we came to our decisions. I'll probably be working the entire weekend. I'm really sorry."

"It's all right. I wish there was something I could do to help you."

"You already have. Just talking to you makes it better."

Work kept Ellen busy the entire weekend. Jody didn't feel like going out. She ran each morning and spent the remainder of the day either reading or puttering around in one of her flower gardens. As she worked, she made mental notes of things that needed attention. At the top of her list, she added the maintenance of her privacy fence. It was in dire need of stain.

Ellen called her twice that weekend. Both calls were rushed, because she was still preparing for the upcoming audit.

By Monday morning, Jody had completed everything on her list, except staining the privacy fence. Unable to sit still she finally called a rental agency and rented a power-washer. Two hours later, she was power-washing the privacy fence around her backyard.

CHAPTER TWENTY-ONE

On Tuesday morning, Jody received the call she had been dreading.

Ellen began talking as soon as Jody answered the phone. "Dr. Chavez called with the biopsy results. The lump is malignant. Dr. Chavez has referred me to a surgeon, Dr. Kenneth Wray, for a lumpectomy. I have an appointment with him at one today."

"Why is he seeing you so soon?"

"I got lucky. Someone canceled just before I called."

Jody felt sick. Everything was happening so fast. She tried to think of something positive to say but couldn't form any rational response. She refused to acknowledge the word that hovered between them. If she didn't think it, maybe it wouldn't exist.

"Say something," Ellen said.

"Have you talked to your mom?" Jody asked, still not sure what to say.

"No. I thought I would wait until after I've talked to Dr. Wray and hear what he has to say."

Jody took a deep breath, trying to control her fear. "You have to tell her."

"I know. I just can't right now. I promise I'll talk to her as soon as I meet with Dr. Wray."

Denise should be told and Ellen seemed determined to keep putting it off. Jody decided not to push the issue until after Ellen talked to the surgeon.

"Can I go with you to the doctor's office? I'll sit outside if you want, but I'd like to be with you."

"Oh, thank you. Would you please? I didn't want to ask, but I'd rather not go by myself."

"Ellen, please don't ever hesitate to ask for my help. I love you. I want you to know I'm going to be here for you, no matter what."

"I know you will be. I'm not used to depending on someone else." She paused. "I don't want to become so dependent on someone that I couldn't survive without them."

Like I almost did with Mia, Jody thought. "If you like, I can pick you up at your office again."

"No. Dr. Wray's office is near you, over in the medical center. It would be easier if I drove to your place and we go from there."

"I'll be waiting," Jody assured her.

Jody hung up the phone. Fear unlike any she had ever known invaded Jody's body. She shook so hard her teeth started to chatter. She stepped into the shower and let the hot water pour over her, but it couldn't remove the chill that had settled deep within her. She moved gingerly, afraid any sudden movement would send her spiraling out of control. She dressed with slow deliberation. Her subconscious remained on constant alert to keep the horrifying word from entering her thoughts. If she didn't think about it, didn't admit it existed, she could avoid facing the possibility of what it could bring.

She got dressed, made a pot of coffee and took her cup to the rose garden. She carefully examined each rosebush until she was satisfied they all looked healthy.

She sat in the swing and stared out over her backyard and patio. Tension was beginning to build in the pit of her stomach. She shifted in the swing, trying to ease the dull ache growing along with her nervousness. Unable to get comfortable, she focused her attention away from the upcoming doctor's visit and back to her yard. During the four years she'd lived here, she'd made several changes. Slowly the yard was beginning to look the way she wanted. She tried to picture Ellen puttering around in the flower gardens with her. Did Ellen even like to work outside? Did she have a green thumb, or was she one of those individuals who couldn't grow a weed?

"I don't even really know her," Jody said aloud.

A butterfly landed on one of the landscaping rocks near the swing. Jody watched as it sunned itself, its yellow and black wings slowly folding and unfolding.

She had once heard butterflies described as God's smallest angels. She stared at the swallowtail. Her Lutheran parents attended church regularly, but after moving away from home, Jody had given up on the institution that worked so hard to exclude her.

"God, if you're listening, please, don't let her die," she prayed.

The butterfly sailed off to a nearby flower.

She thought about Denise and her heart ached. Ellen's decision not to tell her mom was wrong. Denise had a right to know. The longer Ellen waited, the harder it would be.

Jody wondered if Beth was still staying with Denise, and if so, how long she intended to remain there. Jody felt a mild curiosity about her. What kind of woman was she? What was it about her that had attracted Ellen originally?

Jody stayed in the swing until she heard a car door slam. She glanced at her watch. Ellen was a few minutes early. Jody went through the house and opened the door to find Denise, pale and clearly shaken, standing beside a tall, exceedingly beautiful young woman.

"Where's Ellen?" Denise demanded as she pushed past Jody.

"Come on in," Jody motioned to the young woman. "I'm Jody."

"Beth Wilson." The woman extended her hand.

"Where's Ellen? What's happened to her? Has she been hurt?" Denise asked again.

"She's not here yet." It was obvious that Denise knew something was wrong with Ellen, but she seemed confused. "Why are you here?"

"I ran into Myra Bloomberg at lunch and she asked me if I'd talked to Ellen. I could tell something was wrong. She wouldn't tell me anything, but she kept suggesting I might want to call my daughter as soon as possible. I called her office and she wasn't there." Denise began to cry and Beth ran to her.

It took Jody a moment to remember that Myra was a nurse in Dr. Chavez's office. Jody sighed. She didn't want to have this conversation, but there was no choice. "Ellen has an appointment to talk to a surgeon today."

"A surgeon? Why does she need a surgeon?"

Jody took a deep breath. "She's having a lumpectomy. Her mammogram showed a small lump. She had a biopsy. The lump is malignant."

Denise seemed to shrink before Jody. For a moment, she was afraid Denise would fall. She reached for her, but Denise stepped away. "She was going to call you after the appointment today," Jody said.

"I can't believe you didn't call me the minute you found out," Denise cried. "She's my daughter. You're my best friend. How could you keep this from me? What's gotten into you lately?"

Jody started to speak, but was interrupted.

"I asked her not to say anything until I found out more."

They turned to find Ellen standing in the doorway.

"I heard you shouting all the way to the sidewalk, so I let myself in," Ellen said as Denise launched herself across the room and threw her arms around Ellen. Beth was close on Denise's heels.

"My baby, my baby," Denise cried.

"Mom, please," Ellen begged. "Don't fall apart on me. This is exactly the reason why I didn't call you."

Beth clung to Ellen's arm and began to cry loudly.

Denise was sobbing. "It's too much. I can't lose my baby."

Jody saw the look of panic cross Ellen's face. "Denise," Jody snapped. "Stop it. This is not going to help anything. And you." She whipped around to face Beth. "If you want to remain under this roof another minute, stop bawling. This is not a funeral home and no one is dying. In case neither of you have noticed, you're scaring her out of her wits." Jody was shaking.

Denise stepped away. "I'm sorry," she said. "I don't know what came over me." She dug a tissue from her purse and began to dry her eyes. "Of course, everything is going to be all right. There are so many options today. You're young and I'm sure you caught the cancer early enough. I'm sorry, Ellen."

Beth stopped crying, but she retained her proprietary hold on Ellen's arm.

The clock on the mantel announced it was noon. "It's time to go, Ellen. I'll drive you," Jody said.

"I'll drive her," Beth insisted, moving Ellen toward the door.

"I'll drive her," Denise announced.

"I'll drive myself," Ellen growled as she fled from the house and slammed the door behind her.

Jody grabbed her keys and left Denise and Beth standing in her living room. As she backed out into the street, she saw Denise on the porch digging through her purse for her key to Jody's house and smiled. The world could be ending and Denise would still take time to lock the door.

CHAPTER TWENTY-TWO

Jody used her cell phone to call information to get the address of Dr. Kenneth Wray's office. Thankfully there was only one listing for him.

When Jody entered the waiting room, Ellen was staring into space. She looked stunned.

"Is it okay if I sit down?"

Ellen looked up and grabbed Jody's hand. "Thank you for coming. I'm sorry I was such a bitch back there. I kind of lost it when they started crying."

Jody patted her arm. "That's all right, but you need to get prepared. I saw your mom's car behind me in traffic a couple of times. I'm sure they'll be here any minute." She took Ellen's hand. "Before they arrive, there's something I'd like to say. No matter what, I don't want you to be alone during this." She fidgeted in her chair. "After you finish here . . ." She struggled for words, realizing she didn't even know for sure what came next after the lumpectomy.

Suddenly, Denise barged through the door with Beth trailing close behind.

Jody gave herself a mental kick for being so slow in asking Ellen to stay with her. She would have to wait or ask her in front of Denise and Beth.

Ellen groaned. "This is going to turn into a three-ring circus."

Jody held up a hand to ward off Beth and Denise. "Look at me," she said to Ellen. "What do you want from me? If you need me in the background as a shoulder to cry on, I'm there. If you want me—"

Ellen put a finger to Jody's lips. "I want you beside me for the rest of my life."

"I have some say here," Beth insisted.

"Go home, Beth. It's over," Ellen said.

Beth dropped on her knees in front of Ellen and grabbed her hands. "It can't be over. I love you so much. Can't you see how much you mean to me? We're perfect for each other. Don't you remember how all of our friends thought so? I'm nothing without you. How can I leave you? You need me here to care for you."

Denise must have realized that the entire waiting room was now staring at them, because she tapped Beth's arm and said, "Get up. This is not the time or place for this."

Beth was about to protest, but the look of determination on Denise's face left no room for discussion. Beth took the chair on the other side of Ellen. She'd barely settled in when Denise fixed her with a stare. Unable to withstand Denise's glare, Beth moved over to allow Denise to sit next to her daughter. They waited in silence. Denise held one of Ellen's hands and Jody the other.

When the nurse called her name, Ellen said to Jody, "Please don't be hurt, but I want to go in alone. I'm not sure I can explain this, but I feel like I have to do this alone. Whatever happens in there, it's something that I'll ultimately have to face by myself."

Jody swallowed her disappointment and nodded. "I'm not hurt," she lied. Why couldn't Ellen understand that whatever she decided would affect everyone who loved her? But now was not a time for philosophical arguments. "I'll be right here if you need me. Please don't ever think you are alone. You have me and your mom." In a moment of generosity, Jody added, "And Beth. Don't try to face this by yourself, Ellen. Let us help you."

Ellen nodded briefly and stood. Denise and Beth stood with her. "I'm going in alone," Ellen told them. "I need to do this by myself. Mom, please, stay with Jody. She could use a friend."

Jody looked up, surprised by Ellen's observation, but she realized it was true.

Denise gazed at Ellen for a long moment before merely nodding.

Denise didn't speak to Jody, but she did take the chair that Ellen had vacated. The two friends sat side by side as they waited in silence.

A large clock hung above the receptionist's desk. Jody watched the second hand make a painfully slow rotation and realized she would lose her mind if she continued to watch the seconds tick off one by one. She tried flipping through a magazine, reading the posters on the walls and people-watching. She finally gave up and stared at the door that Ellen had disappeared behind.

Almost an hour went by before Ellen emerged. She looked pale, but she managed a small smile for the three women waiting for her.

They trailed out behind her. No one spoke until they were in the parking lot, where they all began to speak at once.

Ellen held up her hand and they fell silent. "I didn't want to have this conversation here in the parking lot, but I guess there's no other option." She grabbed Jody's hand and took a deep breath before beginning. "Dr. Wray gave me a lot of statistics and maybes. As you already know, the biopsy tested malignant."

Denise swayed. Jody grabbed her and held her steady. Denise gulped air for a moment, before she shook her head and pulled away from Jody.

"I'm sorry," Denise said as she brushed a hand over her eyes. "Please, go on, honey."

Ellen glanced at each of the women and said, "Dr. Wray told me it's serious, but because of the early diagnosis and my age he feels certain that a lumpectomy followed by radiation will be all I need. He said he's seen women survive much worse cases. I intend to be a survivor." Ellen squared her shoulders. "I'm having the procedure on Thursday at ten o'clock at the Methodist Hospital. I'll be in the hospital for overnight."

"My God," Denise cried. "Is there no other alternative?"

Ellen patted Denise's hand. "Mom, it's going to be okay. It won't be like it was with Grandma or Aunt Alice."

Jody struggled to assimilate the information. She looked into the grief-stricken faces around her. Denise seemed to have shrunk an inch. Her shoulders hunched forward as if trying to ward off any further blows.

Beth's stepping back caught Jody's attention. She turned and was shocked by the look of disgust on Beth's face. In an effort to prevent Ellen from seeing the look, Jody stepped between them and put her arm around Ellen. As she did so, she felt a tremor run through Ellen's body. Jody held her closer, not caring whether or not Denise approved.

"You'll come home with me," Denise insisted.

"No, Mom. I'm spending the night at Jody's. If that's all right with you," she said, looking at Jody.

It was with mixed emotions that Jody said yes. She knew how much Denise was hurting and how important it was that Ellen be near her during all of this. But Jody wanted Ellen near her, also. She squeezed Ellen's hand gently.

At Ellen's words, Denise's head shot up and she started to protest.

Ellen again held up her hand. "Mom, I love you, but this is not open for discussion. I love Jody. I'm with Jody. I'm staying with Jody. I don't know how else to say this. If you want me in your life, you're going to have to get used to it."

Ellen turned to Jody. There were tears in her eyes, but she brushed quickly them away. "I need to get some clothes from the hotel. I'll be over in about an hour." She kissed Jody's cheek and started to walk away.

Jody followed her. "Ellen."

Ellen stopped and turned around.

"Why don't you check out of the hotel?" Jody asked. "After you're feeling better and all of this is over with, you can start looking for a place of your own, if you still want to, but for now stay with me." She hesitated. "Please."

Ellen cocked her head. "I think you may mean that, Jody Scott."

"I do. I want you near me."

"Is this because of the cancer?" Ellen asked.

Jody looked over Ellen's shoulder and took a deep breath before meeting her gaze. "That's part of the reason, but mostly, it's because I want to be with you." She stopped and shrugged. "I love you and I miss you when you aren't around."

Ellen looked at the ground and took several seconds before answering. "It'll take me a while to pack my things and check out of the hotel." She glanced up at Jody and smiled.

Jody fought the urge to jump up and down and shout. "Do you need any help?" She managed to keep her feet on the ground, but she couldn't keep the smile off her face.

"Just be there when I get home," Ellen said and looked over Jody's shoulder. "I've really hurt Mom. What should I do?"

Jody glanced back at Denise. "I'll try to talk to her. If she agrees, would you mind if I invited her over? She needs to be near you."

Ellen kissed Jody's cheek. "Thank you. I would like to see you two mend fences." Ellen headed for her car.

Jody turned back to talk to Denise, but she and Beth had already left.

CHAPTER TWENTY-THREE

Jody rushed home and changed her sheets. She cleaned off a shelf in the bathroom for Ellen's things. She made space in the closet and was in the process of emptying out drawers when the doorbell rang.

She raced to the door, eager to get rid of whoever it was. She threw open the door to find Ellen standing there with four large suitcases.

"If I stay, do I get my own key, or do I have to keep ringing the doorbell?" Ellen asked and attempted a weak smile.

Jody pulled her inside and kissed her. "I have a spare in my desk with your name on it." She took Ellen's hand and led her through the house to her tiny office. She dug through a drawer looking for the spare key.

"I hope it doesn't have a lot of scratch marks from all those other names you've marked off," Ellen said as she watched Jody.

"Nope, you'll be the first one to own it." Jody finally found the elusive object and held it up in triumph.

"Right." Ellen rolled her eyes and took the key. An awkward silence filled the room.

"Let me get your stuff and I'll help you unpack," Jody said and went back to the living room to retrieve Ellen's luggage.

They took the bags to the bedroom and Jody finished cleaning out the drawers while Ellen unpacked.

When Ellen finished unpacking, Jody stored the suitcases away in the guest-room closet. Ellen was putting away the last of her things when Jody returned.

"Are you hungry?"

"I should be starving. I've been so busy I didn't get a chance to eat lunch."

"Come on. I'll make us a salad."

Jody poured two glasses of iced tea to go with their salads. As they sat at the table Ellen picked at her food.

"Are you all right?" Jody asked.

Ellen nodded. "I was just thinking about Mom. I know she's worried sick. I was mean to her at the doctor's office."

"She left before I could talk to her. You can invite her over if you want."

Ellen hesitated a moment and then shook her head. "This may sound cruel." She touched her breast. "I'm afraid," she admitted, "and seeing Mom so frightened makes it worse."

Jody nodded. She was about to say she understood, then the doorbell rang.

Jody moved her salad aside and stood. "I'll be right back." She went to the door and glanced through the peephole. Denise stood on the other side. Jody opened the door.

"I'd like to talk to Ellen," Denise said. Jody stood back and invited her in, but Denise declined. "I'll wait here."

"Denise," Jody began, "why are you doing this? Ellen doesn't need more stress. If you want to see her, then stop acting like a spoiled brat. We're in the kitchen having a salad if you'd like to join us."

Leaving the door open, Jody turned and headed back to the kitchen. She was almost to the kitchen door when she heard the door softly close. She started to ask if Denise would like a glass of tea, but Denise wasn't there. She had left. Jody hesitated, not knowing what she should do.

"Let her go," Ellen said from the kitchen doorway. "She'll be all right. I'll walk over and talk to her in a little while. But right now, show me your latest creation that you were bragging about the other day."

Jody led her out the back door and onto the patio.

"I've never seen your backyard. It's huge."

Jody beamed. "I actually bought the house because of the yard. Of course, I liked the house too, but I fell in love with this yard. It has so much potential."

"I guess you like birds," Ellen said, pointing to the feeders scattered throughout the yard.

"Birdseed is a big expense. Denise thinks I'm crazy, but I enjoy watching the birds at the feeders. A pair of Carolina wrens nest in an old birdhouse that's attached to the far side of the garage. I love to hear them sing." Jody stopped, embarrassed. "You'll think I'm weird, gushing over birdsongs."

Ellen placed her hand on Jody's arm and leaned into her. "I think it's sweet, or should I say tweet?"

Jody groaned. "That's my latest addition." She pointed out the rose garden.

"I really like the swing," Ellen said as they walked over and sat down in it. "What kind of roses are these?"

"A mixture of hybrid teas and antiques. I just planted them, but look at all those buds. They'll be in full bloom in a few days."

"It's odd, I've spent a large portion of my life around flowers, but I've never actually planted anything," Ellen said.

"That's not so odd. Your mom was never a gardener. My mom and dad both are avid gardeners. Dad grows so many vegetables, he can feed half the small town they live in, and Mom's flowers are the talk of the county."

"Doesn't that strike you as funny, about Mom?" Ellen asked. "She has worked around flowers all these years and she doesn't garden."

"Maybe it's like a butcher who's a vegetarian."

Ellen shuddered. "That I can understand. Now don't get me wrong. I'm a carnivore at heart, but if I had to be around all those animal carcasses all day, I can see where it would be easy to become a vegetarian."

Jody grimaced. "Point taken." She pushed her toes into the mulch. "I need to put some flagstone down so we won't be sitting with our feet in mulch whenever it rains, or after I've watered the plants."

"I like the sound of that *we*."

Jody looked at her and smiled. "It does have a nice ring."

"Tell me about the roses. What color will they be?"

Jody stood and took Ellen by the hand. "Come on and I'll show you. This one," she said pointing to the first rosebush, "is a Mr. Lincoln. It's a deep red. And this one is a John F. Kennedy. It's white."

"Are they all named after presidents?"

Jody laughed and said, "No. In fact this one here is Belinda's Dream."

"How funny."

"What do you mean?"

Ellen touched the tender leaves of the plant. "When I was a little girl, I had an imaginary friend whose name was Belinda. Whenever I was scared or in trouble, Belinda would appear to cheer me up or help me out."

Jody slid her arm around Ellen. "I remember that. You almost drove your parents nuts. Your dad wanted to send you to a child psychologist, and your mom wanted to have another baby."

"Dad always did overreact."

"Do you ever see your dad?"

Ellen nodded. "Yeah, I see him every three or four years. He and Trish, his latest wife, were driving around the country in their RV and drove through Los Angeles a few weeks before I moved. We had dinner together."

"I didn't realize he had remarried."

"Oh, yeah. This is wife number four."

Jody realized the conversation was depressing Ellen, so she changed the subject. "You've not seen the other improvement." Jody turned to the birdbath.

"That's cute," Ellen said as she stuck the tip of her finger into the water. "Do the birds really use it?"

"They sure do. I have to add fresh water each morning."

The sound of the doorbell drifted back to them. Jody stood up. "This place is like Grand Central Station today. I'll be right back." She trotted across the patio and into the house. Maybe Denise had decided to come back. The bell sounded again. "I'm coming," Jody called as she hurried through the kitchen and into the living room. She pulled the door open to find Beth Wilson.

Jody froze. The woman had obviously been crying for some time.

"I have to talk to Ellen."

Jody considered slamming the door, but it wasn't up to her to decide who Ellen did or did not talk to. Instead, she motioned Beth inside. "Ellen's out back." She pointed to the back door. "You can go on out." She watched as Beth walked through the house and out to where Ellen sat. Jody realized she was spying on them and made herself find something to do in the guest room. It was the only room in the house that didn't have a view to the backyard. She was certain she wouldn't able to resist staring out a window if one was available.

Jody sat on the edge of the bed waiting. What did Beth want? She was a beautiful woman. It was easy to see what had attracted Ellen to her in the first place. Her nose was too big, Jody thought with a sense of satisfaction. She probably hadn't been crying at all. Her eyes were just red from allergies created from massive inhalation with that honker.

Jody jumped up, ashamed of her pettiness. There was nothing wrong with Beth's nose. She was just being catty. She glanced at her watch. How long had they been out there? She considered going into the kitchen to see what they were doing. If she got a glass of water, she would be able to see the entire backyard.

"This is pathetic," she growled as she jumped up and went into the guest bath to find a dust rag and a bottle of furniture polish. She dusted the furniture in the guest room and straightened the bed, even though neither chore needed doing. She was scrubbing the sink in the guest bath when Ellen found her.

"I've been looking all over for you. Do you always do so much housework?"

Jody looked up guiltily. "It keeps me out of trouble."

Ellen stepped in and kissed her cheek. "I can't imagine you ever being in trouble."

Jody rolled her eyes.

"I'm sorry about Beth. She says Mom is having a hard time. Beth wanted me to come back to Mom's and stay there." When Ellen stepped away, Jody saw she had her purse.

Jody held her breath. She knew how close Denise and Ellen were. Ellen was going to go back to Denise's.

The sense of sadness that swept through Jody shocked her. She had been so happy to have Ellen here with her, and she wanted her to stay.

"I'm going to go over and talk to Mom, but I'll be back, so stop looking so scared."

Jody looked down at the sink she had been scrubbing. "I'm not scared."

Ellen made a small noise of doubt. "I'll be back soon."

Jody nodded.

"Are you okay?"

Jody hesitated. "I'm in love. Is that ever okay?"

Ellen smiled and said, "This time it is." She gave Jody a quick kiss.

As Ellen left, Jody thought about Thursday and what it could bring. A chill raced over her. She began to scrub the sink again.

CHAPTER TWENTY-FOUR

Jody lay on her queen-size bed and stared at the muted television screen. She had spent the last few hours alternating between worrying about Ellen's health and wondering what was happening at Denise's. It wasn't that she didn't trust Ellen, but there was the chance that Ellen would come to her senses and see the difficulties a nineteen-year age gap could create.

Jody's heart pounded when she heard the unfamiliar scratch of the key in the lock. She clicked the television off and waited as Ellen made her way back to the bedroom.

"There you are." Ellen smiled. "I'm sorry I took so long. Mom had worked herself up into a pretty good frenzy."

"How is she now?" Jody asked, when what she really wanted to know was whether Ellen had talked to Beth.

Ellen shrugged and sighed. "She's worried, of course, but I think I calmed her down a little. Our family history petrifies her. I reminded her that Grandma Murray died almost fifteen years ago and she was in her sixties. Poor Aunt Alice was so paranoid of doctors, by the time she finally went to see one, the cancer was out of control. No one could have saved her."

"I've been meaning to ask you. Are you going to call your dad?"

Ellen shook her head. "No. I wouldn't even know where to look for him, since he's running around somewhere in his RV. Besides, there's no need in making this any harder on Mom. You know, she hasn't spoken to him since the divorce."

Jody patted the bed beside her. "Come and lie down."

Ellen kicked her shoes off and stretched out. She tucked her feet beneath the blanket that lay across the foot of the bed, and placed her head on Jody's shoulder. For several minutes, they lay in silence as Jody slowly rubbed Ellen's back.

Jody had about decided Ellen had fallen asleep when Ellen finally said, "I would understand if you decided to end this."

Jody kissed the top of her head. "You have no idea how many times I've prayed to hear those words come from a girlfriend." She hugged Ellen tighter. "But the thing is, now I don't want to hear them."

"Jody, it's not fair to pull you into this."

"It's a cliché, but life is not fair. I'm not going anywhere, Ellen. I'm in this for the long haul."

"No one knows what's going to happen. You know there's a chance it has spread. They won't know until after the lumpectomy. Even then that slight possibility of a reoccurrence will always be there. I'll never be without that fear."

Jody stiffened. Of course she had known there was a possibility that it had spread and Ellen could die, but to hear Ellen say so cut deep.

"I'm sorry," Ellen said. "I know my speaking so bluntly bothers you, but I have to face the reality of my situation." She rubbed her hand across Jody's stomach.

Jody nodded and took a shaky breath. "Will you tell me everything Dr. Wray told you?"

Ellen hesitated. "I'll try. He recommended a lumpectomy plus radiation. Then because of the family history, tamoxifen. He'll also remove some of the lymph nodes from beneath my arm. He told me he would be injecting a dye, and by following the dye he'll be able to determine which node is the sentinel node. I'm not sure I fully understand the process. The lymph nodes are like filters. If any of the cancer cells have tried to leave the breast area, they would have to go through this sentinel node first. So, if there's no sign of cancer cells there, then Dr. Wray will know it hasn't spread to any other part of my body."

"And if they have?" Jody asked.

"That's what the radiation is for. It'll kill off any of the cancer cells that may have gotten through and are hiding somewhere else."

"What about your other breast? Could they have gone there?"

Ellen shook her head. "No. Cancer cells don't move from one breast to the other. Cancer cells would have to develop on their own in the other breast. I asked him about that and it's not unheard of, but it's rare that it ever happens. The lump is about two and half centimeters, that's about an inch. And I'm in stage one."

Jody pulled the blanket over them and waited for Ellen to continue.

The silence pressed against her. She could hear the small travel clock in the bathroom ticking. A mockingbird called out from the top of the oak tree in her backyard. The sound of a basketball bouncing told her the Johnson boy across the street was shooting hoops.

Ellen sat up. "I'm not sure how much detail to give you. I don't want to gross you out or anything."

Jody sat up and kissed her. "It doesn't gross me out. I admit hearing about it scares me, but I want to know. The more I know, the more I'll be able to understand."

Ellen nodded. "With all three treatments—the surgery, radiation and tamoxifen—I have ninety-eight to ninety-nine percent chance of remaining cancer-free."

One or two percent had never seemed so large to Jody before. She bit her lip and forced herself to remain sitting on the bed. Her legs burned from the effort of keeping them locked in place on the bed. She slipped her hands beneath her legs and grabbed a handful of the sheet and gripped it. "Go on," she prompted.

"The surgery will only be one to three hours long, and I'll have to spend at least one night in the hospital, possibly two."

Jody gripped the sheet tighter. Her stomach burned. She swallowed convulsively to rid herself of the knot growing in her throat.

Ellen leaned toward her and placed a hand to Jody's cheek. "Don't do this."

To Jody's amazement, she realized she was crying. She squeezed her eyes shut, trying to stop the flow of tears.

Ellen pulled Jody into her arms. "Please. Don't cry."

"I'm sorry," Jody whispered. "I'm supposed to be comforting you."

"You are. Come on, let's talk about something else. There's no need for us to get ourselves all worked up over this. There's nothing we can do."

Jody grabbed a tissue from the box on the bedside table. "That makes it harder. There's no way I can fix it for you."

"Your being here has helped," Ellen said. "I know Mom loves me, but there are so many things I can't tell her. She's already scared out of her wits."

Jody felt tears drip down onto her shoulder. She tightened her arms around Ellen.

"Let's talk about something else," Ellen said as she released Jody and sat up. She dried her face with her palms. "Speaking of Mom, she seems to be coming around to our side a little."

Jody's eyebrows went up. "Really."

Ellen crawled out of bed and began to undress.

"She actually spoke your name tonight, and there were no curse words on either side. I think she's missing you."

Jody felt a glimmer of hope spark inside her. "Then indeed, we are making progress. I miss her, too."

Ellen turned with her slacks draped over her arm. "I need to ask a favor."

"Sure. Anything."

"Thursday. No matter what happens, take care of Mom. You're so strong. I know you'll be all right. I'm worried about Mom. She's all alone."

Jody nodded. "I'll do what I can, but don't underestimate Denise. She could very well be stronger than both of us. She has been through a lot. You may not know this, but when your dad left, he didn't just walk out leaving you and Denise. He walked out leaving her with a mountain of debt and no job."

"I know. And I know it was you who bailed us out," Ellen said.

Jody flinched. The statement meant to show appreciation had only served to remind Jody of the age difference and the almost incestuous nature of their relationship.

"Does it ever feel strange to you?" Jody asked.

"What?" Ellen placed her slacks over the back of a chair.

"Us." Jody went to the bathroom to brush her teeth. "I mean, you're almost like a niece to me," she said as she walked back in the bedroom holding her toothbrush.

Ellen turned and stomped her foot. "Don't you dare try to weasel out of this with that lame excuse."

Surprised at the sudden burst of anger, Jody stopped brushing and turned to stare at Ellen. "What did I do?"

"If you want out of this relationship, at least have the guts to say so. Don't try falling back on that 'oh, I'm so much older,' or 'oh, she's Denise's daughter' bull."

"I don't want out," Jody sputtered.

"Then stop asking those stupid questions. You're not my aunt. You're my lover, my partner, my whatever, but you're not my aunt."

Jody held up her hands in surrender. "Okay, okay." She slunk back to the bathroom to finish brushing her teeth. As she put away her toothbrush, she glanced into the mirror and smiled. Ellen might not be Jody's niece, but the spitfire was sure Denise's daughter.

CHAPTER TWENTY-FIVE

On the day of the surgery, Jody and Ellen were both wide awake long before the sun came up. They lay in bed and cuddled while they discussed Jody's plans for the remainder of her backyard. As they talked, Ellen occasionally offered a suggestion. By the time the alarm rang, Jody's backyard had evolved into Jody and Ellen's backyard.

Without speaking the actual words, they had reached a subtle understanding that Ellen was now a permanent resident.

After the surgery, she wouldn't move back to the hotel, and she wouldn't need to search for a place of her own.

"Do you want Denise to ride with us to the hospital?" Jody asked as they dressed.

"No. Beth is going to drive her."

Jody tried to ignore the stab of jealousy that hit her each time Ellen mentioned Beth's name. "I'm going to go check on my roses."

"Can I come with you?"

Jody realized Ellen was nervous and didn't want to be alone. "Sure, but you might want to put some pants on first," Jody said and pointed to Ellen's slacks lying on the bed.

Ellen grabbed the slacks and struggled into them as she followed Jody.

As they walked through the kitchen, Jody looked at the coffeepot with longing. The doctor had told Ellen to fast the morning of the surgery and Jody hadn't made coffee out of respect for her. At the moment, she would have gladly handed over ten dollars for a cup.

The sun had barely cleared the eastern horizon when Jody went out. They went from bush to bush, checking each plant.

"Look. Belinda's Dream is about to bloom," Ellen cried out.

Jody examined the plant. Several of the buds were indeed showing thin streaks of pink. "It'll be a few more days before they burst open."

"It's a sign," Ellen said in a soft voice.

Jody looked at her and frowned. "A sign?"

"I told you. I was always safe as long as Belinda was around. The shadow demons disappeared from the walls. The huge scratchy claws of the ash tree outside my window stopped trying to dig their way in to grab me. All the monsters went away as soon as Belinda appeared."

Jody gazed down at the plant. *If that's all it would take to keep you safe, I'd fill the yard with them*, she thought. She glanced at her watch and her heart began a slow hollow pounding.

"It's time to leave."

Ellen had to be at the hospital early for the last-minute tests and to allow for her prep time.

"I'll get my purse," Ellen said as she again touched the leaves of the rosebush.

"I'll get it," Jody offered, but Ellen shook her head.

Jody walked through the house turning off lights and locking doors. Everything she touched felt cold and foreign. She glanced out the kitchen window as she slipped the chain on the back door. The rose garden looked fresh and crisp. She stared at the hardy little rosebush known as Belinda's Dream.

Belinda, she whispered. *If you're still around, keep my love safe. And God, if you're listening, I sure hope you can overlook my past transgressions. Mom and Pop always told me you would be there when I needed you most. I sure need you now.*

The drive to the hospital was the longest Jody could ever remember. People were beginning to stir. They were going on with their normal everyday lives. How could it be possible she was so miserable while the rest of the world was clicking along at its regular pace?

Jody offered to drop Ellen at the hospital entrance, but she said she preferred to walk in with Jody. After finding a parking space, Jody took Ellen's small suitcase out of the trunk and together they walked across the asphalt-covered lot. As they approached the hospital, Jody stopped and placed a hand on Ellen's arm.

"I want you to know I love you. I'll be here waiting for you."

Ellen kissed Jody's cheek. "I love you too and I intend to keep you around until you're a decrepit old woman."

Jody chuckled and said as she put her arm around Ellen and started walking, "That time may be closer than you think."

"That's true," Ellen said, shocking Jody. "I noticed you didn't make love to me last night or this morning." She tossed her head as the automatic doors to the hospital slid open. "I guess you didn't have the stamina."

Jody snorted, trying to hide the fear threatening to overwhelm her. She had thought about making love to Ellen the night before, but along with the thought came a simultaneous one that it could be the last time they ever made love, and she hadn't been able to do more than hold her. "You wait until you're out of here and well enough to handle it. I'll show you stamina," Jody said.

"Promises, promises, promises."

"Ellen."

They looked up to see Denise and Beth walking toward them.

Ellen turned to Jody. "I love you, Jody Scott."

Jody saw her own fear reflected in Ellen's eyes.

Denise and Beth descended on them before Jody could respond. Ellen gave Denise a long hug before turning to pat Beth's arm. "I have to check in. I'm not sure how long it will take. Find yourselves a place to sit, and I'll join you when I can."

Jody started to sit down, but Ellen grabbed her hand. "Come with me."

"Why does she get to go with you?" Beth protested.

"Because I want her to," Ellen replied. "Beth, I told you last night. You're free to stay in San Antonio as long as you like, but there's nothing between us anymore and there never will be."

"But I want to take care of you," Beth said.

"I don't need taking care of." Ellen stopped and held up her hand. "Beth, I don't want to end things between us like this. Please try to understand. I'm in love with Jody. I want to be with Jody."

Beth began to cry and Ellen's shoulders dropped.

Jody could have kissed Denise when she stepped forward and gave Ellen a quick hug and said, "You two go on. I'll take care of this."

Jody and Ellen walked away.

"I didn't want to hurt her," Ellen said, as she pulled a piece of paper from her purse.

"Stop thinking about her. You have enough to worry about without adding her to the pot."

"This is where I need to go," Ellen said, checking the paper in her hand. They walked into a small waiting room. Jody took a seat as Ellen went to talk to the young woman behind the counter.

Jody tried to control the slight tremors that were beginning to race through her body. She was getting a headache. Probably from the lack of caffeine. There were a dozen things she wished she had told Ellen the night before. Why hadn't she taken the time?

"She said it would only be a minute. They're going to do some tests. There's a room outside the pre-op area for family and friends.

Someone's going to come for us. After I go in would you please go back and tell Mom and Beth?"

"Sure. I don't want you worrying about anything."

Ellen glanced at her. "Actually, worrying about Mom helps me keep my mind occupied."

"Then, I'll go and punch Beth out."

Ellen whipped around. "What?" she asked so loudly the young woman behind the counter looked up.

Embarrassed, Jody shrugged. "I was just trying to give you something else to worry about."

Ellen rolled her eyes. "You're nuts."

"Ms. Murray, Ellen Murray."

They both froze and stared at the young man who stood in the doorway calling for Ellen.

Without speaking, they rose and followed him out.

"You'll have to wait here," he told Jody and pointed to a waiting room to the left of them. "Someone will come for you as soon as she's prepped." Jody nodded as he continued, "It's going to be a while, so you may want to go get some coffee or something. There's a small coffee shop at the end of the hall and there's a cafeteria downstairs." He pointed toward the end of hallway.

"I'll be here," Jody said to Ellen. Before they could say anything else, the orderly whisked Ellen away. Jody watched until they disappeared behind a set of double doors.

She walked across the hall and examined the ten-by-twelve waiting room. Green plastic chairs lined the walls and a double row, fastened back-to-back, ran down the center of the room. Even at this early hour, an older Hispanic woman with two teenagers sat in the far corner. Jody was about to sit down when she remembered she had promised to bring Denise and Beth to the waiting room.

Jody took the stairs down to the first floor. She might have promised to get them, but she hadn't promised to hurry.

The look of relief that crossed Denise's pale face when Jody walked into view made Jody regret her pettiness.

"Where is she?" Denise asked as she jumped up and met her.

"They've taken her back for tests and to prep her. There's a waiting room upstairs where we can sit. They'll come and get us as soon as they've finished."

The trio walked to the elevator and rode up without speaking. The silence held for the next hour and a half, when a nurse finally came out and said they could go back.

Ellen lay on a hospital bed separated from about two dozen other beds by nothing more than thin cotton curtains.

As Denise and Beth talked to Ellen, Jody stood at the foot of the bed rubbing Ellen's cold feet through the heavily laundered sheet. All around Jody came the low, urgent murmur of voices. She imagined she could smell the fear and anxiety that raced around the room, or maybe it was her own fear she smelled. Some of these people might die before the day was over. They would kiss loved ones for the last time before being wheeled away.

"Jody, are you all right?"

Jody looked up. The three women stared at her.

"Are you all right?" Ellen asked again and reached for Jody.

"I'm f-f-fine," Jody said and realized she was shaking. "The room is too cold." She forced herself to smile.

Denise removed her suit jacket and handed it to her. "Here, take this. I'm having so many hot flashes today, I could melt the polar icecap."

When Jody hesitated, Denise placed the jacket around Jody's shoulders. The small act of kindness was almost Jody's undoing. She was saved by the sudden appearance of a tiny woman wearing a smock printed with blue and yellow sailboats.

"It's time for La-La Land," she announced as she hung an IV bag on the pole at the head of Ellen's bed. "If I can just scoot in here," she said, brushing by Beth. The woman tore open a small packet and removed an alcohol pad.

Jody looked away as the woman ripped open a large packet and removed an IV needle. Jody concentrated on rubbing Ellen's feet.

"There we go," the woman said. "Now you may start to feel a little groggy. This is just a mild sedative to relax you, but you won't be completely out." Seeing the look of fear on Ellen's face, she stopped and patted her arm. "It's all right." She placed a piece of tape over the IV needle. "You'll be fine. Dr. Wray is one of the best surgeons I've ever worked with." She gathered up the empty wrappers. "An OR nurse will be here in a few minutes. She'll take you back. Good luck." She disappeared through the curtain.

The frightened group huddled inside the thin cotton cocoon. Jody listened for the footsteps that would take Ellen away.

"Mom," Ellen said in a voice that was already beginning to soften with the drugs being fed into her body.

"Yes, baby?"

"I'd like to be alone with Jody. Can you take Beth to the waiting room?"

Denise hesitated. She clearly did not want to leave, but she nodded. "Sure, honey." She kissed Ellen's cheek. "I'll be right here when you come out."

"Thanks, Mom. I love you."

"I love you, too." Denise started out of the enclosure. "Come on, Beth."

"I'm not leaving," Beth declared, throwing herself across Ellen. "I have every right to stay here. We make the perfect couple. All our friends said so."

Jody had the unkind thought that most of Beth's display of concern was more for dramatic effect rather than concern.

Denise spun around, grabbed Beth's arm and yanked her upright. "You and I are going to the waiting room. Is that understood?"

For a second, Jody thought Beth was going to put up a fight, but something in Denise's face must have convinced her this was a no-win situation.

After they left, Ellen turned to look at Jody. "Come up here."

Jody took Ellen's hand.

"You look kind of disoriented," Ellen said. "Are you going to be all right?"

Jody wanted to shout, "Hell, no, I'm not all right. I'm scared to death." Instead, she nodded and swallowed before saying, "Don't you worry about me. I'm fine. Just a little cold."

"You're not a very good liar."

Jody blinked rapidly to keep the tears at bay. She was not going to break down and worry Ellen further.

"Come here and kiss me," Ellen said, and pulled Jody closer. "You take care of Mom."

Jody forced a smile and said, "I think your mom can take care of herself."

"Then you take care of yourself. Have you eaten?"

Jody shook her head. "I'm not hungry."

"Go eat. You didn't eat breakfast, and I'll bet Mom hasn't either."

Jody shrugged.

"Don't just sit out there worrying. Promise me you'll get something to eat."

Jody started to protest but saw Ellen needed the reassurance. "I'll get something to eat, and I'll make sure Denise and Beth eat also."

Ellen rewarded her with a beaming smile. "Good. I love you."

"I love you, too." Jody leaned down and kissed her.

"Pull that chair over, so you can sit and talk to me."

After moving the chair over, Jody asked, "What do you want to talk about?"

"Tell me about roses."

Jody tried to remember some of the information she had read or learned from Leti but drew a blank. She was about to say so when a nurse pushed the drapes aside and came in.

"It's time to go," she said as she removed the IV bag from the pole.

She turned to Jody. "You can wait in the OR waiting room. If you'll follow us, I'll show you where it is."

Two other nurses appeared, and suddenly the small group was moving. Jody followed them out. She saw Denise and Beth and motioned for them to come. Jody trailed the gurney through a maze of hallways, constantly twisting and turning around corners. She was glad Denise and Beth were there, because she wasn't sure she could have found her way back to get them. The gurney stopped by an open elevator and the nurse turned to Jody.

"The OR waiting room is at the end of this hall, on the left."

Before Jody could say good-bye, the doors closed and Ellen was gone. Jody continued to stare at the closed door until she felt Denise's hand on her arm.

"Let's go find the waiting room," Denise suggested.

CHAPTER TWENTY-SIX

The OR waiting room was a bit more comfortable than the previous one. Instead of the molded plastic chairs, this room had padded armchairs, and rather than the dull white paint of the previous room, this one was painted in relaxing pastels.

Jody removed the jacket from her shoulders and handed it to Denise. "Thanks, for what you did in there," she murmured.

"Don't worry about it. I really was burning up."

"I wasn't talking about the jacket," Jody said. "Thanks for giving me those last few minutes alone with Ellen. I know it was hard for you to leave."

The two friends stared at each other for several seconds before Denise nodded.

Jody sat by a window overlooking the entrance of the medical complex. Beth sat in a far corner by herself, while Denise sat close to the door.

Jody stared out the window where another wing with an identical wall of windows stood facing her. She wondered if someone was sitting behind those windows staring out at the windows on this side, while waiting for a stranger to come with news of a loved one.

She glanced around the waiting room. Seven or eight clusters of people sat scattered about the room. Some watched a vaguely familiar-looking talk show host on the television located at the far end of the room. Jody's attention rested on an elderly man who sat alone. She watched his work-roughened hands as they continuously turned a sweat-stained straw hat in slow, agonizing circles. She wondered who he was awaiting news on. Was it a wife, a child, or a lover perhaps?

A middle-aged woman dressed in scrubs walked in and all eyes in the room turned to her. She went to talk to a young African-American couple. Jody tried in vain to read the woman's lips as she explained something to the couple. She could feel tension tightening her neck as she sat unable to look away from the drama playing out before her. At last, the couple let out a collective cry of relief that echoed throughout the room. From the smile on the man's face, it was truly good news. Jody found her own spirits being lifted by their joy. The couple shook the woman's hand, and the three of them left the waiting room together.

How much longer would it be before someone brought them news? Ellen had said the surgery could last one to three hours. Jody looked at her watch. She had only been in the waiting room for forty-two minutes. It was going to be a long wait.

Twenty minutes later, a nurse appeared and informed them there had been a delay and Ellen had not yet been taken to surgery.

"Can we see her?" Denise asked.

"Since it won't be long before they take her in now, we recommend that you don't. It's less upsetting for her."

"She's back there by herself," Jody said. "I'd think that would be rather upsetting."

The nurse smiled. "Actually she was sleeping when I last checked on her. The mild sedative given in pre-op will help her sleep."

By eleven-thirty, Ellen was still waiting and Jody had a pounding headache. She closed her eyes against the glare on the window. She knew she should go get a cup of coffee but was afraid she would miss the nurse who had promised to let them know when Ellen was taken into surgery.

Jody opened her eyes and watched as Beth walked over and spoke to Denise. She seemed to be trying to convince her of something, but Denise kept shaking her head. Denise pointed toward Jody. Beth turned and saw Jody watching. She seemed to hesitate a moment before she walked out of the waiting room.

Denise frowned as she watched Beth leave. Jody remembered the promise she had made to Ellen to eat, but the thought of food made her stomach roll.

She considered trying to talk to Denise but was afraid Denise would reject her effort. Denise had been civil around Ellen but had said nothing more after Jody returned her jacket. She assumed the temporary reconciliation had been for Ellen's benefit.

A few minutes later, a man in scrubs entered. Jody watched him. Something about him made her decide he was a doctor. Even from a distance, she could sense his exhaustion. He slowly made his way to the elderly man and sat on the edge of the chair next to him. As the doctor spoke to him, Jody watched as the man seemed to shrink before her. The doctor patted the man's shoulder and left. The old man continued to stare into space for several seconds before painfully making his way out of the chair and across the room. As he grew closer, Jody could see the tears in his faded blue eyes. His loss fed her fear. She glanced away, ashamed that she wasn't strong enough to reach out to him and offer him the smallest hint of human kindness.

Was it her imagination or was there a small collective sigh as the old man left the room? Jody glanced around but nothing had changed. The talk show host continued to rave, and Denise was still mad at her. Jody shook off the feeling and looked at her watch.

Jody began to shake. At any moment, a stranger could walk in and tell her Ellen was dying, but the world would continue to whirl around her. Suddenly she had to get out of the room. She couldn't sit here and watch as another family received devastating news.

Jody jumped up so quickly several people turned to stare. Seeing her sudden movement, Denise sat upright and looked around. Jody walked to her. "I'm going to stretch my legs. I'll be out in the hallway."

Jody paced until her feet hurt and there was still no sign of the nurse. She glanced at her watch. It was only twelve-forty. She returned to the waiting room. The television was now showing an old sitcom rerun. Denise was standing by one of the windows gazing out at the same wall of windows Jody had been staring at previously.

She looked up as Jody came in. Jody returned to her original seat and was surprised when Denise came to sit next to her.

"Did you see Beth while you were out there?"

Jody shook her head. "Where is she?"

Denise sighed. "She said she was going for coffee, but I think she may have left."

"What do you mean left?"

"I thought I heard her packing this morning, and I know she made at least one trip to the car before I came out. I heard the car door slam."

Jody couldn't resist the twinge of hopefulness that ran through her.

"After we got home the other night all she could talk about was how beautiful Ellen was, and how horrible it was that Ellen would be scarred after the surgery and how all their friends would know. It was almost as though she cared nothing about Ellen beyond her physical appearance and what their friends would say. I finally had to go to my bedroom to keep from tossing her out on her ear."

"It's hard to believe people can be so shallow." Jody massaged her aching temples.

"Where is that nurse?" Denise asked.

Jody glanced down at her watch and as she did, Denise jumped up and sped off. Jody looked up. The nurse stood at the door searching for them.

Even though Denise had a head start, Jody managed to beat her across the room to the nurse.

"How is she?" Jody asked.

The nurse gave a small reassuring smile. "I'm sorry I took so long in getting back to you, but we had an emergency with another patient."

Jody suddenly recalled the old man. Could that have been the delay?

Denise appeared at Jody's side and clutched her arm.

"Ellen was taken into surgery about ten minutes ago. She is doing great," the nurse told them. "The surgery will take about two and a half hours, barring complications."

"What kind of complications?" Denise demanded.

The nurse placed her hand on Denise's shoulders. "Mrs. Murray, your daughter is fine." She glanced at them both before adding, "I think you both should go eat. You need to be taking care of yourselves." She glanced at her watch. "I'll come back in an hour. That'll give you time to eat. If you'd rather not leave the hospital, our cafeteria is actually very nice."

Denise started to argue, but Jody interrupted her. "She's right, Denise. We need to eat. I'm starting to get a little shaky and I can feel you trembling." She patted Denise's hand that was still clutching her arm.

"If there's an emergency, I'll page you in the cafeteria," the nurse assured Denise.

Denise removed her hand from Jody's arm and nodded.

After the nurse left, Denise returned to her seat by the door. Jody sat down beside her.

"Denise, you need to eat. Making yourself sick won't help Ellen."

"I'm really not hungry. You go on. I'll wait here."

Jody stood. "All right. If they page me in the cafeteria, I'll have someone come by here to tell you."

Denise's head shot up.

"The nurse won't come here looking for us since she thought we were going to eat," Jody said. "So, if there's a page, I'll send someone for you as soon as I have time."

Denise's eyes shot daggers at Jody. "I'll wait in the cafeteria," Denise said as she stomped out of the waiting room.

Jody tried to hide her smile as she followed Denise to the elevator. They rode down in silence.

The minute Jody stepped off the elevator, she smelled the alluring aroma of freshly brewed coffee. She felt as though she were floating as she made her way through the cafeteria line. She ordered coffee and a meal of roast beef with mashed potatoes and peas. She had actually forgotten about Denise until she sat down across the table from her.

"Is it all right if I sit here?" Denise asked quietly.

Jody nodded as she took another sip of her coffee. Denise had gotten the meat loaf platter, but she was more interested in the coffee.

"We drink too much coffee," Denise said as she sipped from her cup.

"Yeah, we do," Jody agreed as she drained the cup.

Jody and Denise looked at each other for a long second before bursting into laughter.

Jody reached for Denise's cup. "I'll go get us some more coffee."

After Jody had returned with the freshly filled cups, Denise shook her head and said, "The lady at the corner table looked at us like she suspected we had just escaped from the psych ward."

Jody glanced over to where Denise had indicated, but the woman had apparently already lost interest in them and was reading her book. Jody dug into her mashed potatoes. "I'm starting to feel like that's where I belong. I'm so tired I can barely think."

Denise took a bite of her meat loaf and chewed it thoughtfully. "Why are you still here?"

Shocked, Jody looked up. "What do you mean? I'm here for the same reason you are."

"Beth left. Why haven't you?"

Jody laid her fork down. "Denise, I know you're having trouble understanding this, but I love Ellen. In fact, I'm not sure I've ever truly loved anyone the way I love her."

Denise pushed a carrot around on her plate. "Beth said she loved her, but she left. Why?"

Jody shrugged. "I don't know. Maybe she didn't feel wanted here anymore. Or maybe she just couldn't face what was happening."

"If you had been in her place, would you have left?" Denise persisted.

"I can't answer that," Jody said, and thought about the question. "But no. I don't think I would have. I think I would have stepped back, but I don't think I could have left until I knew for certain that Ellen was all right."

Denise stared at her. "You really love her?"

"Yes, Denise. I really love her." Jody took a deep breath. "I love her enough to chance losing you, and I've never loved anything that much."

Tears sprang to Denise's eyes. "I've missed you."

"I've missed you, too."

"I'm driving Eric crazy. He's threatened to have the locks on the shop changed and not let me in."

Jody chuckled. "I'm going to miss him when he leaves."

"Me too. I don't know why he continues going to college. You know he hates it."

"No, I didn't know that."

Denise nodded. "His father is an engineer. He has his own business somewhere in Montana and wants Eric to work with him, but Eric doesn't really want to."

"Why doesn't he tell his father he doesn't want to be an engineer?"

Denise looked at her and made a wry face. "How do you think dear old dad is going to react when his only son tells him he'd rather be a florist than join the family business?"

Jody shook her head. "He should tell his father. You never know until you try. He can't spend the rest of his life miserable just because his father has a dream of him carrying on the family business." On some level, Jody knew they were talking about Eric to avoid talking about the more painful issues.

"For all your worldliness, Jody, I swear sometimes you can be so naïve."

"I am not naïve. I'm realistic. I don't understand why parents think they have a right to continue to run their children's lives forever. At some point you have to let them grow up."

"Is that what you think I do?"

Jody hesitated and realized too late that she had painted herself into a corner. She didn't want to destroy the thin line that had reconnected her with Denise. She picked up her fork and took a bite of potatoes to give herself time to choose her words carefully. The wrong ones were certain to upset the fragile truce she and Denise seemed to have achieved.

"I think," Jody started slowly. "That you tend to cling to Ellen."

"Do you know why?"

Jody shook her head.

"I cling because I made Ellen my entire life. She was all I had."

"That's not true, Denise. You have me, Eric, the shop. You have your Bunco friends."

Denise held up her hand to stop Jody. "I know that, but all of you are friends. Any of you could pick up and move away at any given moment, and I'd never see you again. Ellen is the only constant in my life."

Jody reached across the table and took Denise's hand. "You silly woman. I've been in your life for thirty-five years, and I plan to be there for the next thirty-five."

Denise removed her hand and pressed her napkin to her eyes.

"In addition to being your friend, I intend to be your daughter-in-law for the next thirty-five," Jody added.

Denise looked at her in shock, but slowly a smile crept across her face. "I never thought I'd have a daughter-in-law. Maybe I should give it some thought."

"I wish you would, because I'm here to stay. At the very least, can we maintain this truce until Ellen is better?"

Denise nodded.

CHAPTER TWENTY-SEVEN

It was well after four before Dr. Wray came into the waiting room.

Jody and Denise hurried across the floor. Denise began firing off questions before she reached him.

Dr. Wray held up his hands. "Ellen is in the recovery room. She'll be there for a while before they move her to her room. I've requested a private room. I want her to be as comfortable as possible. She needs to rest, but at the same time I want to get her up and moving as soon as she's able. All I can do now is wait on the pathologist's report. It's my gut feeling that we caught it before the cancer spread elsewhere. But it's important that you remember I won't know anything definite until I see those reports. We'll keep her overnight for observation."

"Will she be all right? Is the cancer gone for good?" Denise asked.

Dr. Wray removed his surgeon's cap and scrubbed his hand over the short stubble of a buzz cut. He motioned them toward a small cluster of empty chairs. Jody felt her knees wobble. She felt certain he wouldn't make them sit for good news. After they were seated, he squatted down in front of them.

"I'm going to recommend that she undergo radiation treatments, and follow up with the tamoxifen," he began. "With her family history, I'd rather be overly cautious."

Denise's hand reached out and grabbed Jody's as he continued.

"She's going to need a lot of family support during the next several months. Patients usually experience various degrees of depression. In my opinion, from dealing with hundreds of patients, the speed of her recovery will depend a lot on her state of mind. As far as the cancer returning . . ." He shrugged. "Statistics tell us that there's a strong chance it won't, but unfortunately real life doesn't always respond to statistics. I'm sorry I can't tell you for certain that your daughter will be cancer-free for the rest of her life, but I can't honestly do that. What I can tell you is that if she's careful and has regular checkups, any reoccurrence will be detected early and dealt with." He stood and stretched. "I'll be in the hospital for a while yet, and I'm only a phone call away if problems should arise." Dr. Wray left before they could question him further.

Jody glanced up to see nervous eyes peering at them. She could almost feel the rest of the room pulling away. She and Denise were now the shunned. It was the two of them sitting alone. The rest of the room drew back, afraid Jody and Denise's pain and distress would somehow transfer to them.

Jody didn't know how long they sat staring into space, but at some point a nurse came in and told them Ellen was in her room. She gave them directions and left.

Following the nurse's directions, Jody and Denise made their way through a maze of corridors to Ellen's room. They stood outside the door, almost hesitant to enter.

"Come on," Jody prompted as she pushed the door open and stepped inside.

Ellen was so pale she seemed to be a part of the white bed linen. As they approached the bed, Jody tried to swallow her panic at the numerous tubes that led from Ellen's body to a multitude of machines. Jody brushed a lock of hair away from Ellen's forehead. She longed to hold her, but the wires from what Jody assumed were to blood-pressure and heart monitors intimidated her. The heart monitor emitted a steady *blip* . . . *blip* . . . *blip*. Jody began to find the noise reassuring.

"She looks so small," Jody said as her eyes drifted to Ellen's breast. "How can something so deadly be in someone so young and vibrant? It's not fair. Ellen is so full of life." Jody recalled their trip to the zoo and how animated and playful Ellen had been.

"She's so still and pale," Denise whispered.

"You don't have to whisper."

Jody and Denise both jumped at the sound of the voice. Jody turned to see a nurse. She had not heard her come in.

The nurse took the clipboard from the foot of the bed and moved to Ellen's side. Jody stepped around and stood by Denise. Jody began to fidget as the nurse checked each of the monitors before scribbling something on the clipboard.

"Is she okay?" Jody asked as she gripped the railing on the bed.

The nurse looked up and nodded. "She's doing fine."

Jody slowly exhaled. She hadn't realized she had been holding her breath.

"She may be in pain when she wakes up," the nurse said. "If so, this is a morphine pump." She pointed to a tube-like device near Ellen's hand. "You can pump it for her, or when she's able, she can do it herself."

"How will we know how much?" Denise asked.

The nurse shook her head. "It's regulated. You can't give her too much. If she complains of any pain, go ahead and pump. We don't want the pain to get too severe and get out of control." She hung the clipboard on the end of the bed. "She will sleep for a while yet. If she wakes and needs anything, just ring for us." She pointed to a call button, then tucked the blanket around Ellen's feet. "She may be cold when she wakes up. If so, let me know and I'll bring another blanket. There's a cup of chipped ice here, in case she's thirsty. You can give her a little if she wants it." She started to leave.

"Thank you," Jody said.

The nurse turned and nodded slightly before departing.

Denise and Jody pulled the chairs closer to the bed and waited.

As time crawled by, Jody tried to think of ways she could reassure Ellen. Dr. Wray had warned them that Ellen could suffer from depression after the surgery. Jody made up her mind to do everything in her power to let Ellen know how much she loved her.

"Jody," Ellen called, her voice so raspy it cracked.

Jody and Denise were instantly at Ellen's side. Jody looked down into Ellen's drug-fogged eyes.

"Tell me," she whispered. "Did they get it all?"

"Yes. Dr. Wray said he's confident they got everything."

"Are you thirsty?" Denise asked as she held up the cup of crushed ice that had been replaced each time a nurse came around.

Ellen nodded.

Denise used a spoon to ease the ice between Ellen's lips. Jody had a sudden flashback of watching Denise feed Ellen when she was a baby.

Denise scooped a small amount of ice onto the tip of the spoon. "Can you eat some more ice?"

Ellen turned her head and looked into Jody's eyes. Jody felt the world stop. As she gazed into Ellen's eyes, she realized there was nothing she wouldn't do for her. She'd waited her entire life for this woman.

"I love you," Jody said. "Everything is going to be all right. We'll work this out together. Are you hurting?"

"No. Stay with me," Ellen whispered, her eyes already closing.

"I'm not going anywhere," Jody promised.

They returned to their seats to continue their vigil.

Denise stared at Ellen for several minutes before she spoke. "Jody, you're my best friend, but I feel I have to protect Ellen."

Exhausted, Jody rubbed her hands over her face. Denise's parental need to protect was wearing thin. "I'm not going to hurt her!"

"You're nineteen years older than she is. When you start drawing your Social Security she'll be our age. She'll only be fifty-one when you're seventy."

Jody shook her head and put a rein on her temper. "Denise," she began, "I've done the math a dozen times. I know I'm a lot older. I've come to realize during these last few days that age doesn't always matter. I know you're worried that Ellen will have to wipe the drool off my chin in twenty years, but I've had to accept the fact that Ellen may not even be alive in twenty years. Life doesn't always play by the rules."

Denise flinched and Jody reached out to comfort her.

"I'm not trying to be cruel. None of us knows how much time we have left. Denise, I want to make a life with her, and I need your blessing. We can do it without your acceptance, but I don't want the happiest time of my life tarnished with the loss of my best friend. And she needs you now more than ever. Please. Give us a chance."

Denise stood and gazed down at Ellen. "She's all I have. I know I'm overly protective, but I don't want her to make the mistakes I've made." She took a deep breath and wiped a tear from her cheek. "When Beth arrived at my house, I thought she would be the perfect weapon to fight you with. She's Ellen's age, beautiful, and seemed to love her so much. I thought Beth was a fighter. She had come all the way from California to try and convince Ellen to return to her. I was wrong, Jody. I'm sorry."

Jody felt a flicker of hope shoot through her.

Denise continued, "I have to be honest, I still have some reservations." She shrugged. "Your track record isn't that great, but for Ellen's sake I'm willing to give you the benefit of the doubt."

Jody stood and hugged Denise tightly. "I promise, you'll never regret this. I'll do everything in my power to make her happy."

Denise looked at her and said, "You'd better, I know where you live."

CHAPTER TWENTY-EIGHT

Neither Jody nor Denise would leave the hospital. They slept in the same chairs they had been sitting in most of the afternoon. The morphine pump kept Ellen's pain at bay and allowed her to rest.

Jody squirmed in her chair, trying to get comfortable. She had reached a point beyond exhaustion. Her body was stiff from the endless hours of sitting. The dark circles beneath Denise's eyes made her wonder if she looked just as bad.

It was almost midnight when Ellen opened her eyes and was aware enough to talk. When she moved, Denise and Jody both hobbled from their chairs. Ellen blinked slowly and tried to lick her lips.

Denise grabbed the fresh cup of chipped ice that had been replaced several times already and put some on a spoon. "Eat some of this ice."

Jody tried to smile. She didn't want Ellen to see how frightened she had been.

"You two look like shit," Ellen croaked. She started to move her arm and winced.

"There's always a critic," Jody said. "Are you hurting?"

Ellen nodded and Jody pressed the morphine pump.

"How are you feeling?" Denise asked.

"I don't think I'll be dancing a jig anytime soon," Ellen said, her voice blurred with sleep. "Go home. Rest," she whispered as her eyes closed.

They continued to stand by the bed for several minutes watching her.

"Why don't you go home and rest, Denise? I'll stay," Jody offered.

"I can't leave her," Denise said.

Jody gazed at Denise. She could see exhaustion etched on her face. Jody didn't want to leave Ellen, but she knew she was probably going to sleep as long as they kept pumping the morphine into her. "One of us should go home," she offered. "We aren't going to be doing her any good if we make ourselves sick."

Denise looked at Ellen and slowly agreed.

"We'll toss a coin," Jody suggested. "Winner stays. Okay?"

"How long does the loser stay away?"

"Until eight. That's plenty of time to shower and sleep, and still be back before she's released in the morning."

Denise hesitated but finally nodded.

Jody dug into her pocket for a coin. "You toss," she said. She wouldn't admit that she was so tired, she was afraid she wouldn't be able to catch the coin.

"You call," Denise said as she took the nickel Jody held.

"Heads, I stay with her. Tails, I go home."

Denise tossed the coin. She caught it and cried out when heads appeared. "Best two out of three," she insisted.

"No. You agreed. You're going home. I don't want to see you before eight o'clock."

Denise picked up her purse but continued to stand by Ellen's bed. "You'll call me if there's any change, won't you?"

"Yes, I'll call you. Now go home and try to get some sleep."

"I should stay and you go."

"No. We had a deal. Now get going."

Denise nodded and reluctantly walked out of the room.

After she left, Jody returned to stand by Ellen's bed. She gently placed a hand on Ellen's forehead, the only area free of monitor wires, tubes or bandages. "Ellen, I know you can't hear me," she said. "I swear to you, no matter how long we're together, I'll never take another minute of our happiness for granted."

Ellen had stirred occasionally and cried out in pain each time. When she'd cry out, Jody clicked the morphine pump and prayed that the drug would quickly provide its numbing relief.

Jody was at the window staring out into the night's darkness when Ellen woke shortly before three. She heard her stir and rushed to the bedside. Ellen's eyes appeared less clouded with pain than they previously had been. She tried to move her arms and grimaced.

"Are you hurting?" Jody reached for the pump, but Ellen stopped her.

"No. Please don't do that. I'm tired of sleeping. That stuff makes my head feel as though it's stuffed with cotton."

"Are you sure? The nurse said we shouldn't let the pain get too bad."

Ellen moved her head slightly. "Trust me, I'm no martyr. I'll be the first to yell if I start hurting too much." She tried to lick her lips.

Jody took the glass of chipped ice and fed her some.

"I never thought I'd think something as simple as ice could taste so good," Ellen said, her voice still cracked and rough.

Jody continued to feed her the ice as they talked. "Where's Mom?"

186

"We worked out a schedule of four-hour shifts. She went home to rest. She'll be back around five."

"I'm impressed. It seems like you guys are getting along pretty well."

"We had time to talk and I think we've managed to reach a fairly reasonable agreement."

"What sort of an agreement?" Ellen frowned.

"She gets custody of you on Monday, Wednesday and Friday. I get you Tuesday, Saturday and Sunday and you're free on Thursday."

Ellen started to chuckle but gasped. "Oh. It hurts. Don't make me laugh."

"I'm sorry," Jody said and set the ice down. "Are you okay?"

"Yeah, it just hurts like all get-out." She lay still for several seconds.

"Are you sure I shouldn't be clicking this thing?" Jody pointed to the morphine pump.

"No. Just save your funny stories for a later date. Tell me more about you and Mom. Has she really changed her mind about us?"

"I guess she's still having a few problems, but overall, I think she's going to be fine with it."

"I love you so much," Ellen whispered. "Thank you for not bailing out on me. Even though you probably should have."

"I think my bailing days are over." Jody saw Ellen frown in pain. "Close your eyes. I'll be right here."

"Talk to me," Ellen said.

"All right, but you have to close your eyes and rest. I'll tell you all about my conversation with Denise."

When Ellen closed her eyes, Jody quietly pressed the morphine pump. To cover the noise of the clicking, she told Ellen about the conversation she and Denise had shared. Jody had barely started the story when the frown of pain eased from Ellen's face and she slept.

ᳵ

187

Ellen was sleeping when Denise came back shortly before six. Dark circles smudged Denise's eyes, but her step was a little firmer.

"You're early," Jody said.

"I couldn't sleep. How is she?" Denise asked.

"No change. She was awake for a few minutes but has been sleeping the rest of the time. She's starting to complain about the morphine. She says she's tired of sleeping, but she was still in pain, so I cheated and gave it a couple of clicks when she wasn't looking."

Denise nodded. "I think she'll forgive you."

Jody tried to stand and felt herself sway.

Denise's hand steadied her. "Why don't you go home? I'll stay with her until she checks out and bring her to your house."

Jody shook her head. "No. I want to be here when she wakes up."

"Now who's being stubborn. At least, go home long enough to shower and lie down for an hour."

Jody hesitated. The idea of a hot shower tempted her. "Maybe I will run home long enough to shower."

"You look exhausted. Can you drive?"

Jody nodded. "I'll see you in a couple hours."

She started to walk away, but Denise called to her. "I think I could get used to having you as a daughter-in-law."

"I'll see you later, Mom," she called as she glanced over her shoulder.

Denise's head shot up. She pointed a finger at Jody and opened her mouth.

Jody made a shushing noise and pointed toward Ellen. Before Denise could recover, Jody made a quick escape.

CHAPTER TWENTY-NINE

When Jody returned to the hospital shortly after eight, she felt like a new person. She hadn't slept, but the long hot shower and food had revived her. She had taken time to run by the flower shop and select a dozen pink roses. They weren't roses from Belinda's Dream, but they were the same color, at least. The morning air was fresh and cool. It would be a good day for Ellen's return home.

The minute she walked into Ellen's room, she knew something had changed. Something had gone wrong.

Jody raced to Ellen's bedside and saw tears staining her cheeks. "You're in pain. Denise, why didn't you use the pump?" Jody reached for the morphine pump, but Ellen stopped her.

"I'm not in pain," she said in a voice so low Jody had to strain to hear.

"Then what's wrong?"

When Ellen didn't answer, Jody turned to Denise for an explanation.

Denise shrugged and rubbed her forehead. "When I went home, I found a note Beth left in her room. It was addressed to Ellen, so I brought it back with me. Right after you left, the nurses came in and got Ellen up to walk and I gave her the note afterward. She read it and ..." Denise waved her hand at Ellen and let Ellen's actions finish the rest of her sentence.

Jody was more interested in knowing that Ellen had gotten up than she was in Beth's note. "You were able to walk around?"

Ellen nodded.

"Ellen, that's wonderful. That almost guarantees they'll release you this morning," Jody said and leaned down to kiss Ellen's cheek. She froze as Ellen turned away. A small worm of doubt began to gnaw at her insides. What had Beth said in the note? "Ellen, where is Beth?" she asked.

"California. She left." New tears sprang to her eyes.

Jody took an involuntary step away from the bed, shocked by the extent of Ellen's distress over Beth's leaving. Jody tried to invent excuses for Ellen's behavior: Beth hadn't said good-bye, she had left while Ellen was in surgery. Or had Beth been so angry that she wrote something upsetting in the note? That was it. Beth had written something hateful to Ellen.

Jody looked around on the bed for the note but didn't see it. She glanced at the stand beside the bed and didn't see it there either. She started to ask about it when the door opened and Dr. Wray came in.

"Hello, all," he called. "How's the patient this morning?" He pulled the chart from the end of the bed and began reading. "Everything looks good." He glanced up at Jody and Denise and smiled. "If I could ask you ladies to wait outside for a few minutes."

Jody nodded and followed Denise into the hallway. "What did the note say?" Jody asked as soon as the door closed.

Denise shrugged. "I don't know. Ellen read it and started crying. When I asked her what was wrong, she kept shaking her head and refusing to talk. When I persisted, she folded the paper and slid it beneath her. She's lying on it now."

Jody sat down on the window ledge. "She's pretty upset. She doesn't need more stress." Jody realized she was still holding the roses. She held them up. "I'm losing my mind. I forgot to give these to her."

The door opened and Dr. Wray came out. "Mrs. Murray, we will be releasing Ellen later this morning," he said without looking directly at them. "She would like to talk to you alone." Before they could say anything, he hurried away.

Denise looked at the closed door for a long second. She patted Jody's arm. "It's probably nothing," she said, trying to reassure Jody.

Jody knew better. She could feel it low in her gut. She had been here before. The last time it had been a note on the kitchen table. This time it would come from Denise.

Jody slowly handed the roses to Denise. "Give these to her."

Denise pushed them away. "No. You hang on to them and give them to her yourself. She probably just needs help going to the bathroom and is embarrassed to have you see her so helpless."

Jody nodded, but she knew that wasn't going to be the case. "I'll wait here," she mumbled.

Denise squeezed Jody's arm. She hesitated for the briefest moment and a look of dread crossed her face. She nodded slightly and went inside.

Jody watched the door slowly swing back. The click of the latch slammed against her eardrums. The country sausage and egg taco she had eaten for breakfast began to churn. She sat back down on the window ledge and forced herself to take several deep breaths. There was no way it could be happening to her again. Things had been going too well between her and Ellen for them to go sour. It had to be something else.

Jody jumped as the door to Ellen's room opened. Denise looked at her and Jody stepped back to brace herself against the wall. Denise had tears in her eyes.

"Jody," she began. "Ellen is having a bad time right now. She has decided to come home with me after they release her. Why don't you go home? I'll call you later and let you know how she's feeling."

Jody shook her head. "What's going on?"

Denise looked at the floor and then out the window beside Jody. "She's just confused. Remember the doctor said she might be depressed for a while."

"She's depressed and doesn't want to see me," Jody said and started toward the room. "I want to talk to her."

Denise put her hand on Jody's arm. "Please, sweetie. Go home."

Anger boiled up within Jody. "I don't want to go home. I want to know what the hell is going on. She was fine when I left, and two hours later she doesn't even want to talk to me. What did you say to her?"

Hurt shadowed Denise's face. She looked into Jody's eyes. "I swear to you, I didn't say anything to bring this on. It has to have been something in Beth's note."

"Then I want to see the note," Jody said.

Denise shook her head. "You know we can't do that. She's entitled to her privacy. We have to respect her wishes."

"I'm entitled to know why she no longer wants to see me," Jody insisted.

"I know."

They stared at each other. It occurred to Jody that she could easily push Denise aside and bulldoze her way in, but what would that accomplish? Ellen didn't want to see her.

Jody pushed the roses into Denise's arms and walked away. She heard Denise call after her, but Jody kept going. She forced herself to concentrate on placing one foot in front of the other and to take deep breaths. She counted the spacing of her breathing. Breathe in. One . . . two . . . three. Breathe out. One . . . two . . . three. Over and over she counted until she reached her Jeep. She climbed inside and continued to breathe and count. All the way home, she focused her attention on breathing. She pulled into the driveway and waited for the garage door to open. Breathe in. One . . . two . . . three. Breathe out. One . . . two . . . three. She pulled the Jeep in and closed the garage door before she made her way inside. As she opened the door from the garage to the kitchen, the wave of nausea struck her. She raced to the bathroom, barely making it in time. She had never been so sick in her life. Afterward, she didn't have the strength to make her way back to the bedroom, so she curled up on the bathroom floor and let the pain engulf her. The phone rang several times during the day, but she had no reason to go answer it. She fell asleep, but each time she would jerk awake and force herself to breathe. The room grew dark, but still she remained on the floor. At some point, she heard her front door open.

Maybe it's a mass murderer and he'll put me out of my misery, she thought, but then she heard her name being called. She curled tighter into herself and refused to answer.

The voice calling her name grew more intense, almost frantic. Something about the male voice was vaguely familiar.

Suddenly, light flared, blinding her and igniting an agonizing pain behind her eyes. She tried to cover her eyes, but her hands weren't cooperating. She scrunched her eyelids tighter, but the light still burned through.

"Jody, oh, shit. Jody, wake up. It's Eric. Come on, girl, don't do this to me."

He slapped her cheeks until she opened her eyes.

"That's better," he said. "Come on, stand up."

She closed her eyes. She didn't want to stand up.

"Jody, come on." He slapped her cheeks again. "Come on, girl-friend. You have to get up off this floor. You're freezing."

When she didn't move, he knelt down behind her and placed his arms beneath her. "Why are you making me play Sir Lancelot? You know I don't do the knight in shining armor thing," he grunted as he lifted her from the floor and carried her to the bedroom. He placed her on the bed, pulled the comforter over her and tucked it gently under her chin.

The simple act was her undoing. She began to cry.

He sat on the side of the bed holding her hand for several minutes. "Okay, girlfriend. That's enough. You're going to make your-self sick again."

Jody felt the bed move as he stood. She heard water running in the bathroom. A second later, a cool cloth was draped across her forehead. He sat back down on the side of the bed.

"Jody, sit up. Come on. Sit up." He eased the pillow from beneath her head to encourage her to move.

Feeling like the worst kind of fool, Jody did as he said but covered her face with the wet cloth.

"What's going on?" he asked. "I get a frantic call from Denise telling me to get over here and check on you, and I find you paying homage to the porcelain god. Are you drunk?"

"No. I'm not drunk," she snapped.

"Anger is good. At least I know you're alive." He tried to tug the cloth away from her face, but she held on to it. "Talk to me," he urged. "Tell me what's going on."

"I'm a damn, stupid fool," Jody blurted.

"Ah, a severe case of Cupiditis." He sighed and patted her knee. "Well, that's something I have a multitude of experience with. So tell me all about it. I'm all ears."

Jody wavered, too embarrassed to tell him how stupid she felt.

He pulled the cloth away from her face. "That's better. Now look at me." When she refused, he placed a finger beneath her chin and raised her head until she was looking at him. "Jody, I've been dumped so many times I have a stamp on my back that reads 'Property of the San Antonio Department of Sanitation,' so I can probably empathize with anything you're going through."

Jody hesitantly told him everything.

When she finished, he shook his head. "Girlfriend, it sounds bad." New tears sprang to her eyes. He patted her arm. "I'm sorry. I didn't mean to make it worse." He glanced at his watch. "I have to call Denise before she contacts nine-one-one."

Jody suddenly realized she had heard a key in the door before he came in. "How did you get in?" she asked.

He pulled a key from his jacket pocket and held it up. "Denise made me drive out to the hospital and get her key. Ellen wasn't released this morning."

Jody grabbed his arm. "What do you mean she wasn't released? Why not?" She jumped up. She had to get back to the hospital to see Ellen.

"Whoa, girfriend. She's okay." Eric took her hand and sat her down. "Ellen developed a slight fever after you left. It only lasted a couple of hours, but her doctor decided to keep her there for another night. Denise swore to me, Ellen was doing fine."

Jody tried to relax. If Denise wasn't worried, then Ellen was probably all right.

Eric handed the key to Jody.

Jody bit her lip to stop the tears that threatened. She should be with Ellen now.

"Do you have any Scotch?" he asked as he stood.

Jody nodded.

"Good. Hop up. I left an extremely hot young man to come over here and rescue you, so the least you can do is offer me a drink."

"Eric, I'm sorry. I feel like such a fool."

He leaned down and kissed her forehead. "You're not the first person to feel that way, girlfriend, and unfortunately, you won't be the last."

While Eric made his call to Denise, Jody made his drink. Not trusting her stomach, she settled for a soda.

"I told her you were fine. When she asked why you wouldn't answer your phone, I embellished slightly and said you had turned your phone off and were sitting outside contemplating life when I arrived," Eric explained as he came into the kitchen.

"Is Ellen all right?"

"Denise says she's fine. She has been up and walking around several times today. Denise was concerned about you."

"Thank you for not making me look like a total fool," Jody said.

He shook his head and took the drink she offered. "You're not a fool, Jody. You're in love." He sipped his drink and nodded his approval. "So, what are you going to do?"

"I don't know. I guess I'll try to talk to Ellen and find out what happened."

Eric stared into his drink but kept quiet.

"What? Do you think that's a bad idea?"

He shrugged. "I'm no expert, but maybe you should give her some space. She's going through a lot right now. It's possible it wasn't you at all. The diagnosis and surgery may have gotten to be too much for her to handle."

Jody thought about what he said. "I don't think I can sit here day in and day out and not call her."

"Then don't. You're on vacation. Take advantage of it."

"I can't leave. What if Ellen—or Denise—needs me?"

"Then opt for the second-best thing."

"Which is?" she asked.

"Work. Tell Denise you're going to go back to work. I'm sure she'll jump at the opportunity to stay home with Ellen for a few days. You come back, tell Mrs. Jimenez you want to buy her shop and start the renovations. That'll really turn your life upside down."

"I don't know anything about renovating."

"That, dear heart, is where you're about to get very lucky. Not only did I excel in woodworking shop, but that hot young stud I stood up to come and rescue you happens to be one of the most talented, up-and-coming interior designers in the city. Of course, no one but me knows it so far, but give him time."

Jody frowned. "What is this hot new talent going to cost?"

"That's the best part. He's still a student. He not only works cheap, but his calendar is free for the summer."

Jody pinched her lower lip and considered the offer. She would like to go back to work. It would also allow Denise to take off if Ellen needed her. Dr. Wray had told Ellen she could go back to work in a few days.

"I would have to talk to Denise," she said.

"That's why I told her to call you at the shop tomorrow afternoon."

Jody looked up and gasped. "You told her to call me! I can't believe you just assumed I would do whatever you suggested."

"We both know you love the shop. Expanding it is the logical thing to do, and Mrs. Jimenez isn't going to wait around forever until you two make up your minds. Besides, you can't hide for the rest of your life."

"Couldn't I hide for a week or two?"

He shook his head and drained his drink. "No. Tomorrow your new life begins. Try and get some sleep. I'll see you bright and early tomorrow morning." As he was heading out the door he stopped. "Listen. If, you know, the night starts getting too long, give me a call. I'll be home."

She hugged him. "Thanks, Eric."

She watched him drive away, then turned off the lights. She made her way through the darkened house and settled into her recliner where she spent the rest of the night agonizing over what had happened to make Ellen change her mind.

CHAPTER THIRTY

The phone rang early Saturday morning as Jody put her backpack behind the counter. It was good to be back at Petal Pushers. She hadn't slept much the previous night, but she knew the next few hours would keep her too busy to think about Ellen. She answered the phone and reached for a sales pad, then froze at the sound of Denise's voice.

"Is Ellen okay?"

"She's fine. She was released this morning. She's in her room sleeping."

"Have you heard anything from the lab?"

"No. She has an appointment with Dr. Wray next week. He's supposed to go over the results with her then, and set up a schedule for radiation."

Jody bit her tongue to keep from asking if she could go over.

"How are you?" Denise asked.

Jody took a deep breath. "Confused, hurt, stupid and pissed off. I think that about sums up my feelings."

"Jody, I'm sorry. I don't know what's going on. I've tried talking to her about Beth's note, but she won't discuss it. She's so angry, but I can't get her to talk. I don't know what to do."

"There's nothing you can do." Jody squeezed her eyes to stop the tears that threatened to start again.

As she struggled to maintain her composure, her anger started to grow. She had stood by and done nothing when Mia left. She had never even attempted to contact her, but she wasn't going to let Ellen go so easily. Deep in her heart, she refused to believe that Ellen could have stopped loving her so quickly.

Jody squared her shoulders with a new sense of determination. "I'm going to give her time, but I have to know how she's doing. I need you to help me. As long as I know she's all right I can wait. But I don't think I could stand not knowing how she's doing. Can you do that for me?"

"What if she asks me not to?"

"It won't even occur to her, if you don't mention that I want to know."

Denise hesitated. "You're probably right. I'll be back to work Monday morning. She's talking about going back to work either Tuesday or Wednesday. I'll let you know what's going on with her."

"Thanks, Denise. I know I'm asking a lot."

They remained silent for a moment before Denise changed the subject. "Thanks for rescheduling your vacation and going back to help Eric this weekend."

"That reminds me," Jody said. "I wanted to talk to you about us going ahead with trying to purchase the building next door. Are you still open to expanding the shop?"

"Jody, I don't think I can commit to a project that time-consuming. With Ellen and all, I'm not sure I could promise the hours needed."

"You won't have to do anything but be available to sign the paper-work. I'll run everything by you before I do it, but I really want to do this now." Her voice dropped. "I need this."

They fell silent. "What happens after I come back to work Monday?" Denise asked. "Is seeing me every day going to be a reminder?"

Jody's newfound determination disappeared. What if Ellen really had dumped her for good? Could she see Denise every day without it tearing her apart? She couldn't let this destroy everything she and Denise had worked so hard for. If Ellen chose not to see her again, she'd have no alternative except to get over it and move on with her life. Jody forced a vitality that she didn't feel into her voice. "I'll be all right, Denise. Hey, it's not like it's the first time I've been dumped, right?"

"Oh, sweetie." Denise sniffed.

"Don't you dare start crying, Denise Murray. I'll get through this. You were right all along. I'm too old for Ellen. She would have moved on eventually." Jody rushed on before Denise could interrupt her. "It's better that she did so right away. I don't want to talk about it anymore. Are you prepared to expand the shop or not?" Jody quickly started telling her about the interior designer Eric knew, and about Eric's offer to help with the renovations.

"Do you think this designer is any good?" Denise asked. "I mean, he's still in college."

"I don't know. I trust Eric's opinion, but we can ask him to draw up some preliminary sketches and see what he suggests. Of course, we have to actually buy the other building first," Jody reminded her.

"Go ahead. Start talking to Mrs. Jimenez. If we get the building, then we can talk to Eric's friend," Denise said.

Eric came into the shop just as she was hanging up with Denise. "How are you feeling this morning?" he asked as he gave her a hug.

"Ready to start over. I'm going to talk to Mrs. Jimenez today and try to buy the shop."

Eric nodded his approval. "Good. That's what you need. Loads of work to keep you busy." He started gathering supplies to begin filling orders.

"I'll make the deliveries," Jody said as she flipped on the display lights.

"Fine with me. It's getting hot out there already. You know I hate it when my face gets a sheen," he called from the workroom.

Jody shook her head and started dusting the displays. She kept a watch out until she saw Mrs. Jimenez come around the corner to unlock her shop.

"Eric, I'm going next door. I'll be back as soon as I can."

Jody put the dust rag away and took a deep breath. She had to convince Mrs. Jimenez to sell them the shop. Otherwise, what would she do with herself until she found a way to deal with Ellen's rejection?

As she went next door, she tried to think of how she would bring up the subject of buying the shop. If she sounded too eager the price would probably go up, but if she sounded nonchalant, Mrs. Jimenez might decide it wasn't a serious offer and sell the shop to someone else. Since no great words of wisdom hit her in the twenty-five or so steps from the doorway of Petal Pushers to the doorway of the card shop, she decided to play it by ear.

Mrs. Jimenez looked up from behind the counter and smiled. "Jody," she called out. "Have you come to buy my shop?"

Shocked, Jody nodded. "How did you know?"

"Your friend Denise has been dropping hints for weeks."

Jody looked around and noticed that most of the inventory had been sold. "You're almost out of inventory," she said, feeling foolish for stating the obvious.

Mrs. Jimenez motioned to her. "Come and have some iced tea with me, and I'll sell you this store."

That was exactly what she did. Jody left the store an hour later feeling confident that both she and Mrs. Jimenez had gotten what they wanted. There was still paperwork to draw up, lawyers to consult and bankers to convince, but those were just annoying details.

She stopped at the approximate point where the two shops came together and closed her eyes. She would make the new Petal Pushers the finest flower shop in all of south Texas.

Thoughts of Ellen tried to push in, but she turned them away. Ellen had made her decision, and Jody would have to find a way to live with it.

CHAPTER THIRTY-ONE

Jody stood outside the lawyer's office and waited for Denise. The humidity of late June was beginning to make her wish she had waited for Denise inside. It had been almost five weeks since Ellen's surgery. Noninvasive ductal carcinoma *in situ* had been the final diagnosis. The lab report on the lymph nodes had come back negative, but Dr. Wray had still prescribed a series of radiation treatments.

Ellen was in her second week of those treatments. She would have to go for treatments five days a week for six weeks. Each treatment lasted thirty minutes. Her appointments were scheduled for three-thirty. Because the treatments left Ellen feeling tired and washed out, Denise had been leaving early to take her. Denise had been true to her word of letting Jody know how Ellen was progressing, but Jody quickly discovered it wasn't enough. During the first week after Ellen's surgery, she would reach for the phone to call Ellen several times a day. Her low point came when she found herself driving past Denise's house, hoping to catch a glimpse of Ellen.

Disgusted by the desperation she felt, Jody had driven home, determined to never think of Ellen again. Of course, that resolution had only lasted until the next thought.

"Sorry," Denise said as she came out. "I swear I have a bladder the size of a Ping-Pong ball."

"Do you want to grab some lunch before we go back to the shop?" Jody asked.

Denise glanced at her watch. "I guess Eric can handle things for another hour. Where do you want to go?"

"How about Burger Barn. It's on the way and their service is fast."

"Sounds good."

They started toward Denise's car. They had ridden over together to sign the closing papers on the card shop. The building inspection and loan application had gone smoothly, allowing them to close quickly.

"I can't believe we actually did it," Denise said as she unlocked the car. "We're really going to expand the shop."

Jody smiled as she climbed into the car. She knew Denise would now start to second-guess their decision.

Denise slid the key into the ignition. "You don't think we made a mistake, do you?"

Jody laughed and it felt good. It seemed like it had been a long time since she had really laughed.

"What's so funny?" Denise demanded.

"You're so predictable," Jody said, fastening her seat belt.

"I just want to be sure. I know the shop's revenue is up ten percent from this time last year, but you never know."

Jody reached over and squeezed Denise's hand. "It was the right thing to do. We'll be fine." Jody sat back and heard Denise's sigh of relief.

"You're right. It's time. The shop is so cramped you can't cuss a cat without getting hair in your mouth."

Jody looked at her and frowned. "Where do you come up with these weird sayings?"

A look of confusion crossed Denise's face. "What weird sayings?"

Jody shook her head. "Never mind. I interrupted you. What were you about to say?"

Denise paused while she gathered her thoughts. "Oh," she said and rushed on. "We need to hire another full-time employee. I don't know about you, but I'm getting tired of working every other weekend."

Jody thought about how empty her life had felt since she last saw Ellen. Free time didn't seem so important to her. Suddenly she felt an overwhelming need to see Ellen.

"Does Ellen ever ask about me?" Jody inquired, embarrassed at having to ask.

Denise didn't answer right away. Her silence told Jody more than she wanted to know.

"Sweetie, don't take it personally, but all of her energy is focused on recuperating."

Jody felt like a whiny brat. "That's all she should be thinking about," she agreed. "I thought, maybe . . ." She let the sentence trail off.

"Every evening at dinner, I tell her about my day at the shop," Denise said.

Jody looked at her. "What do you tell her?"

Denise shrugged. "Everything. I just ramble on. She seems to enjoy hearing the stories. I tried to ask to her about the note a couple of times, but she refuses to discuss it." She stopped talking long enough to negotiate a turn. "She spends her spare time reading or sitting on the patio watching the birds."

"Birds?"

"Yeah, she asked me to buy a bird feeder and birdseed. I fill them for her each afternoon. She seems to enjoy watching them."

Jody suddenly had an idea. "Denise, would you mind if I planted a rosebush in your backyard? I'll do it during the day while Ellen is at work."

Denise glanced at her and frowned. "A rosebush?"

"It's a long story, but I think Ellen would enjoy it."

"If you think it'll make her feel any better you can fill the back-yard with rosebushes."

"I think one will be enough," Jody said, feeling better than she had in days.

Eric wasn't alone when Jody and Denise returned to Petal Pushers.

"Here they are," Eric called as they came in.

"We stopped for lunch," Denise said.

"How did the closing go?" Eric asked.

Denise waved the envelope full of paperwork. "All signed, dated and stamped."

"This is Oscar Zamora." Eric nodded toward the young man beside him. Oscar was only a few inches taller than Eric. His long, black hair was pulled back into a ponytail.

"The fabulous interior designer we've been hearing so much about," Jody teased, as she extended her hand to the ruggedly handsome young man. "It's nice to finally meet you."

Oscar shook Jody's hand and then Denise's. "I've heard so much about you two, I feel as though I know you already."

"Oscar has been working on some preliminary designs to show you. Wait until you see what he has done," Eric said, clearly unable to control his excitement.

Jody pushed her backpack beneath the counter. "Well, let's see them. I, for one, am ready to get this baby started."

Oscar took a notebook from the counter and flipped it open. "I have two different designs to show you. Of course, these are only meant to acquaint you with my work. If you decide to allow me to design your new space, we'll sit down together and talk about what you two had in mind."

Jody sensed his nervousness. "Let's see what you have."

Oscar cleared his throat. "The first one is a classical look." He revealed a drawing that had been done in colored pencils. The design was beautiful, but the Greek columns and flowing drapes were too elaborate for Jody's taste.

Denise took the design and studied it closely. "Oscar, this is beautiful, but I think we need something simpler."

Jody looked up to see Eric practically jumping up and down. "Show them the other one," he said, patting Oscar's arm.

Oscar looked at him and smiled, shaking his head. "You're so obvious."

"I can't help it. Hurry up and show them."

"Well, with that buildup I can hardly wait," Denise said.

Oscar flipped a page over to display the second design. Even before she had fully viewed it, Jody felt her breath catch. She turned to Denise and saw she was staring at the sketch. Denise took the drawing and held it so both she and Jody could see it. The plan was simple but still managed to portray a sense of elegance.

The design would turn the shop into a garden. There were several individual groupings that suggested flowerbeds. Rustic benches served as display tables, and strategically placed ficus trees gave the overall scheme a park-like feel.

"Is this a stream?" Denise asked.

"Yes, it's made from a molded plastic sealed with polyurethane. You won't have to worry about it leaking, and a pump keeps the water circulating, so it'll remain fresh-smelling. Here"—Oscar pointed to where the stream ended— "is a pool where the water will run into and allow it to be recirculated. The runoff won't be very high, so it won't be too noisy, but I thought the sound of running water would be soothing for you and your customers. Eric told me that a lot of your walk-ins are people who are picking up an arrangement or plant to take to a loved one in the hospital."

"You're right," Jody said. "What is all this going to cost?"

"That's the beauty of it all," Eric said, again patting Oscar's arm.

Denise and Jody both laughed. "Eric, I've never seen you so excited about anything," Denise said.

"We can do most of the work ourselves," Eric jumped in, too excited to wait for Oscar's more studied explanation. "Look at this." He pointed to the design. "We won't have to knock out the entire wall. We'll remove sections, frame them out for additional support, and then Oscar's plan trims them out to resemble arbors. So instead of the customers walking through doorways between the buildings they can go through the arbors that will have live plants growing around them."

"But what is all this framing and stuff costing?" Jody asked again.

Eric rolled his eyes at her question.

"Calm down," Oscar told him. "You've had more time to look at these than they have."

Eric took a deep breath and ran his hand over his cropped hair. "Okay, okay."

"The cost will be less than half of what it would cost you to tear out the entire wall and install support beams between the buildings," Oscar said. "You're lucky that the two buildings share a common wall. Eric was so sure you'd love this design, I went ahead and drew up a rough estimate."

Jody took the sheet and studied it. The figures were much lower than she anticipated. With a glance at Denise, who was also frowning, she cleared her throat. "Oscar, I don't mean to look a gift horse in the mouth, but these figures seem awfully low to me."

"That's because they don't include labor costs," he said.

Eric piped up, "We're going to be the labor."

"We?" Denise asked, clearly horrified at the idea.

Jody had a vague memory of Eric's talking about them doing the work themselves, but with everything that had been going on, she had forgotten about it.

"We can do it," Jody said.

Denise looked at her skeptically. "How? What do you know about ripping out walls and building things?"

"Not a lot," Jody admitted. "But it doesn't look that complicated."

"We can," Eric said and motioned between himself and Oscar. "You two will continue to run the shop and help out with the manual labor. Oscar and I can do the carpentry work."

"Aha!" Denise said. "There's the problem. I don't do manual labor."

Jody chuckled. "Denise, do you like this design?"

"I love it," Denise admitted.

Jody turned to Eric. "Do you two have enough experience to handle this?"

"I can certainly handle the designs," Oscar said.

"I worked as an assistant carpenter with my uncle, every summer until I joined the Marines," Eric assured her. "This is not brain surgery. We'll have to have an electrician come in to complete all of the electrical changes, but the construction is actually minor."

"Then let's do it," Jody said and held out her hand.

Eric quickly placed his hand on top of Jody's hand. Oscar covered Eric's hand with his own.

Denise looked at them and shook her head. "I'm surrounded by crazy people." She laid her hand over Oscar's. "I'm not doing manual labor," she insisted.

CHAPTER THIRTY-TWO

While making deliveries later that afternoon, Jody decided to stop by Leti and Maricela's nursery to pick up the rosebush she would be planting for Ellen.

Inside the nursery, several customers were shopping. She glanced out the large window that filled most of the back wall and spied both Leti and Maricela outside helping customers.

"I'm surprised to see you here."

Jody turned to a familiar voice and saw Sharon. She braced herself for more of Sharon's anger.

"Don't worry, I'm over it," Sharon said and smiled.

Still leery, Jody gave a weak smile. "It's good to see you. I didn't know you were a gardener."

Sharon shook her head. "We didn't learn too much about each other, did we?"

Jody blushed at the memory of why they never talked. Sharon laughed outright at Jody's obvious discomfort.

"What's so funny?" a voice called out.

Jody froze. She could never forget a voice as distinctive as Pat Rodriguez's. Jody held her breath, certain she had stumbled into some version of ex-lovers' hell.

Sharon laughed even harder.

Pat stepped from behind a display of wind chimes. The tall, long-haired Amazon was the complete opposite of her short, stocky sister, Maricela. "Well, would you look at who's here? Long time no see, Jody." Pat gave Jody a quick hug.

Sharon wiped tears of laughter from her eyes. "Oh, Jody, the look on your face is absolutely priceless." She gave Jody a long, hard hug.

Jody began to recover her wits. "What are you doing here?" she asked Sharon.

"You wouldn't believe it if I told you."

"Try me," Jody prompted.

"Well, after I left your house that day"—Sharon looked at Jody and grimaced, leaving Jody with no doubt as to which day she was talking about—"I went to Artie's to cry in my coffee."

Jody nodded. Sharon was addicted to coffee. She and Sharon had gone to the coffee shop several times while they were dating.

"I was sitting there feeling sorry for myself and Pat walks in," Sharon said. "The coffee shop was packed. I watched her looking around for a table, and there weren't any, so I invited her to sit with me. One thing led to another, and guess whose name came up?"

Jody cringed, which made Pat and Sharon smile.

Pat picked up the story. "After we had a really good Jody Scott bashing, we went for walk, and then to dinner, and the rest, as they say, is history."

They looked happy and Jody felt a small sense of relief rush over her. "So, you two are together?"

"Yeah," Pat said as she put an arm around Sharon's shoulder. "Ironically enough, we have you to thank."

"I'm glad," Jody said. "You're both wonderful people, and you deserve to be happy."

"What about you and the teenybopper?" Sharon asked.

Caught off guard by her question, Jody hesitated just long enough for Sharon to shake her head and sigh.

"Jody, don't tell me you've already dumped that poor girl."

Jody shrugged. "Actually, she dumped me." To Jody's horror, tears began to stream down her face. She tried to turn away, but both women saw her tears.

Sharon reached over and put an arm around her. "Honey, I'm so sorry."

Tears flowed down her cheeks. The more she tried to control them, the harder she cried.

Customers were beginning to look their way when Pat took Jody's arm and said, "Come on." They led her to the back of the shop, to a small break room furnished with a sofa.

"Get her a glass of water," Sharon said as she pushed Jody down onto the sofa. "Tell us what's going on."

The need to talk overwhelmed Jody. She told them everything that had happened since the day Sharon had arrived to find her and Ellen in robes. After finishing her story, she felt a small sense of relief. She closed her eyes and rested her head against the back of the sofa.

The room was silent for several seconds, before Sharon finally spoke. "I don't know what to say."

"Is there anything we can do to help?"

Jody's eyes flew open. She turned to find Leti and Maricela standing in the doorway. She hadn't heard them come in. Leti was waiting for Jody to answer her question. Afraid the tears would return if she opened her mouth, she shook her head.

Leti came over and sat on the arm of the sofa next to her. "My sister had breast cancer," Leti said. "That was about eight years ago, and she's fine now. She just celebrated her fiftieth birthday."

A bell dinged in the shop, letting them know they had a customer. Maricela patted Leti's shoulder. "I'll go," she said and went out.

"What are you going to do?" Sharon asked.

Jody shrugged. "What can I do? If she doesn't want to see me, then I have to respect her wishes."

"Are you sure she doesn't want to see you?" Leti asked.

Jody looked at her and frowned. "I think I can be safe in answering yes to that."

Leti shook her head and said, "I don't know, Jody. Sometimes we say one thing but mean something totally different. I remember when Rachel, my sister, was diagnosed. She withdrew from everyone. Later, she told me, she couldn't bear to see the fear in our eyes. Our fear became an extra burden for her. It was easier to avoid us completely. Solitude provided her with the luxury of focusing totally on herself. We grow up believing that it's selfish to dwell only on ourselves, but I think sometimes we have to."

"How did you get her to start talking to you again?"

"We waited and gave her the space she needed. It took time, but she eventually found her own way back."

The chime on the shop door rang again. Jody glanced at her watch and said, "I've got to get going. I still have deliveries to make." She looked up as Maricela came back in. "Sorry I blubbered all over everyone."

Sharon patted her shoulder. "We all need to blubber sometimes."

Jody smiled and started to leave. "I almost forgot why I came. I wanted to buy another Belinda's Dream rosebush."

Leti instantly went into her gardener's mode. "Did something happen to the other one? If it died, we'll replace it."

"No," Jody said. "My roses are fine. I wanted to get one to plant in Denise's yard." She suddenly felt embarrassed by what she was about to do. She looked up to find Sharon peering at her and smiling. "What?"

Sharon chuckled and said, "Jody Scott, you really are a romantic at heart. I don't believe it. You're not planting this rosebush for Denise, are you?"

Jody shook her head and told them the story about Ellen's childhood imaginary friend named Belinda and how Ellen had felt protected whenever Belinda was around. By the time she finished her story, tears glistened in everyone's eyes.

Maricela rubbed her hand roughly across her face. "I'll go get the rosebush," she said.

Jody hugged the remaining three women and pulled out her wallet.

"No," Leti said, pushing the wallet away. "This one is on the house. You just make sure you don't let Ellen slip away from you."

Jody tried to speak around the lump in her throat caused by Leti's words. All she could manage was a nod. She left quickly before she started crying again.

Maricela was standing by Jody's delivery van with the potted rosebush on the ground beside her. She picked it up as Jody approached. "I watered it earlier this morning, so it'll be fine while you make your rounds. Just make sure you don't leave it in the van afterward."

Jody nodded. "Thanks for everything," she said as she took the plant.

Maricela slid one hand into her back pocket and rubbed the other one over her short black hair. "Call if you need anything," she said.

Surprised, Jody looked at her. "I thought you didn't like me."

Maricela shrugged. "Until I met Leti, Pat was the only family I had. Our parents were killed in a car wreck when I was twelve and Pat was five. An aunt took us in, but she was always kind of cranky, and two kids didn't do much to improve her disposition. I always sort of looked out for Pat."

Jody nodded and placed the plant in the back of the van.

As she walked back around to get in the truck, Maricela gave her a small slap on the shoulder. "You take care of yourself."

Jody smiled. "You too, Maricela." She crawled into the van and rolled the window down. "Pat's a lucky woman. The world could use more sisters like you."

A blush raced across Maricela's face, but she smiled slightly and nodded.

As Jody drove away, she looked into her side mirror. The four women stood in a small huddle staring after her. A few hours ago, she wouldn't have considered any one of them a true friend, but something had changed. They had all come to support her in a moment of need. Suddenly, she didn't feel quite so alone, and a tiny spark of hope flared within her. If her differences with these women could be resolved, maybe there was still some hope with Ellen.

CHAPTER THIRTY-THREE

Jody was in bed watching television later that night when the phone rang. She snatched it up, hoping it was Denise, who hadn't returned to the shop after taking Ellen for her radiation treatment. Jody had been out on deliveries when she called the shop to say she wouldn't be back.

"Hi, it's me." Denise sounded tired.

"Is Ellen all right?"

"Yes. She wasn't feeling well after the treatment and I didn't want to leave her alone. She's doing better now. I'm sorry I'm calling so late, but I waited until she went to bed."

"How much longer is she going to keep me away?" Jody asked, frustrated.

Denise sighed. "Sweetie, I don't know. You got her attention with the rosebush though."

Jody sat up. She had gone to Denise's house and planted the rose-bush by the far edge of the patio. Ellen would be able to see it from her bedroom window. "Did she like it?"

"She sat out there and cried until I made her come in," Denise said. "I swear that girl is so stubborn. I tried to get her to call you and work this thing out, but she won't do it. I know she misses you, and I'd bet my last dollar that she's still in love with you."

Jody's heart soared. "Maybe I could drop by tomorrow and see her."

"I don't think that's a good idea, Jody. You can't push her. She's thinking about joining a support group. She was talking to a woman in the waiting room today who told her about a breast cancer sup-port group she has been attending. Ellen seemed pretty excited about it."

"Ellen is never going to change her mind," Jody said. "Why can't I accept that and move on?"

"Don't you start feeling sorry for yourself," Denise snapped. "I don't have enough energy to take care of both of you at once."

Jody felt ashamed for whining. "Denise, I'm sorry. I know you must be out of your mind with worry."

"I'm so tired. The emotional pounding she's taking is wearing me out. I see her struggling, and there's nothing I can do to help." Denise drew in a long shaky breath. "And now we're starting the renovations on the shop. You're working seven days a week. I know it's hard for you and Eric when I have to be out with Ellen. I feel like I'm letting everyone down."

"You're not letting anyone down. I'm working seven days a week because I choose to. You're tired. You're trying to work, plus take Ellen in for her treatments, and I know you've stayed late several times to complete orders." She heard Denise sigh as she continued. "You need to start taking care of yourself. We shouldn't have agreed to give up our vacations this year because of expanding the shop. That was a mistake."

Denise yawned. "You're probably right, but what choice did we have? The renovations have to be completed before the guys go back to school in August. I'm going to bed. We can talk tomorrow."

Long after Denise had hung up, Jody continued to lie across her bed and stare at the ceiling. If only there was some way she could convince Ellen to let her back into her life, Jody thought. She could be a help to Denise. Suddenly it hit Jody what she could do to help Denise. She would make the call tomorrow. Smiling, she switched the light off and finally drifted into a restless sleep.

The following day, Jody called the temp agency and made arrangements to hire a temporary full-time employee who would be in charge of making deliveries and filling in wherever needed.

Two hours later as Jody, Eric and Oscar were going over their plans on how to begin the renovations, the new hire arrived. Jody took in the wide, purple streak that ran through the girl's hair, the nose ring, and the sun tattoo that peeked from beneath the sleeve of her T-shirt.

"I'm Ra," the girl said around an enormous wad of orange gum.

"Ra?" Jody asked, unable to tear her gaze from the orange mass.

"Yeah, as in sun." She looked at Jody as though Jody were a cretin and raised her shirt sleeve to expose the sun tattoo.

Jody rubbed her hand over her hair and noticed Eric look at Oscar and roll his eyes. She hadn't slept well after Denise's call last night and was exhausted. "Ra, are you old enough to drive?" she asked.

"Like, yeah." She managed to drag the latter word out into three syllables. "How do you think I got here?"

Jody nodded. "Good. Lose the gum, and the attitude. The next few weeks around here are going to be hectic and hard on everyone. You'll be making the deliveries by yourself. Do you know your way around the city?"

Ra started to express her three-syllable answer to life, but she caught herself and simply nodded.

"Good," Jody said. "Eric will help you load the van for the first couple of days, to give you a feel for the most efficient way to place the arrangements. After that, you're on your own."

Eric appeared at Ra's side. "Come on, I'll help you load the van," he said.

Jody watched the two until they disappeared into the workroom.

"Were we ever that young," Oscar said at Jody's elbow.

Jody turned to him, struck a pose and said, "Ye-ee-ah."

It was the first of July before they were finally able to start the actual renovations. Oscar had proven himself invaluable in showing Jody how to wade through the paper maze of city hall. He had helped her obtain the necessary permits to begin the renovations. Jody swung the sledgehammer with all her strength. She was already looking forward to the larger workspace the remodeling would provide. In addition to the showroom's garden display, Oscar had drawn up plans to tear out a smaller section from the back portion of the wall. The opening would be become a double-wide entrance between the two shops. The card shop was much larger than the flower shop had been, so its back portion would become the new workroom. The old workroom would be converted into an office and a small kitchenette.

Jody continued to pound out chunks of the wall. It felt good to push her muscles to their limit. She was beginning to appreciate why Sharon enjoyed lifting weights. Jody was working in the now-empty card shop, attempting to break through the wall. The vast emptiness of the room made the hammering reverberate loudly.

At Oscar's suggestion, they were going to start the demolition from the card shop in an attempt to help keep the noise and dust to a minimum. They had also hung a curtain of heavy black plastic across the end of the flower shop. The curtain hung about five feet from the wall to allow them a small working area and to help stop the dust that would be present when they finally broke through the wall. Jody suspected dust was going to become a major issue before the construction ended.

She and Eric were taking turns helping Denise and Ra in the shop when needed. Ra had quickly proven herself to be a valuable asset. Despite her less-than-professional appearance, she was a hard worker, often staying after closing to watch Denise prepare arrangements and help with cleanup.

As day after day had slipped by and Ellen continued to make no effort to contact her, Jody began to lose hope. Nights were the roughest. After a long day in the flower shop, she would go home and find enough chores to keep her busy through the lonesome hours until it was time to go to bed.

On the good nights, she was too tired to worry about anything or anyone. On the not-so-good nights, she paced the floors and tried not to think of Ellen. Then there were the horrendous nights when nothing could drive away the images and memories of Ellen. On those nights, she cried herself to sleep.

A chunk of plaster slapped against Jody's cheek and snapped her attention back to her demolition work. She set the sledgehammer down and wiggled her nose, trying to ease the pressure of the safety glasses. They irritated the backs of her ears, but Eric was adamant that she wear them. It had only taken a couple of swings of the hammer and the resulting explosion of drywall and plaster fragments for her to see the wisdom of his decision.

She stretched her back before resuming her work. A few seconds later, she shouted in exhilaration as the head of the hammer penetrated the drywall on the opposite side of the wall. She stopped hammering and peeked through the hole and saw Eric and Oscar on the other side.

"Hey, guys. I did it," she called through the opening.

"Only thirty more square feet to go," Eric said.

Jody stuck her tongue out at him. "Party pooper. Step back. I'm on a roll." She gave them time to move away from the wall and resumed her destruction with renewed vigor.

An hour later, the wall opening had been enlarged to Oscar's specifications. Jody rested while Eric cut through the wall joists with a reciprocating saw.

They were hammering in the new frame when Ra returned from making the deliveries. "Cool," she exclaimed as she peeked behind the plastic barrier and saw the hole in the wall. "Can I help bust out a wall?"

Jody's arm muscles were still quivering. "Oscar will be glad to show you the next spot he wants demolished."

The door chimed and Ra turned to see who it was. "It's only Denise," she reported.

"Only Denise, is it?" Denise said as she pulled the plastic aside and appraised the group.

Dust and drywall fragments covered Jody's faded work shirt and jeans. The guys, decked out in work boots, painters' overalls, hard hats and safety glasses looked prepared to handle whatever came their way. Eric had rounded out his wardrobe with a pair of leather work gloves.

"You two look like creatures from outer space," Denise said as she pointed to Eric and Oscar.

Oscar took a few tiny steps and whirled. "Honey, this is the latest in macho male attire."

Eric rolled his eyes and said, "Give him a hard hat and suddenly he thinks he's one of the Village People."

"Who's that?" Ra asked.

Without warning, Denise and Jody began to sing "YMCA." Eric and Oscar quickly joined in. Within seconds the four had a flamboyant rendition going.

Ra shook her head as she watched them cavorting among the dust and debris. "And you think I'm weird."

CHAPTER THIRTY-FOUR

Jody made the last delivery of the day and headed back to the shop. The renovations had taken three weeks, but they were finally finished. Setting up the final inspection had taken almost a week, but at last everything was complete and signed off on. The shop was so beautiful, Denise and Jody had decided to have a full-blown celebration for the new Petal Pushers.

Jody ran advertisements in all the area papers and sent out flyers, and posters announcing the event had been dropped off at dozens of businesses. She and Denise arranged for a caterer and hired a local jazz ensemble to entertain the crowd of guests they hoped would attend.

Jody pulled into the empty parking lot. Despite the energy-stealing humidity of early August, she stood in the parking lot and gazed at the newly painted building. She experienced a burst of pride when she thought of all the work they had been able to accomplish by themselves. It hardly seemed possible that over two months had passed since she talked to Mrs. Jimenez about purchasing the building. It was hard to believe such an amazing transformation could have occurred with the two buildings during that time.

Thanks to Eric and Oscar, the demolition and renovation had moved along relatively painlessly. The first couple of inspections had made Jody nervous, but she quickly realized that as long as the work met the legal standards, the inspectors didn't hassle them.

Jody locked the delivery van and went inside to get her backpack. She walked through the entire shop. Eric and Denise had everything prepared for tomorrow's celebration. The shop was as ready as it would ever be. She retrieved her backpack and headed home.

Jody lay in bed waiting for the alarm to go off. She had been too excited about the celebration to sleep much. She glanced at the clock; it was only seven. The alarm wouldn't ring for another thirty minutes. Impatient and knowing she wasn't going to be able to go back to sleep, she shut off the alarm and showered.

Afterward, she poured a cup of coffee and went outside. August was always horrible in San Antonio, but the last few days had been worse than usual. She was relieved to find when she stepped out that the humidity was low. It looked as though even the weather was going to cooperate today.

As she did every morning, she checked the progress of each of the rosebushes. After assuring herself that the plants continued to thrive, she sat on the swing and gazed at Belinda's Dream. The plant was covered in large, pink roses. Jody had sat by the rose and repeated her prayer for Ellen's complete recovery every single day since Ellen's surgery.

During that time, Jody finally admitted to herself that the only way she was ever going to be able to move on with her life was to erase as much of Ellen as she possibly could from it. The cleansing was proving much more difficult than she had anticipated, because no matter where she looked she saw something of Ellen.

Sometimes it was nothing more than the beauty of a sunset or the song of the wrens that pulled Ellen to the forefront of Jody's thoughts. But not a single day went by without memories of Ellen working their way into her heart.

Jody had briefly considered moving away from San Antonio, but she quickly realized she couldn't. There was too much of herself in the city, and she couldn't leave Denise with the shop now that it had been renovated. She accepted the fact that she would have to find a way to live with Ellen's memories.

As she drank her coffee, she allowed her hand to gently brush over the petals of the roses. They would always remind her of Ellen. Tears burned her eyes as the memories grew too painful. She escaped into the house and began to clean until it was time to get dressed.

Jody chose a soft pastel-blue shirt and a pair of navy blue slacks. The clothes would be dressy but comfortable enough for the long day ahead of her. On her way out, she picked up a package and a folder. The item in the package had been her idea, but the items in the folder had been a joint decision between her and Denise. She smiled. If the paperwork in the folder was met with approval, as she hoped, today would indeed be a grand day.

Jody was the first to arrive. She opened the register and prepared the cash drawer for the day, started a pot of coffee, and began to remove the displays from the cooler.

Denise came in while she was pouring her coffee. "It's me," she called out as the bell rang to announce her presence.

"I've made coffee," Jody called back.

Denise came into the new kitchenette. She was wearing a new gray suit that she had bought for the grand opening. She gazed around and shook her head in amazement. "I still can't believe it's finished. I'm so happy with the changes."

Jody handed her a cup of coffee.

"Did you bring the paperwork?" Denise asked.

"It's in the blue folder on the desk."

"Jody, do you really think he'll agree?"

Jody shrugged. "We won't know until we try." The bell rang again. She looked at Denise and smiled. "Speak of the devil." She grabbed the package and the folder and followed Denise into the showroom. Eric and Oscar had come in together.

"What a beautiful shop," Oscar cried out. "Oh, I do wish I had the name of the extraordinary designer who created this master-piece."

"I have something here that might help you with that," Jody said, handing him the package.

"What's this for?" he asked as he ripped it open like a kid at Christmas.

"Just a little something extra to tell you how much we appreciate everything you've done for Petal Pushers," Denise said.

"Honey, the check you wrote out yesterday told me that," he teased.

"Then consider this a small bonus," Jody said.

Oscar opened a box and pulled out one of the cards. "Look." He turned it to Eric. "Embossed business cards." He held up a card and read it aloud. "Oscar Zamora, Interior Designer. I like the sound of that. Thank you." He hugged Jody and then Denise.

"We realize you have another semester before you graduate, but there's no doubt you're well on your way," Denise said.

Jody saw the look of sadness in Eric's eyes. He also had only one more semester before he would graduate and leave to help his father.

As if sensing his thoughts, Oscar hugged Eric. "I don't want you to move to Montana."

Denise nudged Jody, who picked up the folder and offered it to Eric. "We thought that maybe . . . What I mean is, if you're not dead set on moving back to Montana . . ."

Denise took the folder from Jody. "For heaven's sake, Jody, he'll be gone six months before you even give it to him." Denise handed the folder to Eric.

The small group grew silent. Oscar was practically bouncing on his toes with curiosity.

Eric opened the folder and read for several seconds. He stopped once to look from Jody to Denise, then continued reading.

"What is it?" Oscar asked, unable to keep still any longer.

Eric suddenly closed the folder and turned his back to the group.

"What?" Oscar demanded again.

Finally Eric rubbed a hand over his face and turned to them. His eyes were red, but he had regained control of himself. "It's partnership papers for one-third interest in Petal Pushers," he said to Oscar.

Oscar's jaw dropped, and for once he was speechless.

"I don't know what we would have done without your help these past few months," Denise said.

"This is too much." He tried to hand the folder back to Jody.

She pushed it away. "I know you have some kind of offer with your father, and if it's something you want to do, then you should take it. But if not, we would like you to sign your name on the bottom of that contract."

"I can't," Eric said. "It's too much."

Jody shook her head. "We don't think so. You're as much a part of this shop as either of us. You've never once complained about the extra hours or the last-minute calls to come in and work. You did almost all of the carpentry work on the renovation. We think you deserve an equal share."

Eric looked from Jody to Denise and finally at Oscar, whose eyes were gleaming with hope.

Jody held her breath as Eric reached into his jacket pocket for a pen. The scratching of the pen across the paper was the only sound in the room.

Eric closed the folder and looked at Jody and Denise. "Thanks," he said, his voice thick with emotion.

Before they could respond, Oscar grabbed Eric and spun him around the room in a hug.

"I'm getting dizzy," Eric cried, laughing.

Oscar stopped and gave him a kiss that lasted long enough to make even Jody blush.

Oscar released Eric and grabbed first Denise and then Jody. He danced them around in an extravagant waltz.

They were still celebrating when the bell on the door rang.

Jody pulled away from Oscar and felt the floor drop from beneath her. Ellen was standing in the doorway.

CHAPTER THIRTY-FIVE

Eric caught Jody and held her to keep her from falling. She clung to his arm as blood raced through her veins so hard her ears began to roar.

Ellen was as beautiful as ever. She was pale and had lost weight since the last time Jody had seen her. Seeing her now made Jody's heart ache with love.

She had almost convinced herself she was over Ellen, but in that moment, she knew it was all a lie. Ellen's presence was almost more than she could handle. She pulled away from Eric and rushed to the kitchenette, where she stood at the sink and gasped for air. Why hadn't she prepared herself for the possibility that Ellen would attend the celebration? It made perfect sense, but why hadn't Denise warned her?

"I'm a damn fool," Jody said, pounding her head against the overhead cabinet.

"I think I hold that title."

Jody turned to find Ellen standing behind her. "Hi." It was all Jody could think to say.

"Hi, back." Ellen gave a crooked smile that nearly tore Jody's heart apart.

Jody turned away. The silence that followed hurt Jody's ears. "How are you feeling?" she asked.

"Good. It's such a relief to have the radiation treatments over with."

Jody nodded. "I heard you'd taken the last one a couple of weeks ago."

"Jody, I'm sorry."

Jody shook her head. "There's nothing to apologize for."

"Yes, there is. I should have talked to you at the hospital," she said. "But I couldn't handle that look of disgust."

Jody spun around. "Disgust? When did I ever look at you with disgust?"

Ellen lowered her eyes. "It would have happened after the surgery or during the radiation treatments." She paused. "I love you so much, I couldn't bear to see it."

There they were, the three tiny words she had been longing to hear again, and now that they were out, all Jody could do was shout, "Damn you, Ellen Murray."

Ellen said nothing.

"Who do you think you are? What gives you the right to decide how I'll feel?" Jody's body shook with anger. "Did it ever occur to you to ask me how I felt?"

"I didn't have to," Ellen said. "Beth told me in her letter how she felt just thinking about the way my body would look and feel afterward."

"*Beth*!" Jody slapped the counter with the flat of her hand. "You used the opinion of that spineless ninny to decide how I would react?"

"What else did I have?"

"You had my word. You could have asked me, given me a chance," Jody said, trying unsuccessfully to rein in her anger.

Tears began to stream down Ellen's face. "You were always saying how beautiful you thought I was. Well, now, my breast is disfigured. It's scarred, and the cancer could come back."

Jody shook her head. She suspected the fear of the cancer's returning was affecting Ellen more than the scar. "Ellen, I told you once before. I'm not in love with your looks. My body no longer looks like it did twenty years ago. Did it ever occur to you that maybe I was self-conscious when I first undressed in front of you? Look at me. I'm forty-four. I run three times a week, but trust me I'm very aware that I'm fighting a losing battle with time. It's a part of being alive."

"But you're whole."

Jody's anger wilted. "No, Ellen. I stopped being whole the day you sent me away. Without you, I'll never be whole again. I loved you."

Silence hung between them there for several seconds.

"You used the past tense," Ellen said as she began to fidget with the collar of her blouse. "Have I completely destroyed whatever feelings you had for me?"

No, I love you more than ever, Jody thought, but her pride kept her from saying the words aloud. "It's been two months. You dump me without so much as a *thank you very much*, and now you expect to be able to just waltz back in and pick up where we left off?"

"I'm sorry," she said, her voice little more than a whisper. "I was wrong. Beth's note left me so . . ."

"To hell with Beth's note," Jody snapped. The mere mention of Beth rekindled her anger. "You never answered my question. Did I ever give you a reason to believe that I would be disgusted at the sight of you?"

Ellen shook her head and left. Jody wanted to call to her, but she couldn't. To think that Ellen had judged her by the actions of the mealy-mouthed little twit Beth was almost more than she could tolerate. The memory of all the long nights of waiting and praying that Ellen would call fueled her anger and confusion.

Forgive her and move on, the voice of reason pleaded. *Are you serious?* her pride hissed. *She dumped you and didn't even have the courtesy to do it herself, she sent her mom to do it.*

"What happened?" Eric said from the doorway.

She shook her head and sat down at the small kitchen table. She put her head in her hands.

"We thought you two would be in here making up, and the next thing we know, Ellen is running out of here crying her eyes out."

"She was crying?" Jody asked, feeling like an ogre. "She left?"

"Yes, Denise went after her." Eric took a seat across from her. "What happened?"

Ashamed of her behavior, Jody slowly told him what had transpired. When she finished, he placed a hand over his forehead and sighed.

"Why did you do that?" he asked.

"I don't know. I was angry." Jody traced the design on the table with her finger. "Eric, I have some pride. I can't just roll over the minute she walks back in and says she's sorry."

Eric shook his head. "Well, no, you can't just forgive and forget and get on with your life. It's so much better to be miserable and wallow in your self-pity."

Jody's head shot up. "Don't you start in on me too."

"Jody, I'm going to be completely honest with you. I've watched you mope around here for two months just waiting for a single word from Ellen. And now she comes in and tells you that she's still in love with you, and you decide to get on your high horse and show her the door." He threw up his hands in frustration. "What do you want?" He walked out before she could answer.

His words hurt. The worst part was she knew he was right. She loved Ellen. Why couldn't she forgive and forget?

She was still sitting at the table trying to sort out her feelings when Denise came in. "Are you going to chew my butt, too?" Jody asked.

Denise took two cold sodas from the refrigerator and sat down in the chair Eric had vacated. "No," she said, placing a soda in front of Jody and popping open the other one for herself.

Jody endured the silence between them as long as possible before she said, "Well, say something."

Denise looked at her and sighed. "What can I say that you don't already know? Shall I give you the 'life is too short' speech, or how about the one on swallowing foolish pride?" Denise took a sip of her soda. "What good would it do? You're hurt and angry, and you have every right to be. What Ellen did was inexcusable."

Surprised, Jody asked. "Why aren't you defending her? You always defend her."

Denise shrugged. "Why should I? She's wrong. I don't blame you in the least for telling her to fuck off." She calmly took another sip of her drink.

Jody was stunned. In their thirty-five years of friendship, she had never heard Denise use the word *fuck*. "Denise, you of all people should be defending her," Jody said when she recovered.

Denise shook her head. "Not this time."

Jody's anger found a new target. "I don't believe you. Ellen was sick and she made a mistake. Denise, think of what she must have been going through. How would you have felt if you had been facing breast cancer? Not to mention the surgery." Jody's indignation was growing.

"And your point is?"

Exasperated, Jody looked at her. "My point is, she deserves a second chance."

Denise stood. "Good, she was headed home. Why don't you go on over and tell her you think she deserves a second chance?"

Jody was dumbfounded. "Denise Murray, you set me up."

"No, ma'am, you set yourself up." Denise stopped and turned back to Jody. "You once told me life is too short to waste. I think you two have wasted enough time."

Jody went to Denise and threw her arms around her and hugged tightly. "When did you get so damn smart?"

Denise hugged her back and said, "I've been smart enough to keep you around all these years. Now go find Ellen and bring her back. We're going to need all the help we can get."

CHAPTER THIRTY-SIX

Jody pushed the speed limit all the way to Denise's house. She parked the Jeep at the curb and raced up the walkway. She had no idea what she would say when Ellen answered the door.

For a moment, she faltered. What if Ellen refused to talk to her? Jody pushed the thought away and pressed the doorbell before she could change her mind. After what seemed like an eternity, Ellen appeared. Her eyes were puffy from crying.

"I'm sorry," Jody said. "I let my stupid pride get in the way. I love you and always will."

Ellen moved back slightly, and Jody's heart took over as she stepped inside and took Ellen into her arms. Their lips met in a tender embrace, but two months of fear and longing stirred a hunger in Jody that she had nearly forgotten. Her kisses grew more demanding, and Ellen's answered with a hunger of their own. Jody kicked the door closed, and before she knew what was happening they were on the carpet. Somehow during the turning and tumbling Jody ended up beneath Ellen. She tried to roll Ellen over, but Ellen was proving hard to move.

Ellen fumbled with the buttons on Jody's blouse. She could sense Ellen's frustration with the uncooperative buttons. She was about to offer help when Ellen gave a small cry of desperation and grabbed the material and yanked. There was a sound of material ripping and Jody heard a button ping off something nearby. The act turned Jody on so, she nearly came before Ellen ever touched her.

Jody reached up to unbutton Ellen's blouse but Ellen froze. Fear raced through Jody. "Ellen, please don't do this. I want to make love to you. I want to see you." Jody watched a series of emotions play across Ellen's face. "Please," she whispered. She kissed Ellen softly.

Ellen's hands trembled as she slowly raised herself until she was kneeling between Jody's legs. She unbuttoned her blouse, and hesitantly opened it. Even though Ellen was still wearing a bra, Jody could see the scar at the top of Ellen's breast where the wedge-shaped piece of breast tissue had been removed. Jody knew this wasn't the only physical scar. Denise had told her about the two-inch scar across Ellen's armpit where Dr. Wray had operated on the lymph nodes.

"How can anyone ever think this is beautiful?" Ellen asked as she reached back and released the clasp on her bra, allowing Jody a full view. The removal of the breast tissue during the surgery had caused the breasts to appear asymmetrical.

Jody traced her fingertips alongside the path of the scar before she said, "It's simple. I'm not in love with your body. I'm in love with you."

"But it's so ugly." Ellen tried to tug her blouse closed.

Jody grabbed her hands and held them. "Do you love me?"

Ellen nodded.

"Will you love me less as I grow older and my body continues to decline?"

"No, of course not."

234

"Then give me the opportunity to show you that I love you for who you are here." Jody placed her hand over Ellen's heart.

Ellen gazed into Jody's eyes. Her lips trembled. "I'm scared," she whispered.

"We'll take it slow." Jody used her thumb to wipe away Ellen's tears. She pulled Ellen down beside her and held her. She knew it would take time before Ellen would feel comfortable with her body again, but she intended to be there beside her during the journey.

ABOUT THE AUTHOR

Frankie J. Jones is the author of *Rhythm Tide, Whispers in the Wind, Captive Heart, Room for Love,* and *Midas Touch*. She enjoys fishing, traveling, outdoor photography, and rummaging through flea markets in search of whimsical salt and pepper shakers.

Authors love to hear from their readers. You may contact Frankie through Bella Books at www.BellaBooks.com, or directly at FrankieJJones@aol.com.

Be Your Own *Breast* Friend!

IN THE SHOWER OR LYING DOWN:

Examine each breast and armpit from top to bottom, keeping your hand flat and using the pads of the fingers. Learn what *your* breasts feel like.

Some women have breasts that have lumps naturally. Look for any physical *changes* like knots or thickenings.

Reprinted with permission from:

The Mautner Project
The National Lesbian Health Organization

Special Thanks to Alison Bechdel

1707 L Street NW, Suite 230 ❤ **Washington, DC 20036** ❤
Voice: 202-332-5536 ❤ **Fax:** 202-332-0662 ❤
mautner@mautnerproject.org ❤ www.mautnerproject.org ❤
Combined Federal Campaign #2675

Publications from
BELLA BOOKS, INC.
The best in contemporary lesbian fiction

P.O. Box 10543, Tallahassee, FL 32302
Phone: 800-729-4992
www.bellabooks.com

BACK TO BASICS: A BUTCH/FEMME EROTIC ANTHOLOGY
edited by Therese Szymanski—from Bella After Dark. 314 pp.
ISBN 1-931513-35-X $12.95

SURVIVAL OF LOVE by Frankie J. Jones. 236 pp. What will
Jody do when she falls in love with her best friend's daughter?
ISBN 1-931513-55-4 $12.95

DEATH BY DEATH by Claire McNab. 167 pp. 5th Denise
Cleever Thriller.   ISBN 1-931513-34-1 $12.95

CAUGHT IN THE NET by Jessica Thomas. 188 pp. A wickedly
observant story of mystery, danger, and love in Provincetown.
ISBN 1-931513-54-6 $12.95

DREAMS FOUND by Lyn Denison. 201 pp. Australian Riley embarks
on a journey to meet her birth mother . . . and gains not just a family
but the love of her life.   ISBN 1-931513-58-9 $12.95

A MOMENT'S INDISCRETION by Peggy J. Herring. 154 pp.
Jackie is torn between her better judgment and the overwhelming
attraction she feels for Valerie.   ISBN 1-931513-59-7 $12.95

IN EVERY PORT by Karin Kallmaker. 224 pp. Jessica's sexy,
adventuresome travels.   ISBN 1-931513-36-8 $12.95

TOUCHWOOD by Karin Kallmaker. 240 pp. Loving
May/December romance.   ISBN 1-931513-37-6 $12.95

WATERMARK by Karin Kallmaker. 248 pp. One burning
question . . . how to lead her back to love? ISBN 1-931513-38-4 $12.95

EMBRACE IN MOTION by Karin Kallmaker. 240 pp. A
whirlwind love affair.   ISBN 1-931513-39-2 $12.95

ONE DEGREE OF SEPARATION by Karin Kallmaker. 232 pp.
Can an Iowa City librarian find love and passion when a California
girl surfs into the close-knit dyke capital of the Midwest?
ISBN 1-931513-30-9 $12.95

CRY HAVOC A Detective Franco Mystery by Baxter Clare. 240 pp.
A dead hustler with a headless rooster in his lap sends Lt. L.A.
Franco headfirst against Mother Love.   ISBN 1-931513931-7 $12.95

DISTANT THUNDER by Peggy J. Herring. 294 pp. Bankrobbing
drifter Cordy awakens strange new feelings in Leo in this romantic
tale set in the Old West.   ISBN 1-931513-28-7 $12.95

COP OUT by Claire McNab. 216 pp. 4th Detective Inspector
Carol Ashton Mystery.   ISBN 1-931513-29-5 $12.95

BLOOD LINK by Claire McNab. 159 pp. 15th Detective
Inspector Carol Ashton Mystery. Is Carol unwittingly playing
into a deadly plan?   ISBN 1-931513-27-9 $12.95

TALK OF THE TOWN by Saxon Bennett. 239 pp.
With enough beer, barbecue and B.S., anything
is possible!   ISBN 1-931513-18-X $12.95

MAYBE NEXT TIME by Karin Kallmaker. 256 pp. Sabrina Starling has
it all: fame, money, women—and pain. Nothing hurts like the one that got
away.   ISBN 1-931513-26-0 $12.95

WHEN GOOD GIRLS GO BAD: A Motor City Thriller by
Therese Szymanski. 230 pp. Brett, Randi, and Allie join forces
to stop a serial killer.   ISBN 1-931513-11-2   12.95

A DAY TOO LONG: A Helen Black Mystery by Pat Welch.
328 pp. This time Helen's fate is in her own hands.
ISBN 1-931513-22-8 $12.95

THE RED LINE OF YARMALD by Diana Rivers. 256 pp.
The Hadra's only hope lies in a magical red line . . . climactic
sequel to *Clouds of War*.   ISBN 1-931513-23-6 $12.95

OUTSIDE THE FLOCK by Jackie Calhoun. 224 pp.
Jo embraces her new love and life.   ISBN 1-931513-13-9 $12.95

LEGACY OF LOVE by Marianne K. Martin. 224 pp. Read the whole
Sage Bristo story.   ISBN 1-931513-15-5 $12.95

STREET RULES: A Detective Franco Mystery by Baxter Clare.
304 pp. Gritty, fast-paced mystery with compelling Detective
L.A. Franco   ISBN 1-931513-14-7 $12.95

RECOGNITION FACTOR: 4th Denise Cleever Thriller by Claire McNab. 176 pp. Denise Cleever tracks a notorious terrorist to America.   ISBN 1-931513-24-4 $12.95

NORA AND LIZ by Nancy Garden. 296 pp. Lesbian romance by the author of *Annie on My Mind*.   ISBN 1931513-20-1 $12.95

MIDAS TOUCH by Frankie J. Jones. 208 pp. Sandra had everything but love.   ISBN 1-931513-21-X $12.95

BEYOND ALL REASON by Peggy J. Herring. 240 pp. A romance hotter than Texas.   ISBN 1-9513-25-2 $12.95

ACCIDENTAL MURDER: 14th Detective Inspector Carol Ashton Mystery by Claire McNab. 208 pp. Carol Ashton tracks an elusive killer.   ISBN 1-931513-16-3 $12.95

SEEDS OF FIRE: Tunnel of Light Trilogy, Book 2 by Karin Kallmaker writing as Laura Adams. 274 pp. Intriguing sequel to *Sleight of Hand*.   ISBN 1-931513-19-8 $12.95

DRIFTING AT THE BOTTOM OF THE WORLD by Auden Bailey. 288 pp. Beautifully written first novel set in Antarctica.   ISBN 1-931513-17-1 $12.95

CLOUDS OF WAR by Diana Rivers. 288 pp. Women unite to defend Zelindar!   ISBN 1-931513-12-0 $12.95

DEATHS OF JOCASTA: 2nd Micky Knight Mystery by J.M. Redmann. 408 pp. Sexy and intriguing Lambda Literary Award–nominated mystery.   ISBN 1-931513-10-4 $12.95

LOVE IN THE BALANCE by Marianne K. Martin. 256 pp. The classic lesbian love story, back in print! ISBN 1-931513-08-2 $12.95

THE COMFORT OF STRANGERS by Peggy J. Herring. 272 pp. Lela's work was her passion . . . until now.   ISBN 1-931513-09-0 $12.95

CHICKEN by Paula Martinac. 208 pp. Lynn finds that the only thing harder than being in a lesbian relationship is ending one.   ISBN 1-931513-07-4 $11.95

TAMARACK CREEK by Jackie Calhoun. 208 pp. An intriguing story of love and danger.   ISBN 1-931513-06-6 $11.95

DEATH BY THE RIVERSIDE: 1st Micky Knight Mystery by J.M. Redmann. 320 pp. Finally back in print, the book that launched the Lambda Literary Award–winning Micky Knight mystery series.   ISBN 1-931513-05-8 $11.95

EIGHTH DAY: A Cassidy James Mystery by Kate Calloway.
272 pp. In the eighth installment of the Cassidy James
mystery series, Cassidy goes undercover at a camp for troubled
teens.   ISBN 1-931513-04-X $11.95

MIRRORS by Marianne K. Martin. 208 pp. Jean Carson and Shayna
Bradley fight for a future together.   ISBN 1-931513-02-3 $11.95

THE ULTIMATE EXIT STRATEGY: A Virginia Kelly
Mystery by Nikki Baker. 240 pp. The long-awaited return of
the wickedly observant Virginia Kelly.   ISBN 1-931513-03-1 $11.95

FOREVER AND THE NIGHT by Laura DeHart Young. 224 pp.
Desire and passion ignite the frozen Arctic in this exciting
sequel to the classic romantic adventure *Love on the Line*.
                                          ISBN 0-931513-00-7 $11.95

WINGED ISIS by Jean Stewart. 240 pp. The long-awaited
sequel to *Warriors of Isis* and the fourth in the exciting Isis
series.   ISBN 1-931513-01-5 $11.95

ROOM FOR LOVE by Frankie J. Jones. 192 pp. Jo and Beth
must overcome the past in order to have a future together.
                                          ISBN 0-9677753-9-6 $11.95

THE QUESTION OF SABOTAGE by Bonnie J. Morris.
144 pp. A charming, sexy tale of romance, intrigue, and
coming of age.   ISBN 0-9677753-8-8 $11.95

SLEIGHT OF HAND by Karin Kallmaker writing as
Laura Adams. 256 pp. A journey of passion, heartbreak,
and triumph that reunites two women for a final chance at
their destiny.   ISBN 0-9677753-7-X $11.95

MOVING TARGETS: A Helen Black Mystery by Pat Welch.
240 pp. Helen must decide if getting to the bottom of a mystery
is worth hitting bottom.   ISBN 0-9677753-6-1 $11.95

CALM BEFORE THE STORM by Peggy J. Herring. 208 pp.
Colonel Robicheaux retires from the military and comes out of
the closet.   ISBN 0-9677753-1-0 $11.95

OFF SEASON by Jackie Calhoun. 208 pp. Pam threatens Jenny
and Rita's fledgling relationship.   ISBN 0-9677753-0-2 $11.95

WHEN EVIL CHANGES FACE: A Motor City Thriller by
Therese Szymanski. 240 pp. Brett Higgins is back in another
heart-pounding thriller.   ISBN 0-9677753-3-7 $11.95

BOLD COAST LOVE by Diana Tremain Braund. 208 pp.
Jackie Claymont fights for her reputation and the right to love
the woman she chooses.   ISBN 0-9677753-2-9 $11.95

THE WILD ONE by Lyn Denison. 176 pp. Rachel never
expected that Quinn's wild yearnings would change her life
forever.   ISBN 0-9677753-4-5 $11.95

SWEET FIRE by Saxon Bennett. 224 pp. Welcome to
Heroy—the town with more lesbians per capita than any
other place on the planet!   ISBN 0-9677753-5-3 $11.95